DAPHNE

Will Boast

GRANTA

Granta Publications, 12 Addison Avenue, London W11 4QR

First published in Great Britain by Granta Books, 2018
This paperback edition published by Granta Books, 2019

First published in the United States by Liveright Publishing Corporation,
a division of W.W. Norton & Company, Inc., New York, in 2018

A CIP catalogue record for this book is available from the British Library.

1 3 5 7 9 10 8 6 4 2

ISBN 978 1 78378 151 5
eISBN 978 1 78378 150 8

Offset by Avon DataSet Ltd, Bidford on Avon, B50 4JH

Printed and bound by CPI Group (UK) Ltd, Croydon, CR0 4YY

www.granta.com

WILL BOAST was born in England and grew up in Ireland and Wisconsin. His short story collection, *Power Ballads*, won the 2011 Iowa Short Fiction Award and was a finalist for a California Book Award. He is the author of *Epilogue*, a memoir (2014). His fiction, essays, and reporting have appeared in the *New Republic*, the *American Scholar*, and the *New York Times Magazine*, among other publications.

'Engaging . . . *Daphne* makes us coolly contemplate how and why we feel' *Guardian*

'Sleek and artful . . . touching' *Literary Review*

'Just like that, Boast seems to have captured today's cultural zeitgeist' *New York Times*

For AJB, RJB, and NPB
yours and yours and yours

A heavy numbness seized her limbs,
thin bark closed over her breast, her hair turned into
leaves, her arms into branches, her feet so swift
a moment ago stuck fast in slow-growing roots,
her face was lost in the canopy.

—*The Metamorphoses*

DAPHNE

ONE

When I was thirteen, I used to stay up all night with Thomas Hardy.

That home feels so long ago now. Yet sometimes I hardly seem to have moved an inch. I'm still in my old twin bed, legs gangling off the end. Just thirteen and I was as tall as any of the boys in school. I'd scrunch and bury myself under my comforter and two heavy blankets on top of that. Mom and I lived near the river. The winter wind yowled off the floodplain, shaking the windows, making the frames slab-cold to touch. The shag carpet in my room was moldering to dust, the wood paneling warping away from the walls. I could hear my mother in the other room tossing and turning. Every sigh and groan in that house, every draft and whimper, every scuff on the linoleum and worn-down wale on the corduroy couch—they all seemed eternal.

But that was not my old home.

Youth is a wilderness. The mind buds and flowers too

quickly to tame. A boy I liked said hi in the hall: a tiny sprout that, by the time I reached my bed, had exploded into lush forest. Even when exhausted from volleyball, I traveled miles before sleep, my feelings snarling brambles, soaring glades, chasms without bottom, the pain always endless, the joy just too much to contain. Christ, adolescence—even the word is ungainly.

It wasn't just Hardy. The stack on my bedside table was like geologic strata, layers of girl detectives, wayward babysitters, and dragon-riding heroines compressed under the solemn tomes that, on the cusp of high school, I'd started checking out from the town library. *Of Human Bondage*, *Middlemarch*, *Far from the Madding Crowd*. My best friend, Brook, was already devoted to *Sassy* and *NME*, but I felt I had an older, more timeless sensibility, one I was discovering in all of those sonorously titled books.

Somehow I got stuck on Hardy. Thirty, forty pages could go by, and he still seemed to be describing the same field or the noble visage of a shepherd. But the plots pulled me along: intercepted letters, mistaken identities, sudden riches, groveling poverty, scorned proposals, vows of vengeance. *The Mayor of Casterbridge*, that one had almost as many coincidences and twists as my old fantasy novels. Elizabeth-Jane—first she was the mayor's daughter, then the sailor's, then the mayor's again. Or was she, finally, crushingly, the sailor's?

I read in a state near compulsion, my tired brain skittering on to each new page. I shivered with anticipation, tingled with dread. When all the calamities crashed down at once, I wept. I knew Wessex was made up. Yet it felt more real than anything outside the cocoon of my bed. Arcadia, Indiana, was a distant murmur, one dim streetlight bleeding through the curtains. Only when I heard my mother's own quiet sobs was the spell broken. I tightened my cocoon, kept on reading.

I remember one night in eighth grade, the depths of February—I'd come to the part where Elizabeth-Jane and Farfrae, the clever young farmer, were falling in love. In Casterbridge, they never seemed to have occasion to talk, shy of each other and the eyes of the other villagers. But Elizabeth-Jane's mother arranged to have the two, unawares, meet at the granary of a nearby farm. When they realized they'd been tricked, they were awkward and overly polite, and Elizabeth Jane somehow managed to get herself covered in wheat husks. As they were about to say nervous goodbyes, Farfrae said it wouldn't do—it was raining, and wet chaff would ruin her clothes. Blowing was best, he said. And Elizabeth-Jane trembled as, carefully, one piece at a time, he blew the husks from her bonnet, her dress, "O," she said, "thank you," her hair, her neck, her—

The book dropped from my hands. Nested under my heavy blankets, I felt it: my skull buzzing, icy, electric, like I'd touched my tongue to a battery or bonked my funny bone, though it seemed to come not from outside but within me. I shook my head to clear it, reached for my book. I couldn't get hold of it. It kept slipping from my fingers.

What did I think it was, way back then? Maybe exhaustion, all the sleep I missed. Or growing pains, my arms and legs still throbbing and twitching at night—maybe that prickling electricity had migrated to my head. My body seemed so foreign, so unwieldy, this all seemed more or less plausible.

But I wasn't convinced. That night wasn't the first time I'd felt it. In school, someone slammed a locker or popped a blown-up lunch sack in the cafeteria—I startled, the buzzing came. Faintly, ghostly, but it was there, and stayed just long enough for me to miss a step or drop my fork into my spaghetti. Then it was gone.

Now, lying in bed, I didn't know whether to worry or treasure an inner secret. The girl detectives who always acted on a hunch, the dragon-riders in humming vibration with the very skies, Hardy's tempestuous, willful, yearning women—maybe I was like them, more sensitive, more attuned than the rest of the plodding world. Call it hormones. Call it fear, an overheated imagination, a longing to be somewhere, anywhere else. Call it simple teenage delusion. Still, I felt, then, so weirdly, fiercely alive.

Yet somehow, for ten then twenty seconds, as both Elizabeth-Jane and I trembled on the verge of either ecstasy or disaster, I just couldn't pick up the book.

I couldn't move at all.

TWO

WAKE, 5:40. BLEATING ALARM, WOOLLY HEAD. Fog-gray light through the windows, fog outside and in. Creak down from bed, espresso almost in my sleep. Shower hot as I can stand. Empty, weary calm before the day yawns open. Oatmeal.

Out the door, out on the street. Damp, chilly almost-rain. Whiff of the Pacific. Dodge the hypodermics, the human shit, Capp onto 17th onto Mission, the slumbering human zoo. A lump under heaped-up blankets. A beard and half a broken-veined face nestled in a filthy sleeping bag. Someone under a blue tarp, facedown, trembling. Don't linger—*white smoke drifting, cattails bobbing in the breeze*—slip briskly by.

BART to Millbrae to Caltrain, the 7:04. Get a seat upstairs. Earbuds in, white-noise app. Bury myself in apartment websites. Insulate. At Sunnyvale, the company shuttle, long circuit of MedEval's campus. Last stop, my lab. In through the side door, three card swipes, past the bio-waste bins, into the break room, coffee. Don't think about the bio-waste bins. Don't.

Lab quiet. Knock on the glass, wave to the night-shift techs as they finish up. Scattered yips from the pens. Earbuds back in. Bury myself in yesterday's data, sift, compile, bug hunt. Steady, rhythmic thinking—sweet balm to the condition—until nine o'clock, when my day techs arrive, immediately start making their needs and grudges known.

Seven, quitting time, hour in the company gym, climbing endless stairs. Skip the shower, stink up the train, maybe no one will stand next to me. Someone always does. White noise up. If I'm tired, touchy, then *smoke, cattails, sun-bleached picnic tables, diamonds of light, light making diamonds on the river.* Home. Reheat something, two glasses of Moscato. Repeats of *The Grand Design,* couples and families sledgehammering through cabinets, walls, old and awful habits. Lives torn down, rehabbed every twenty-two-and-a-half soothing minutes. Creature comforts, snack-size redemptions.

A quarter drunk, my bath. Hot as I can stand. The knot between my shoulders unwinds. My vigilant, chattering mind goes blank, and for upwards of ten, fifteen minutes, it just cannot touch me.

Then I climb up to the loft and sleep, and the river rises. The current pulls me along, pulls me down—shoves me back up. I'm awake and lie there limp, sweating, unmoving. Slowly, I sink back down. Giddy joy, almost smiling in my sleep, then jags of terror, then something amorphously sexual, hands fluttering over my body, caressing, smothering—everything I stifle during the day coming back to ravage me in dreams.

Wake, 5:40. Bleating alarm, woolly head. Creak down from bed. Repeat.

Same old grinding, deadening routine. But it got me through. I could, at least, guess what might be coming. I could prepare. On a good day, just a little flutter or slump in my private moments. I was, at least, surviving.

And then, at the end of another endless week, I walked into the bar.

THREE

I WALKED RIGHT OUT.

Even on a Friday night, the Pit Stop should've been dead. That's why Brook and I met there. Instead, a crowd of twenty-somethings dressed for the weekend. My one go-to dive in the Mission had been "discovered."

It was January, a wet month in a dry year. I stood out in the rain, watched the streetlights streak and smear across the dark, gleaming streets. Brook was late. Two months since I'd seen her. Work, we both kept saying. I texted in one rush—*Hey here where you at ETA?*—thought about going home. But, no, I wouldn't back out. What was worse, soaked misery or the crowd inside? I got rained on some more. I went inside.

It was loud, the jukebox playing Bob Seger, everyone shouting above it. I grimaced my way to the bar. All elbows, body heat. A wash of self-consciousness as I inched out of my coat—I'd come straight from work, in pantsuit and flats.

A group of friends were laughing at a joke, one guy doubled over like he'd been socked in the gut. The sudden wallop of his pleasure—*cattails, willows, diamonds of light*—I needed to insulate myself against him.

An open stool at the bar, I got myself into it, grasped the rail. The bartender came over, poured me a glass of white, menthol between her fingers. ABSOLUTELY NO SMOKING sign above the bar, and everyone was. "Looks like your ship came in," I said, gesturing at the crowd. "Hope they tip big."

She exhaled a burnt minty cloud. "And how long before the boss cans my ass for some young thing?"

I murmured in commiseration, left my wine to sweat down its sides, my fingers slightly dead. Across the room, the pool table was free. The Pit Stop was too tight to really play. Still, I could rack one up, play myself, a couple of rhythmic, distracting games. But, no, safer over here. Too shitty, too unpredictable a week to take more risks.

All that week the trains had run late. A drop of rain on the tracks, they ran late. Morning and evening, I'd stood eyes closed in the packed, rattling car, everyone's irritation pulsing around me, amplifying my own. Secondhand pain, mirror neurons, automatic responses in the supramarginal gyrus, empathy—whatever you call it, I needed to be wary. I'd already had two bad attacks that week.

The first had been uncomplicated: Tuesday, coming home late from work, a car whipped around the corner, blasted its horn at me. I crumpled to the curb, went down on my ass, hobbled home. Sudden, blunt surprise—it wears off quick. But the second attack . . .

Early Thursday morning on Mission, I'd passed a torso in a wheelchair: stub legs, stub arms, paper begging cup in what he had for a lap, plastic rehab bracelet around his tiny wrist. "Hey, lovely lady, spare some . . ." He slurred off into a bleary smile. Jesus, to see him . . . I had to get down on a bus bench, sit awhile, my head bobbing. A cop came by—"Ma'am? Can't sleep here!"—poked me in the leg with something, his nightstick maybe, then just moved on. I heard the torso roll past, the whir of his motorized chair. My eyes were still closed—*willows, cattails*—but I couldn't unsee him. I had to sit on that bench another fifteen minutes. Even now, at the end of my week, glass of wine between my dead fingers, I had to labor not to add his pain to my own.

"YOU'RE GOING TO HAVE to educate everyone," Dr. Bell said when he diagnosed me. "Everyone." So here's the short version: I'm paralyzed by emotion.

Mostly, ninety percent of the time, the big ones trigger the bad attacks. The big, primal stuff: rage, ecstasy, sorrow, disgust, laughter, horror, our friend surprise. All of them can land me on my ass. Or worse.

The more subtle things, the shades between the bright, primary colors, they're easier. Embarrassment, apprehension, melancholy, grudging admiration, conflicted trust . . . How many should I list? The delight soured by envy when Brook tells me about yet another amazing party? The lazy, luxurious serenity that washes in after a huge meal? The oddly poignant remorse and self-reproach I feel whenever I *just* miss a train? Our heads paint with every pigment on the wheel. Small mercy, then, that the smaller, in-between stuff tends not to trigger me. Or, when it does, only minor attacks.

The severity, the duration, it all depends on how strong the emotion, how sudden, how tangled up with other emotions. "You're a puppet dancing around on your strings," Dr. Bell once told me. "Cut one string, what happens?" A sudden loss of muscle tone, partial paralysis. A minor attack is usually benign: My eyelids flutter, my jaw sags, my knees go a little weak. My fingers quit working; I keep dropping my pen or something. An annoyance, a few weird looks if anyone else is around to see.

But bad attacks . . . "Now cut *all* the strings," Dr. Bell said. Total collapse.

And what causes all of this? I was sixteen when Mom and I found Dr. Bell. I had questions. I asked and asked. "So, when are you getting *your* neurophysiology PhD?" he'd answer with a pedant's sigh. "All you need to know: The human brain is the universe's most implausible chemistry experiment."

I SIPPED MY WINE carefully. The room kept pushing in: the group of friends busting up at another joke; a clutch of blond Marina girls hooting about something, all loud and elated; a guy waving a twenty to get the bartender's attention, way too surly about being ignored. *Cattails, willows, sunbleached picnic tables, white smoke*. I'd spent all week looking forward to catching up with Brook. My goal for the week now: just stay vertical.

Skunky beer, pool-cue chalk dust, the bartender's menthols—the dank familiarity of the Pit Stop calmed me a little. And the taste of the wine, cheery, sweet stuff that reminded me of grad school, when I could, briefly, drink myself into equilibrium. I signaled for another.

As I did, a guy nestled up to the bar. He immediately pulled back to check the sleeves of his chambray shirt for stains. Dark Japanese denim, sweetly scented Moroccan-oiled hair—he was attractive, yes, and the clothes beautiful. He ordered three Anchor Steams, three shots of Fernet, glanced over, smiled at me, shook his head.

"I can hardly believe it."

"Sorry?" I said.

"There are still places like this in the hood."

"Oh," I said.

"I'd say it's totally unpretentious, but that sounds really pretentious."

"Right," I said.

"Okay, wait, dumb question, but who are you with?"

"Who?" I said.

"If it's a start-up, no way I'll be able to guess. There's a new start-up every half-second. But you seem *way* more recruitable than that."

A compliment, sort of, that he'd intuited I was an engineer, in my past life anyway. And he was trying to push past my one-word answers. All of this could've been, I don't know, fun?

"Sorry," I said, "but you really don't want to know what I do."

"We do what we have to do." He shrugged philosophically, narrowed his eyes, and said in a mock-sultry murmur, "So, another drink here? Or should we just skip right to mimosas tomorrow morning?"

Oh, thank God there was no reason to talk to this guy now. He was trying for ironic and hadn't quite sold it. Well-oiled as he was, there was something melancholy about him. All of these young guys—and, yes, girls, too—who could buy and maybe even do whatever they wanted yet still couldn't fulfill all the things San Francisco and its heavy legacy of liberation promised—even on the train, I felt all their desperate energy. Lord knows a little irony gets us all through. Still, I just . . .

"I can't," I said.

"What?"

"Please, I just can't."

He smirked again. "Can't what?"

I needed the fastest way out. "That line," I began, "that's not even the slimiest thing you just said. You asked where I work but just so I'd ask *you*. So, you want me to guess what you make? Three hundred grand a year? Five hundred? Why don't you write it on the back of your card, and I'll . . ." I ran out of steam. "Please," I mumbled, "go back to your bro-grammer buddies looking on over there. Truly, don't waste your time."

He laughed uncertainly, muttered a perfunctory "bitch" at me, and retreated to his friends. I felt so shitty I drooped in my stool, and probably looked like a lunatic in front of all of them.

When I came back, I looked up and saw Brook threading through the crowd. The girl I met the first day of fifth grade, the one in dungarees and snap bracelets, was now the twenty-nine-year-old in ankle boots, sheer black tights, and, somehow, leather lace-up shorts and a camouflage jacket. She wore one half of her dark hair long, the other half shaved, a look every other edgy girl in the city seemed to be trying but Brook actually pulled off. Her inhibitions sat in the junk drawer of the past, somewhere back there with the midwestern deference and the novelty bracelets.

"Hey, lady." She gave me a light hug, brushed her lips against my cheek. "Shit, sorry I'm late. Had a last-minute event to get off the ground." She signaled the bartender, who started mixing Brook her usual Manhattan, ignoring at least five people waiting for drinks. "Jesus," Brook said, glancing around, "what happened to the good old Armpit?" She looked at me with concern. "You okay? We could go to your place?"

"Don't worry, it's just . . . We can't give up our shithole without a fight."

Nothing drooping now, but Brook didn't need any obvious signals. She reached out, brushed a snarl out of my hair. I flinched, then thought of middle school sleepovers, giggling in the bathroom as we streaked each other's hair purple with Manic Panic.

"I had a lovely little spill on Tuesday," I went on, giving her the condition update despite myself. "My ass is still sore. Good thing I've got all this padding."

"Please, all that stair climber you do, I could bounce quarters off that thing. I'm about to get a roll off the bartender." Brook paid for her Manhattan, sipped off the top third in one go. "And everything's okay at work? Been staying on your feet?"

"Zero accidents on the job," I said.

"You could tell your staff. I don't think they'd mutiny."

"They think your head's a mess, they start questioning everything you say."

"Hmm," Brook said, not agreeing or disagreeing. Over the lip of her raised drink, her eyes briefly settled on a guy in bright orange Tiger sneakers and a rumpled but immaculately cut sport coat. A CEO or CTO or "founder"—she had a radar for them.

"What was your thing tonight?" I said.

"I'm going to have to switch champagne suppliers. There's such a run on the stuff, they think they can charge whatever."

Since Brook graduated Berkeley, she'd run her own events business. She'd started out herding Miller Lite girls around Pleasanton sports bars and ended up running high-end restaurant launches and huge private parties down on the peninsula. In a world where everyone was trying to radiate success while praying for actual profits, Brook's margins narrowed and narrowed. I was proud of everything she'd built. But I hated all the flirting and promising and haring around she did to keep it up.

"You should've seen this guy." I pointed out Moroccan Hair Oil. He and his friends were now mixing with the Marina girls. "He dropped this godawful line on me."

"At least he's kind of cute."

"Objectively."

"Good enough, isn't it?" Brook said. "Come on, lady, if I hadn't seen you pee your pants in gym, I'd be all over you right now."

"Stop trying to make me laugh."

"Is it that bad? Lame jokes are going to put you on your ass?"

"No, it's just—"

Someone bumped my elbow. More people were jostling for a spot at the bar. One of the Marina girls started whooping again. "What?!" she shouted at Hair Oil. "You're buying mimosas for *everyone*?" I felt an involuntary, uneasy smile stretch my lips. My teeth were on edge, like I'd chomped down on tinfoil.

"How about some pool after all?" I said tightly. "Some breathing room."

Brook knocked back her cocktail. "Want one? I can't let you drink that cheap white." She measured me up again. "If you'll be okay?"

I hesitated. "I'll try to be okay."

"We are going to have ourselves a night. Okay?"

"Okay," I said. "Okay, okay."

Everything Brook and I said these days sounded performed, like we were playing some bad cover version of our friendship. Distance, always distance, but never, I thought, between my best friend and me. "I'll just be at the bar," she said. "I'll be right back."

I worked my way to the corner, dug out some quarters, racked up a game. I'd spent too much of my early twenties circling pool tables in empty dives, drunk enough it was like a glass barrier had slid between me and the world. I drew the cue back, relished the long shatter of the break. A stripe went in. I sank another, then another, didn't have to police my thoughts, just move, find a rhythm, insulate myself inside of it.

When I finally looked up again, Brook was at the bar with the guy in the sport coat. I couldn't blame her for it. I wasn't going to. I really shouldn't—*white smoke, cattails*. I looked away, saw the group of friends guffawing again. From a distance, it looked so theatrical. Still, part of me reached out, yearned to laugh along. Next to them, Hair Oil and Marina Girl were making out. I watched their slow deliriousness, their smiling and murmuring, sealed off in their own world, brains flooded with dopamine, an ache that kept pulling you back, his lips, his neck, his—

"Shit, they should sell tickets."

"B-rook, p-lease . . ." I took a moment, got my tongue back. "Don't sneak up like that."

"You were so lost in the show, I couldn't resist. Here, drink up. I find a breath of menthol gives it an extra something."

I took a long sip of my Manhattan, but a gummy, saline taste still sat on my tongue. Well, I could deal with embarrassment. *White smoke drifting*. Except when it made all the riskier stuff flare up.

"Look at those two. The thing about skinny jeans, you don't have to read a guy's mind."

"Christ." I had to put down my drink.

"Sorry, I had to work him a little." Brook was locked on Sport Coat again, calculating. "He said he wants to do something huge for Halloween."

"You're planning that far ahead?"

"Always."

"Take a night off. Help me finish this game."

"You know I suck at this. You'll be scraping *me* off the floor for a change."

I couldn't help a little laugh, had to prop myself up with my cue. Brook reached out, touched my arm, just to tell me she was there. For a few minutes, as we knocked balls around the table, telling dumb almost-jokes, we slipped into some version of how we used to be. Then Sport Coat started settling his bar tab. I felt Brook stiffen. Business was about to walk out the door.

"Go ahead."

"You sure?"

I palmed a pool ball, bounced it off the cushion. "At least he's kind of cute."

Brook looked at me skeptically. "What?"

"Nothing."

"No, what does that mean?"

It meant that it drove me crazy when she led with her sexuality, especially in her work. And that she was even more sensitive about it than I was. But neither of us wanted to get into that. "Just don't let him walk without your card," I said.

Brook crossed the room, the girls and boys in tight jeans parting before her, heads turned in her wake. Even in a roomful of strangers she moved like the host of the party. At the bar, she clamped a hand on Sport Coat's arm. I focused on the table: the calm green baize, the light ringing off the balls, making them stand out starkly in their little pools of shadow, the dented cue bumping through my fingers, the thunk of balls dropping into pockets, the angle, the spin, the—

I shanked the eight and clattered the cue down in sudden, ridiculous frustration. The buzzing, between a headache and a shiver, started at the top of my skull. I found myself staring around the room again. Longing, envy, remorse, hair-trigger rage—for once couldn't I just give in? Never mind the pain, I could just thump down in a heap, my strings trailing around me. These people wouldn't even pause, just keep on with their headlong Friday nights. *White smoke, picnic tables, cattails, the willows shaking their ribbony leaves, noon light on the river, diamonds of light on the . . .* My concentration kept scattering, the buzzing rising. My knees went soft. God, I just wanted to let go! Still, I sank slowly. The cue slipped from my fingers, knocked into the balls. I watched the eight roll into a pocket as my head drooped forward. I began to fold, squatting down into my heels and, thinking I might tip back, just had the control to tilt forward, my forehead against the side of the table, sticky from several million spilled beers, shit, my skin sticking to the fake wood, shit, shit, I would never get up from here, they'd just have to sweep me up in the morning, with the cigarette butts and shattered glasses, but at least, Jesus, at least, I was in the corner where no one could—

"Hey, you all right down there?"

A male voice. Not Hair Oil, mercifully. From my less than commanding vantage, I could only make out gray jeans with what appeared to be sawdust peppering the cuffs.

"Um, excuse me, need any help?"

"Fine," I managed to get out. "Fine. Just look-ing for my quart-ers."

"You dropped them? Where?"

I went one syllable at a time—"I'll fin-d th-em. Just nee-d a sec to"—ran through my visualization as fast and clean as I could, and by some miracle managed to lever myself back up to standing or, anyway, leaning against the table.

"Ah, okay . . . You get them all?"

I forced my fluttering eyelids fully open. He wore a tan work jacket and a black shirt, also dusted with sawdust. His hair was shoulder length, dark, shot through with silver. But he seemed young, twenty-five maybe, three or four years younger than me. I'm five-eleven. He was several inches taller, wiry with broad shoulders, though he was trying to stoop his way out of them. His eyes had a muted, oyster-shell glimmer, between gray and blue. His fingers were scraped and scratched, his features blunt and masculine. Yet he wore a tentative, inquisitive look. And the smile he gave me then wasn't so much shy as oddly private. He seemed already to know something secret about me.

"Don't worry about it"—I was back in myself again,

more or less—"they're probably permanently glued to the floor." Faux casual, I leaned further into the table.

"Think maybe I got next game," he said hesitantly.

"Aren't you supposed to put *your* quarters on the table?"

"That's me up there." On a small chalkboard with all the other names rubbed off, I read OLLIE. His script was surprisingly florid. "You have to put your name up here."

I hesitated, too. "Fine. But you rack. My break. I beat myself."

"So, uh," he said, doing everything he could not to seem as bashful as he obviously was, "what's yours?"

"What's my what?"

"Your name."

"Sorry, I can't . . . It's Daphne. What are we playing, house rules? Slop?"

"Either way," he said, "I bet you'll crush me."

He put in quarters. The balls thundered out of their cage. My break was clumsy. Nothing went in. Ollie took down a cue. The walls made him hitch up his shoulders and strike the cue ball at a high, awkward angle. A solid trickled into a corner pocket. He looked up at me, grinned toothily. "You here with friends?"

"Sure," I said, too brusquely.

"And, uh, what do you do? You work downtown? The peninsula?"

"You don't want to know what I do. You really don't."

He scrutinized me again. "We calling shots?"

"Whatever you want."

"Okay, um, sorry, excuse me, I . . ."

As he circled the table to line up his next shot, he brushed against me. Over the years, I've gotten used to tracking the slightest signals from my body: The lingering tastes and tiny twitches. The tightening of my muscles—stomach, throat, bowels—heat rising in my face, my scalp beginning to tingle. The buzzing in my skull. These are my early warnings, the ripples that can become waves. But something else rang in me as his hip brushed mine. I smelled him, and he was not exactly fresh from the shower. Still, it wasn't his slight musk but something I couldn't place, a resonance across the senses, a steady hum, a thin, liquid sweetness, like nostalgia, vibrating right through me.

I put out a hand for the table. But whatever it was, in the crush of that bar, had faded. My turn. "Nine ball"—I drew back the cue—"side pocket," and in a daze sank the shot.

At the bar, Brook was laughing/grimacing at something Sport Coat was saying. I tried to catch her attention, but she was hard at work. "Fifteen," I said, "in the corner."

Ollie and I played in silence, only the clicks of the game passing between us. The bar clock read ten. The crowd was elbow to elbow. "You been watching what's happening in Egypt?" he said. "Tahrir Square and everything?"

I'd only caught bits of coverage at the gym, before flipping to reruns of *The Grand Design*. "The Middle East?" I said. "Too fucked up for me." I made a hasty shot, caromed into the eight, and scratched. "Rules say that's game."

"We're playing slop, though, right? Come on, let's finish

up right." He placed the cue ball on the spot, lined up an easy shot, missed it, shrugged. "Your turn."

I sank two more, sank the eight, and felt a catch at the base of my esophagus. Game over. At the bar, Sport Coat raised his hand for two more drinks. I saw Brook crumple a little. I failed again to catch her eye. Fine. I needed a clean escape anyway.

"Another?" Ollie said gently, picking up, perhaps, on my turmoil.

"No, I'd better flee for the night. It's way past time."

"You live nearby? It's just, I was heading out, too, if you wanted someone to—"

"Okay. But, really, it's not far."

Outside, it'd stopped raining. Fog cast a glimmer over the parked cars, an obscured moon giving everything the dim luster of tin. The thump of the jukebox inside made out here blessedly quiet, and I felt a moment's relief at getting out on my own two feet. But then he was standing so close I was overwhelmed all over again. I reached into my bag for my phone, to distract myself. It was dead.

We set off. There was hardly anyone on the streets. The damp had driven the homeless and the junkies to their SROs and shelters. I walked briskly, one arm clamped over my bag, the other swinging like a soldier's. Turning onto Capp, I accidentally knocked my hand against his. A crackle of anticipation went through me, a couple of drinks enough to make me skittish, my emotions like horses that wanted to surge ahead.

We came to my building. "See, really not far."

He whistled, low and strangely mournful. "You live *here*?"

"I know, I know. My broker said this block was 'on the edge.'"

Meaning I got a deal, and that my building looked aggressively resplendent among the peeling-paint Victorians and auto body shops, the dingy corner store where you could blow dust off the Nutter Butters and chicharrones. Ollie and I stood considering my building's four-story bamboo-and-glass façade, the hanging boxes of primrose and calla lilies that softened its lacerating sheen. THE GROVE, read the sans-serif aluminum nameplate the developers had hung above the entrance.

"So, hey," Ollie stammered, "I should let you go. But I wanted to, you know . . ."

He looked like he might kiss me. My mouth went cottony and slack. My legs twitched to flee. But my feet were rooted like stumps. *The willows shaking their heads.*

"I mean, if it's okay with you, maybe we could—"

"I really should go up."

"—trade numbers."

Relief, buoyancy, gratitude—he wasn't going to kiss me. "Why?" I said. "I've been a bitch all night."

He gave me a quick piccolo squeak of a smile. "Well, I'd be annoyed, too, if I'd lost seventy-five cents."

"Okay, okay, got your phone?"

He dug an ancient flip phone out of his pocket. I heard myself giving him my actual number while my thoughts rioted with what might still be possible. Maybe I'd surprise us both, ask him upstairs, get half of a quick thrill on the couch, kick him out before he started noticing my lapses. Maybe I'd ask him to stay the night, just a warm body encircling mine. I'd make us omelets in the morning, be blithe and brisk, make it clear he wasn't coming back. Or there was the route we were already on: an awkward dinner date or two, the explanations—the educating—his sympathetic/panicked questions, eyes darting around the restaurant, wondering when exactly would be appropriate to get the hell out. Or, shit, maybe it could work for a while . . . Ask him upstairs, omelets, climb back into bed, we could spend all day . . . Shit, shit. The buzzing, a faint, menacing glimmer—I had to close my eyes as I came to the last digit. *Willows, cattails.* My lips parted, and I heard myself changing it, from a four to a six.

"Want me to call you?" he said. "So you have mine?"

"Phone's dead," I mumbled. "Won't get it. Not till la-ter."

A ripple of concern passed over his face. "I'll try you later, then."

"Tex-t." I could hardly get the word out. When I'm having a mild attack, or trembling on the edge of a bad one, I can't always predict what will go first: eyelids, tongue, fingers, knees . . . Every emotion is a different chemistry, a different electricity shot down a different part of the nervous system. This particular encounter—desire, fear, self-thwarted triumph—was making my tongue as thick as taffy. "Tex-t is bes-t," I finally finished. "I on-ly do tex-t."

He looked at me with curiosity. Or was it freaked-out confusion? "Okay, no problem." He held up his phone, grinned again. "I think this does text."

I could still give him the right number. Things didn't

have to go the way they had before, the few times in the last decade I'd actually tried to date. "Hold on. Ollie . . ." The buzzing subsided; my drooping eyelids came slowly up. Maybe it looked like I was batting my eyes. Or like I was drunk. Or tired. Or insane. "Ollie, I . . ."

"Yeah?" His concern was thickening.

"I owe you a game." I couldn't own up to it, the fake number.

"Next time!" As he turned to leave, an impulse flashed up from the depths. I grabbed his jacket collar, pulled him to me. The buzzing leapt back up, rogue current prickling down to my fingers and toes, my whole body shimmering. I'd call it deadening, but that's not quite right—it's not anesthetic, I feel everything. It's just that things switch off, stop working. My fingers curled into loose fists, my shoulders slumped, my knees once again started dissolving. *Cattails, picnic tables, willows, diamonds of light, a man, a man waving.* I stayed up. Only just.

In fact, I had to lean into Ollie a little. Which meant I didn't so much kiss him as mush my face into his. "*Hmmggh,*" he murmured—with pleasure or, more likely, surprise at my amorous little head butt. Clumsily, I pushed him away, separated us. "Tex-t me," I said, my voice ripe and slurred.

He didn't ask what was wrong, thank God. Puzzled smile on his face, he turned and slipped off into the moon-tinged fog. I stood watching him go, still rooted in place. Then I went in and took the stairs up to my apartment. Carefully, one at a time, clinging tightly to the rail.

FOUR

"YOU'RE GOING TO HAVE TO EDUCATE EVERYONE."

Over the years, I've come to understand that not everything Dr. Bell told me was right or even particularly responsible. In this pronouncement, however, his prescience, and his ego, have been vindicated.

If anything, the condition is closest to narcolepsy. You know: People fall asleep right in the middle of the day. Their brain commands them to nap—they nap. The cop who thought I was sleeping on that bus bench, who poked me like I was just another sack of human misery, he was far from the first to make that mistake. I used to have a little speech: "I might *look* like I'm dozing or passed out drunk. But I'm awake. I can hear everything happening around me, everything you're saying. When it's really bad, I can hardly move a muscle. But I'm *awake*. I'm not here, but I'm here." A warning—a plea—to new friends, roommates, professors, potential employers. Before I learned to corral my feelings, I had to make that speech all the time.

So, narcoleptics sleep during their episodes. I, on the other hand, am simply paralyzed. Most narcoleptics feel their naps arriving and know to get ready. I get less notice. If I can sense a particular feeling shoving its way in, I'll kneel or sit down, get myself into a safe position. In a pinch, I'll lean against a wall. This sometimes works for joy or sadness or fear—emotions that can emerge slowly, from a generally brightening or darkening mood. But anger? Laughter? Surprise? Those usually burst on us too quickly. Anger is too volatile and sudden. Laugher is spontaneous. And how—Jesus, how—do you prepare yourself to be surprised?

Somewhere in the tangle of the brain's wiring, there's a connection between the two syndromes: In narcolepsy, deep REM sleep suddenly clamps down on the waking day. Have you ever woken from a dream and found yourself unable to move? That's REM sleep shutting down your body—everything but the vital systems—so you don't act out a dream, don't thrash around or hurl yourself out of bed or punch your bedmate in the face. It's thought, with my condition, that the brain somehow confuses strong emotion with that trigger for deep sleep, that sudden command to switch off the muscles. It's thought, with my condition, that this has to do with the absence of a certain neurotransmitter in the hypothalamus. It's thought that this is caused by an autoimmune disorder, that around puberty my body launched an all-out attack on that part of my brain and wiped out this rather key mechanism.

It's thought.

Because, in the hierarchy of human frailties, there is so much other research to pursue. And so much of it is sexier/more lucrative. Dr. Bell and a handful of other specialists published a new study or paper every few years, attacks on each other's work, theories that were never verified, seeming breakthroughs that could never be repeated. For a time, I tried to educate myself, tried to keep up with the literature, the impenetrable discourses on "excitatory neuropeptide hormones" and the "homology of hemagglutinin epitopes." In college, I thought I was going to be an English and bio double major, a neurology researcher who understood the entire human animal. I kept at it, B minuses right through junior year, when I finally dropped both and switched to com-sci. But I tried so hard. I was going to educate them all.

In the end, I just didn't have the head for it.

I WOKE LATE on the Saturday after the Pit Stop, muzzy, wrung out, trying to swallow down a coppery burr in my throat. The outlines of a dream—two men sitting on a raft on a river like diamonds—dissolved into the sunlight blitzing through my windows. I rolled heavily out of bed, creaked down from the loft, tried to slot myself into my Saturday routine:

Pack my Bialetti, fill it with Volvic. High heat with the top open, just till it starts to boil, then very low heat, get some *crema* in the espresso. Squeeze the oranges for juice,

Cara Caras or blood. Omelet, nothing complicated, I want to *taste* each ingredient: a soft cheese, a cured meat, whatever vegetable curiosity comes in the CSA box each week. Micro-green salad, oil, balsamic, sprig of thyme, one twist Himalayan pink, one twist Indian black. Set the table, wake up the apartment a little, TV on mute, NPR aw-shucks-ing over some almost-funny quiz show, fork in one hand, phone in other, thumbing through new apartment tours on Interior Life. Little hits of admiration and irritation—I'd been submitting my own apartment photos for years and still nothing—keep thumbing anyway. Pattern, repetition, small, comforting tasks—with the constant low buzz of stimuli, there just isn't time or space enough to really feel.

I sent an exploratory text Brook's way. *Sorry to run out on you just couldn't deal with crowd text me okay?* But Brook wouldn't be up for hours. And, truly, did I want to hear about the club or SoMa penthouse where she'd ended the night, partying to get more business throwing parties? I tossed my phone aside, went over to my bookshelf, reclaimed pine dredged up from the wreck of a Lake Superior steamboat, ran my finger along the spines of my books—Koolhaas, Hadid, Smithson, Serra—flopped on the couch, and read Le Corbusier saying something about space and light and order.

At two-thirty, I started pacing. I didn't need to go. What was the point in going? No one ever made any progress. There was no progress to even be made. I flipped channels on TV, skirted past the news. Aerial shots of writhing public squares. Shaky footage of young men in stiff-fitting jeans shouting, waving flags, hurling bottles and stones at riot squads. Bloodied faces. Police dragging a beaten woman by her coat, her clothes torn open, one of them with his boot poised above her, about to—

I turned the TV off and called my car service. "371 Capp," the dispatcher said brightly, "thought maybe you wouldn't be needing us today!"

The car arrived. I tried to do my hair and makeup on the way. In my compact, my face bobbed up and down with the car's suspension. Classical, slightly humped nose, broken from a fall junior year and set as well as the campus ER cared to do. Full, rosy cheeks that taper into a pointed chin—my mother's. My eyes are my dad's, an icy, riverine blue that people often call "disarming." "Inscrutable," that's another I get.

Outside the side entrance to the church, men were blowing over cups of coffee and smoking. A few were broken down and frazzled, but others were tanned and muscular, V-necked tees showing off biceps and chests, smiles weary but gleaming white. An all-gay AA group. "Late again to the temple of penance," I said as an action-figure-handsome guy held the door. "We forgive you," he whispered. "It's in our contract."

The church was Korean Methodist. I'd never actually seen the church proper, only the rented basement meeting rooms. The bulletin board in the stairwell was a catalog of vice and frailty: Pills Anonymous, Gamblers Anonymous, debt management, video game and internet addiction, another group for gamblers who only did scratch-offs. Half of human life seemed to be backsliding, compulsions, near-automatic behavior—people flailing against the frantic imperatives of their addled minds. The hallway stank of the vinegar they used to flush out the big coffee urn in the kitchen. Nose wrinkled, mood contorted, I eased open the second-to-last door.

The group, seven of them that day, all turned to watch me come in. Sherman's eyes fluttered, his head dipped. I'd taken him, very mildly, by surprise. Sherman, our organizer, our beacon of optimism. He wore white linen trousers and a pressed checkered shirt, and his brogues were buffed to a high shine. He always dressed up for meetings. As his head bobbed back up, he lit up to see me. "Daphne, so glad you could make it!"

"Sorry, everyone, sorry."

I dragged a desk over to the circle. To those who didn't know I was habitually late, when I came at all, I mugged a presidential level of contrition. Many in our group had been coming for years, though it wasn't uncommon for someone to drop out for months at a time, only to return looking even more desperate. In this metropolitan area, our numbers might well have been larger. The condition isn't so astoundingly rare, one in ten thousand (it's thought). But getting a diagnosis remains a total crapshoot. It's a half-paragraph in a med school textbook, a quirky human-interest piece that crops up maybe a couple of times a decade. Most of our group, it had taken them years to find out what the hell was wrong with them, why they kept falling down when someone told a good joke, or wilted like a drunk if something blindsided them or pissed them off. A lot of people with the condition may never even make that connection. Emotion, after all, suffuses and influences everything we do, everything we think, everything we are. We're absolutely pickled in it. Who would guess it could, quite literally, paralyze you?

I looked around. There was Russell, a jumpy young guy with his arm in a sling and a livid scar across his forehead. Driving can be so rhythmic and calming. But Russell is a case in point why so few of us actually get behind the wheel; a couple of months ago a jag of road rage landed him in SF General. Worse, he kite-surfed, mountain-biked, free-climbed, did other lunatic things. He'd only recently been diagnosed. The limitations hadn't sunk in yet. He didn't seem to realize just how easily they could get him killed.

Then there was Miranda. She taught poli-sci down at SF State. A sharp one, Miranda, hard to bullshit. And so depressed that, as a bonus curse, she'd eaten herself into type 2 diabetes. She worried constantly about switching off in front of her students. We were always telling her just to come clean with them. But she couldn't, she said, not when she had to command a lecture hall full of squirrely undergrads. I agreed with her. A woman just couldn't relinquish that control.

Next to her sat Teshawn, who came over from the East Bay. He did shift work at a cold-storage warehouse, picking orders and loading trucks. It was the kind of work, people and forklifts flying around, where a slip-up meant getting yourself or someone else hurt or worse. So Teshawn medicated himself, hard. There is no cure for the condition, and the cocktail of pharmaceuticals that seems to suppress attacks dulls everything, turns you vacant, affectless. The world dims to a shadow play. All of us had tried the drugs at one point or another and found that no amount of coffee or pep pills brightened the picture. Teshawn had no choice but to take them. Now and then we glimpsed his charm, his true playful, funny, outgoing self. But only in glimmers.

The rest of the circle were part-timers, faces that came and went. Only Sherman showed up every single week, devoted as he was to organizing our little group of headbobbers. Almost anything could trigger him: the dumbest little joke, a weepy song on the radio, sunlight playing prettily on the floor. His bonus curse: an exquisitely sensitive soul.

"I'll catch Daphne up on business at the end," Sherman was saying. "Bill, you were talking about your son's birthday party?"

How could I forget Bill? Tanned, crew cut, early forties, polo and khakis, acting the part of the FiDi trader with a fat watch around his wrist and the world by its neck. But we all knew who drove him to every meeting. Bill depended on his overburdened wife for everything, yet cast himself as both the hero and victim of every story.

"Well, it started out so perfect," Bill said with a tight smile. "Danny's at that age when everything's a discovery. He's just perfect to me, like his mother. But seeing him with all his friends, all those cute little five-year-olds, I just couldn't take it. My heart was practically bursting. And that's when I started to worry."

Murmurs of recognition and concern flitted around the circle. My phone vibrated in my bag. Brook. *Hey, lady, don't*

blame the crowd. I saw you walk out with that young fella.
Holding my phone under the swing-top of the desk, I tapped
out a reply.

*He just walked me home no big deal how'd it go with
Halloween?*

"For the first half hour, I was good," Bill said. "Just a
few funny faces." Funny faces, our shorthand for fluttering
eyelids or a sagging jaw, minor attacks. "Then Carianne
brings out the cake. You should've seen Danny's face. Plus,
all the kids have kazoos—Carianne bought a bunch of them
somewhere—and they're all playing 'Happy Birthday.' What
a sound! Me, I'm hanging back, working the camcorder, videoing it all. For some reason, it helps. Maybe I'm like the
observer, not the participant?"

"Interesting." Sherman made a note of this, as if it were
useful advice: You could self-treat by carrying a goddamn
camcorder around the rest of your life.

*Halloween, yeah, maybe something there. He dragged
me to this thing. Everyone was on DMT. Sort of fun. You
see elves.*

Jesus Brook . . .

*But, come on, who was your guy? Bass player? Acad-
emy of Art student? Rainbow Grocery bulk foods guy? At
least he was cute.*

"But the kids, Danny, the kazoos, it's all too much," Bill
was saying. "I'm videoing away, but I feel the *joyousness*
welling up in me. It's going to break loose any minute, and
I'm going to face-plant right into the cake or something. So
I put the camcorder down, leave it recording. I run for the

bedroom, flop down on the bed, and just have to lie there, listening to them all singing and kazoo-ing."

Sure he was okay—I hesitated to tell Brook about the kiss—*I gave him fake number would've been shit show anyway.*

"I let myself go, just let the damn episode happen. I'm sprawled on the bed, I don't know how long, and all I can do is listen, just listen while they're all having a blast out there. Christ, the kid only turns six once, and I only get to fucking *listen* to it!"

Bill was getting worked up. No self-control. A wonder he didn't slide right out of his desk. I could hear the despair in his voice, and the resentment, not just of the condition, but of his wife, his son, all of his son's little friends, everyone who didn't have to worry about face-planting in the cake.

Brush it off, lady. Mezzanine, this Thursday. We'll go early, get set up with a booth. I know a couple really sweet guys who DJ there. It'll be chill, really.

"Carianne said Danny didn't even ask where I went off to. He knew I was having 'daddy time.' Normally, we would've watched the video later on. We would've at least had that to share. But I left the goddamn thing pointing the wrong way."

More sympathetic murmurs from the circle. I cringed at the sound. The vinegar from the hallway had drifted into the room, curdling my stomach again. My thumbs flew. *B that's YOUR life what the hell am I supposed to say to a DJ or do at a club especially if you're working again I mean Christ I WANT to but really*—

"What do you think, Daphne?" Sherman said. "How do you respond to Bill's experience?"

"Sad," I said, dropping my phone into my bag. "Very sad. It's like you're not even there for your own life. You're there, but you're not there, you know?"

Bill gave me a sour look; he'd seen me on my phone. But the others nodded. The ones like Bill, with spouses and families to look after them, they did all right. The others had to get by with help from friends or neighbors. Some of them got disability, checks from the government, assistance from hired carers. A lot of them—including Sherman, who did web design—worked from home. Telecommuting and the internet had been a godsend for them. My company offered me at-home days a few years ago. But I wouldn't be shuffled into a corner. I wouldn't let the condition run my entire life.

"Come on, Daphne," Miranda broke in. "That's easy enough to say. Let's talk about strategizing. You should've discussed with Carianne before the party," she said to Bill, "come up with a real plan."

"God, I don't even pick Danny up anymore!" Bill said. "I'm too afraid I'm going to drop him!"

The emotions of others affect us unpredictably. Sometimes they resonate like a struck bell. Just as often they clank and mean nothing at all. Bill's story *was* sad, yet, today, it couldn't reach me. His mouth was gaping. The snack tray was just behind me; I could've reached over and popped in a cookie.

"Bill, sorry to cut you short," Sherman was saying, "but we'll have to continue this next session." I'd come so late the meeting was already over. "Anything before we go?" Sherman said. "Anyone?" He always got an eye-fluttering thrill from what he said next. "Until next time, everybody, stay safe, stay open."

As I got up to leave, Sherman called to me, "Daphne, I'll give you that info I mentioned." The rest of the group trickled out, chatting and checking in with one another as they went down the hall of frailties.

"What info?" Then I got it. "Ah, another study."

Sherman pushed a hand through his shaggy, rather beautiful brown hair. He adjusted his shirt, smoothed out a wrinkle. "Yeah, a new one down at Stanford."

"The pay good?" I asked to be polite.

Sherman had made the condition his crusade. He wrote letters—to politicians, drug companies, universities, research centers—laying out the case for more funding, more awareness, more everything. He truly believed something could be done. "The pay?" he said. "Better than usual. And the guy running it worked with your Dr. Bell."

"No kidding." Dr. Bell, now that was some recommendation. "Well, wish I could. I'm just so busy right now."

"Yeah, wasn't sure you were going to show today."

Sometimes I thought I came for a little boost in self-esteem. Comparing my own life to theirs made me feel better, made me feel like I actually had some control. But, really, these people were my weird little family. Not even Brook, not even my mother knew what it was to live with the condition. I often hated the group wallowing, the automatic sympathy. But maybe I needed to share in a little blind, dumb hope, too.

"Things have been crazy lately," I said lamely. "Work and everything."

"You don't let it affect your career. We all admire that." We started stacking desks. "And thanks for your contribution today," Sherman said, an uncharacteristic wrinkle of sarcasm in his voice.

"I was moved by Bill's experience, and I wanted to—"

"You know"—Sherman cut me off, *very* unlike him—"you could be an inspiration to them. The way you hold it all together on your own. They all think you know the secret or something." He stood for a moment, letting his head bob. A desk started to slip from his fingers. I grabbed it. "Sorry," he said, "it's just, watching you disappear into your phone in the middle of a meeting . . ."

"The lab," I lied, "they find me wherever I go."

"You know what you should do? Get yourself a pet. Get your mind off work. Make you relax a little, think about another life." A reasonable enough suggestion, but I bridled at the hint of scolding in it. "I've got a cat," Sherman offered. "A Sphynx. Prince Hairy. He has FAS, feline aging syndrome. He ages at three times the normal rate. He looks like a purse of bones, and he can't eat a thing except tuna from the blender."

Of course, the wounded caring for the wounded. "Sounds like a lot of work."

"Are you kidding? He takes care of me."

We finished stacking the desks and stood there, at a loss for what else to say.

"Anything new with the site?" I asked, pointing at Sherman's wrist.

He wore a red rubberized bracelet with the URL of the website he ran. A lot of the group wore them. If they had a bad episode out in public, went down and weren't getting up, then hopefully someone would check the bracelet and look up the condition. I kept a card in my wallet but otherwise didn't go around advertising my frailty.

"You haven't been visiting the forums?" Sherman said.

The discussions and testimonials on the site were just too depressing. You had to consider that those who made it to group were well enough to actually leave the house. We all tended to be homebodies, but a lot of people with the condition were virtual shut-ins, even worse than Sherman. Too much out in the world to startle, upset, sadden, disgust, or thrill them to risk just traipsing outside on a sunny day or a cheerful whim.

"I'd get too obsessive. I can't think about the disease every hour of the day."

Disease. Sherman didn't like it when anyone called it that. But now he just sighed and nodded his head. Or maybe bobbed it. It was hard to tell the difference.

MY CAR SERVICE was waiting outside. As we wound back down to the Mission, the late afternoon sun slanted gauzily over the candy-floss Victorians, and the golden dome of City Hall shone like a crown. It was one of those glorious days that pop up even midwinter in California: bedheaded couples in hoodies and canvas sneakers reclining in the park, the concerned faces of joggers striving through the gathering twilight, everything burnished and glowing. "Us midwesterners have a hard time adjusting to paradise," Brook warned me before I moved out here. But I'd loved this tiny motherboard of a city immediately. Three years ago, the entire economy collapsed, but in San Francisco everything just kept going up. On the streets, there would be fewer and fewer addicts and lunatics, more and more kids with perfect haircuts and four-thousand-dollar bikes. Fewer rehab clinics and community centers, more half-occupied, investor-friendly, live/work lofts. Fewer mad outbursts and fevered rants, more calm luxury and detached bemusement. Less abject despair, more bored anxiety. Besides an earthquake, you almost always knew what was coming here—sunny, seventy degrees, seven days a week, and a new brunch place every month. Throw in some decent public transport, and San Francisco was the perfect place for a headbobber—this one anyway—to survive.

As the Panhandle flitted by, I checked my phone. No messages, just the one I'd been typing to Brook. *I mean Christ I WANT to but really . . .* I deleted it, typed instead: *Darn have to work late Thursday thanks anyway have fun say hi to the DJs have fun for me.*

FIVE

Alarm, coffee, shower, oatmeal. Blouse, blazer, a pair of low-heel boots—I needed to feel even taller walking out the door on a Monday. I turned onto Mission, and there he was, the torso. This time, he only froze me in my tracks. He tapped himself forward with his wheelchair's joystick. "Hey, pretty girl, got a twenty for me?"

"Twenty bucks?" I got out. "That's am-bitious."

"It's for surgery. I need some surgery."

I couldn't help sweeping my eyes over him: tiny hands and feet, withered narrow waist, sunken chest, greasy blond hair drooping in his eyes—if I looked him in the eyes, it was maybe a little easier. "How far is a twenty getting you for surgery?"

"Twenty bucks closer than I am now."

I got a glimpse of the track marks just above his waxy white elbows. "I don't know, that a sound investment?"

He grinned wolfishly. "Safer than stocks these days."

I fumbled in my purse, managed to dig out a five, bent

over carefully, dropped it in his cup, and somehow—maybe the release from guilt—this unlocked my legs. "Call me Jeff," he said. "For next time you make a deposit in my fund."

I continued on, lurching only a little. On the next block, a neon sign for a body shop flickered out of the fog. Its P was fizzling out. ERFECT DETAILING. My bonus curse: to only notice the flawed and the damaged.

BART to Caltrain to the company shuttle. We made our circuit of MedEval's campus, rolling greens and bucolic ponds, before arriving at my lab, concrete and razor wire. Hidalgo, one of my technicians, was outside on a smoke break. He wore a black and orange Giants cap and chunky red headphones, his head slowly nodding to blaring heavy metal. As I reached for my ID to swipe in, he looked up, quickly dropped his cigarette, and ground it out. I caught a whiff. Shit, pot. I didn't blame him—whatever got him through another day. Still, if anyone else caught him . . .

"You good to clean out the pens this morning?"

"Yeah, I'm good."

I hesitated. "Hidalgo, you look pretty beat." I knew he had a two-year-old daughter and that she was sick, something about her not being able to swallow, and that he worked a second job to pay for all her doctors. But what exactly was wrong, the finer details of his worries, I didn't pry into. His privacy, my insulation. "Listen," I said cautiously. "I'll get Staci to do the pens."

"Nah, I'm cool."

I swiped inside, went past the bio-waste bins, through the second and third security doors, and into the lab and its familiar dull, high-pitched yipping. Staci, my other tech, waved from behind the glass and mimed putting her latex-gloved fingers in her ears. Pin, my veterinary surgeon, was at her desk, earbuds in, hunched over a stack of charts. Byron, my researcher and failed PhD, looked up, squinted like he was trying to squeeze me out of existence. "What do we have today?" I asked him, like every other Monday. "Fancy coffee or shitty coffee?"

"I believe it's 'shitty.' But you could send Hidalgo out."

"Hidalgo's on break." One dog was barking full-tilt, and it was rattling my skull. "And he has actual work to do."

"Know what they'd give that dog where Pin's from?" Byron said, with what he thought of as irascible mischief. "A nice marinade."

"Christ." It was all part of the tiresome script, but I couldn't help an eye-flutter. "At least your jokes never get any better."

I went over to the scrub station, washed up, pulled on a white Tyvek clean suit, and stepped into the air shower. Tiny jets buffeted me. They weren't cold, but I felt iced over, imprisoned. *Cattails, willows, cattails, willows.* Finally, the inner door sighed open.

The pens gave off a meaty, damp smell overlaid with bleachy anti-flea shampoo. Yips and barks volleyed around the room. As I went down the aisles, inspecting, some dogs perked up, poked their noses through the wire, sniffed eagerly at me. Some were busy gnawing on bones, squeaking toys. Some drowsed in their beds. A few, new arrivals, shivered with fear or confusion. God, what we asked of these dogs. Sometimes I couldn't even . . . I came to a little salt-and-pepper terrier barking his head off, Staci trying to quiet him.

"Good boy, Oscar. Come on, boy. Shush now." She brought out the treats. "It's not like I've been stuffing him," she said. "He's just freaking."

I flipped through the dog's folder. I didn't prohibit my team from naming them. I didn't encourage it either. The scheduling page said Pin was implanting R39466 with one of the new pacemakers the next day.

"Oscar, quiet now," Staci said desperately. "Shhhhhh."

I saw that the door to the operating room was open and went over and shut it. Oscar stopped barking.

"How does he know?" Staci said. "He only got here last Thursday. We haven't even done a surgery yet. Maybe he smelled something he didn't like in there? Or the other dogs were talking." Staci smiled bravely, as if someone had just broken her heart. The girl wore her feelings like bangles; they glinted and jangled. MedEval had a program that subsidized vet school for lab techs after two years on the job. I shouldn't have hired Staci, but in the interview she'd kept on about "her dream," and I didn't want to be the one to trample it.

"Don't overuse the treats," I told her now and headed back to the air shower.

"Sorry, Daphne," Staci called out, "could you take a quick look at Biscuit?"

I let her lead me over to his pen. A medium, tan-and-white beagle, not unlike half of the other dogs bred for lab use. He refused to eat wet food, only biscuits, the reason the techs had given him his name. But now he wasn't eating biscuits either.

He lay on his stomach, muzzle on his forelegs, ears over paws. I could just see the shaved strip of fur and zigzag of stitches where his access tube poked out. He was a defibrillator dog. Once a week, we induced cardiac arrest and used the device to start his heart again—what the ICDs were built for, after all. I tapped lightly on Biscuit's cage. He slowly opened his eyes, peered up at me with what seemed enormous effort.

"He looks like he's frowning," Staci said.

"Dogs don't frown or smile. Eyes, ears, that's their body language."

"I know. He's just not happy about his ICD. He might be allergic. We could give him a coated device. Or maybe it's an infection."

We cared for the dogs, tried to make their lives comfortable and meaningful. It was just that, after the first few rounds, some withered. It might have been better for the team, better for the dogs, to have sacrificed Biscuit then. But Staci nudged me, her smile quivering. "I can recheck all the settings," she said, "see if it's calibrated?"

"All right, fine. Run another check and give Byron the output."

When she turned back to the other dogs, I slipped Biscuit

a couple of treats. He sniffed one cautiously and slowly, very slowly, began to eat.

At my desk, I tried to find a rhythm, clicking between the compiler, the debugger, and email. The higher-ups were always emailing me about the budget. It was the reason, I understood, they'd brought me over from hardware in the first place—my "discipline." I'd done my bachelor's in com-sci, my master's in electrical engineering, and even in school my peers considered me aloof and analytical. Getting hit on by every awkward boy certainly helps that. But I found cod-ing and hardware—refining a design, tightening thresholds, tolerances—gratifying, soothing. Medical devices weren't like an iPod or a phone, filled with old, junk code, dispos-able. They had to be built and programmed to last twenty years on one battery and never once crash—the elegance, the purity of a well-made device. MedEval circulated a newsletter each month with testimonials from heart patients surviving because of our work. I still read it front to back.

When the higher-ups asked me to run the lab, they'd intimated it'd only be for a year or two and then they'd be grooming me for upper management. The position came with a substantial pay bump; I'd been able to buy my apart-ment. And, I don't know, on some level I'd thought it might be good practice. If I could train myself, intellectually, to see ten beagles hanging in the slings that calm them pre-surgery and respond as if it were merely routine, then maybe nothing out in the wide world could fell me either. But almost three years had gone by, without a murmur of promotion out of here, and I still took a long walk whenever Pin and Staci were prepping for implants.

An alert sounded on my computer. The pen I'd been twiddling between my fingers dropped to the desk. *Daph, how are you today?* read the chat window.

Fine good just another Monday

But, honey, really, how are you today?

Why what's today I'm fine really what's up?

Dad's birthday. He would've been sixty. Hit me harder than I thought it would.

~~Mom please it's been twenty-four years~~ Before I hit ENTER, I deleted this and typed instead: *Thinking of you hoping everything's all right with you today*

Remember the year we went to La Petit Maison? He let you blow out the candles on his cake and you singed your hair. God, the smell! They almost cleared the restaurant.

~~Don't remember that I was only five what were we even doing at a nice restaurant?~~ *Sorry I forgot would've called but so swamped right now*

You used to mark these dates in your diary. Maybe you were too conscientious about it actually.

Haven't kept diary in a decade at least

Why not try it again? Could be a healthy release for you?

~~Dear Diary remember when my mother stole you to spy on me?~~

That was when I was sixteen, in the months after my diagnosis, when I was first beginning "treatment." Dr. Bell had suggested I keep the diary, though he saw it more of a record book, a ledger, raw data for his research: my symptoms, my thoughts, my feelings, my feelings about my feelings, my thoughts about my feelings about my feelings . . . Of course my mother couldn't resist.

Here I am, thinking about your dad again. Arcadia isn't paying me to mope around all day!

No problem mom I'm here listening real busy but I'm here

I'd learned to step carefully around her grief. At twenty-nine, I was the age she was when she lost him. She raised me alone, then had to share the nightmare of my peculiar vulnerability. For my mother, strength had become reinforcing yourself for the worst yet to come. My leaving home for college and then San Francisco knocked the tremble back into her stoicism. Even now, the little we talked on the phone, I could hear a stifled sob.

We signed off. She said stay safe, I said of course and love you. I closed the chat, tried to concentrate again. But my rhythm was in tatters. "Going to lunch," I told Byron. "This data is still compiling. Log me out when it's done?"

He squinted at me, and I saw the contempt—that he should have to work under a woman, a young woman no less—he thought he hid behind that pinched look. And the disappointment. He'd been with MedEval thirteen years to my five; they perpetually passed him over to run the lab. "As long as I get to read your voluminous personal correspondence," he said.

"You know what?" I mumbled, my tongue suddenly thick.

Smoke, cattails, smoke— Fuck it, I was lucky the words came out garbled. "Tru-ly, scr-ew you . . ."

"I'm sorry," Byron said, feigning confusion, "I don't think I caught that."

Since he was in charge on the rare occasions I was out sick, the execs had made me tell Byron about the condition. He hadn't told anyone else on the team, but he held his discretion over me like a guillotine about to drop. At least he never bothered to proffer his sympathy. He took too much pleasure in never letting me off the hook.

SIX

EVERY EVENING FOR THE REST OF THE WEEK—THE lab quiet, dogs prepped for the night-shift techs—I went to the company gym and climbed and climbed stairs. On Friday, both the Caltrain and BART were jammed, but my exhausted thoughts stayed blurred, diffuse. At Balboa Park, a woman got on, crying into her phone. "The repo man come, took our things. My boys had to watch it all. They took they Xboxes and they DVDs. They took everything!" The other passengers stood stiffly, trying not to listen. I cranked my white noise, thought about my night: pajamas and slippers, grilled branzino and polenta, a half bottle of Riesling. The BART braked into 16th Street. I patiently pushed my way out onto the platform—and found myself in the middle of another crowd, all churning confusion and shouting, and my mind now scrambling to sieve it all out:

Protestors, kids mostly, in their early twenties, canvas

backpacks, Baja hoodies; a handful of middle-aged people in Patagonia zip pants and bucket hats, picket signs aloft; some tired-looking Filipino women in cleaning smocks just waiting for the train; journalists snapping photos, swiveling TV cameras; "Cops, pigs, murderers!"—chants echoing off the arched ceiling—"Cops, pigs, murderers!" Among the crowd, white masks, white masks with black slashes for features, gaunt, sinister, black-mustached faces from every direction; the commuters jostling to break out, the chants growing louder, a spastic, muscular pulse of disorder cannonading around the low tunnel, I tasted fear, rough, metallic, like licking a pipe, my skull already buzzing, I reached for the businessman next to me, tried to hang on to him, he brushed me off with an indignant grunt—*white smoke, picnic tables, white*—protestors holding the train doors open, stopping it from leaving the station, BART employees in yellow vests trying to shunt everyone upstairs, someone barking through a megaphone, "No justice, no peace, disband the BART police!" I tried to make for the escalator, my legs weak, the crowd pushing me back, thinking I heard someone calling my name, "Daphne! Hey!" concentrating on *smoke, the river, the willows*, the train driver let out a deafening blast of his horn, the buzzing leaping up, bursting out of my skull, shooting down my spine, I started melting—jaw, neck, shoulders, arms, knees—only the tight-packed bodies holding me up, on the brink of puddling, and at the core of my panic, once again, the impulse to let go, just let it happen already, let them trample all over—

"Daphne!" A hand reached out, grabbed my shoulder. I

tried to shrug it off. Strangers mauling me when it's happening just makes it worse. But then his face appeared before my fluttering eyes. His eyes close to mine, full of concern and astonishment. "It *is* you! Hey, you okay?!"

"P-lease," I said. "Get me . . . out of . . ."

I don't know if he understood, but he got an arm under mine. We made it through the turnstiles, to the escalator. "Keep going," I mumbled. Aboveground, the plaza was boiling with people. I didn't trust myself to get free of them. "Re-mem-ber where I . . . ?"

He got me there, got me home. Maybe I would've been able to make it by myself. Then again, maybe I would've taken a header into the sidewalk. By the time we got to the Grove, I had my body back. But I kept a cautious hand on him.

"Um, should I help you to your apartment?" Ollie said.

"Fourth floor. Please."

Once we got through my door, I made a dash for the couch, dropped onto it. My apartment, its familiarity, wrapped around me like an old, soft quilt. Ollie stood on the threshold, glancing around. "When I saw you . . ." He shuffled in place, unsure of himself. "I wasn't sure if you needed, if you were maybe having a—"

"Come in," I said, more composed now. He looked down at his work boots. "Don't worry, I'm not one of those . . . Actually, yeah, if you could." He padded into the apartment in white socks, the right one with a hole in it. "What were you doing down there?" I said. "Taking the train, or raising hell?"

"You didn't hear? The transit cops shot another guy, some homeless guy they thought had a knife or something. Fucking murderers."

"Maybe they were just defending themselves."

"You shoot a guy three times point-blank for *maybe* having a knife?"

"Were you in one of those masks?"

"Hell no. If they want to shoot me, they'll have to look me in the eye." He was glancing around again: my repro Noguchi table, the vintage Knoll sofa a guy had nearly strangled me over at a Laurel Heights estate sale, the blue-cheese marble countertops I spent half my life trying not to scratch. "Wow, this place should be in a magazine or something."

"Tell that to those smug pricks at Interior Life. Shit, you must have to know someone there."

"Huh?"

"How about a glass of Riesling?"

"Um, if you want," he said. "Or I could go?"

"In the fridge, right side. Corkscrew's in the first drawer. Sorry, I'm going to hang out here on the couch." Whenever I brush up against a bad episode, I'm exhausted afterward. Worse, all my built-up trust in myself, my ability to manage the condition, drains away, too. Maybe that's the cruelest part of it; you're never comfortable in your body, never fully insulated.

Ollie brought over two glasses of wine. I had to gesture for him to sit. He fit himself awkwardly into the opposite corner of the couch. Though I was always preparing the apartment to be admired, it was odd to actually have company. I smelled him again, a whiff of salt breeze or dried sweat. And that deeper, mysterious thing, too, like an echo across a subterranean lake. "Branzino," I said. "You like branzino?"

He looked, understandably, puzzled. "Sure you want me to stay?"

"The wrong number, that was rude of me."

"To be honest, I thought it was about a fifty-fifty."

"I should thank you. You are hungry, right?"

"What happened down there? Was it a seizure?"

"Polenta and white asparagus on the side? Any food allergies?"

"Sorry, I don't mean to intrude, but—"

"Food first," I begged. "Please."

As I cooked, we creaked our way through forty minutes of conversation: Muni delays, the hierarchy of burrito joints in the Mission. Twice he brought up the protests that had just begun in Wisconsin, but I changed subjects, asked about him. He worked in construction, he said, whenever he could get on a job, filled in the gaps fixing up old radios and gramophones and selling them to antiques dealers. He'd grown up on a communal farm way up in Trinity County. There'd been forty other families, and he'd torn around the fields and the looms and the wellness center with the other kids, playing hide-and-seek and freeze tag. He'd gone to a high school that started each morning with ujjayi breathing, then did two years at UC Santa Cruz before dropping out to spend the next five years roaming, Oregon, Washington State, and BC, reading philosophy and building grow houses, before finally moving down to the city and going semi-legit. "I guess I've met all kinds of people," he said, and I didn't know if it was a point of pride or a cue to me to divulge whatever kind I was. As I pan-seared the polenta, I found myself distracted by his large, callused hands wrapped around the dainty wineglass. The oil popped out of the pan, and we both jumped back like I'd set off a firecracker.

"Okay," I said, "let's eat!" Ollie took dainty bites, as if at a formal event. I ate quickly, ravenous. He helped clear the table. We stood in the kitchen, close together. The central air ticked on, brushing my steadily warming cheeks. The colors in the room deepened. I gulped my wine and tasted the minerals of the earth the grapes had grown in. We moved to the couch. I scrunched against the arm. He was looking at me with unmistakable intent. Very likely I was doing the same. I went for my remotes. The TV played some cop show, a woman being zipped into a body bag, a too resonant image.

"I wonder if they do auditions for corpses," Ollie ventured. " 'What's my motivation?' 'Okay, so you're dead . . .' "

I smiled tightly, turned off the TV, took another gulp of wine, swallowed hard.

"You okay?" He radiated concern, his special talent.

"You're probably a great guy."

"You say that like it's a crying shame."

"If you weren't, this would maybe be easier."

"I'm interested in you. I guess that's obvious." He blushed to say this. "But, yeah, I've been feeling you stressing since dinner. Not saying you have to talk about it . . ."

"What, dinner? Quite a feat. I think we broke the land speed record for branzino."

I blushed, too, my cheeks tingling pleasurably, menacingly. The last guy I met—online, where the people-shopping is less fraught—was handsome in a nondescript, collegiate way, though he wore a beard that made him look like the evil twin of himself. After four very polite dates, I let him make out with me in the back room of Skylark, propped myself in the corner, as rigid as a telephone pole. He tasted awful to me, like body spray and regret. There wasn't much danger of even a headbob; I was more embarrassed than anything. After thirty excruciating minutes, I got in a cab and never spoke to him again. A week later, he sent me drunken texts calling me "ice queen" and other unimaginative things. That was almost a year ago.

"I'm up for kissing again," I said. "Just don't spring anything on me."

"Want me to do a countdown or something?" Ollie said.

"Actually, that would be kind of perfect."

"Okay, then—three, two, one . . ."

My eyes were closed, but I somehow found his mouth. Mine was constricted in a half-grimace, half-grin. We swiveled our heads this way and that, trying to find the right choreography around noses. My kisses grew more forceful, less precise; I think I kissed him on his eye and, somehow, his teeth. "Oops," he said but didn't stop. My fear and pleasure mounted together, but I kept going, too. I felt myself high up, teetering on my soaring feelings, a frightened diving horse, about to take the plunge.

SEVEN

To look back on it from the cynical reaches of adulthood, it seems impossible. But there I am, beaming out of every school photo. The hairstyles change—perms, crimps, middle parts, clips everywhere—and just before high school I start trying unfortunate things with turtlenecks and plaid. But, other than being taller than a lot of the boys, I hadn't developed quickly enough to draw any special attention. That was Brook's burden. To everyone in the new, daunting hallways of Arcadia High, I appeared happy and, for a time, aggressively normal.

In classes, I mostly stayed quiet and wrote papers on which teachers scribbled "insightful" and "Tell me more!" but which, thank God, they never read aloud. Though I'd started to shy away from my late-night Hardy, I still loved English. I thought I might study abroad, imagined myself wandering the cobbled streets of some Casterbridge-like village, lingering in old churches with stained-glass sunlight dappling my face, falling calmly asleep at night, a leather-bound edition of *Tess* or *Jude* on my chest, far, far away from the girl who lay tensed up in bed, listening for her mother's crying, waiting for the tingling to come.

It hadn't gone away. Worse, it'd started to creep further into my life. The slammed lockers or popped lunch sacks—surprise, that blunt force emotion—were already bad enough. Once, Brook rushed up behind me in the hallway and clapped me on the butt—"Yo, sweet cheeks!"—and my chemistry book slipped out of my hands, shooting worksheets all across the floor. In the chaos between classes, no one much noticed, and Brook picked everything up while I just stood there. Maybe she thought I was pissed at her idea of a fond prank. Well, yes, that, too. But from that day I started carrying all my stuff in my backpack.

One afternoon in Mr. Jukes's health class, Kyle Magolski, who always sat diagonally from me, started snoring. He was a junior repeating a freshman class, and Mr. Jukes had pretty much given up on him. But that week was sex ed week, when Mr. Jukes put out his "Questions about Intimacy?" jar, an old commercial-size tub of mayonnaise wrapped in construction paper, a slot cut in the lid.

The way Mr. Jukes used the word—intimacy—it sounded like some uncomfortable, embarrassing disease. "When you *have* intimacy," he'd say, "always, always be careful." I was aware that Brook had been stricken, five or six times even, though she was oddly quiet on the subject. Me, I'd never even had a boyfriend. I'd kissed a few middle school boys, and one tried to fumble off my bra playing

Seven Minutes in Heaven at Brook's and later apologized by buying me a Dr. Pepper. Otherwise my Questions about Intimacy had largely gone unaddressed. As for asking Jukes, with his male-pattern-bald ponytail, Teva sandals, and moose socks, most of us would've paraded naked through study hall before dropping an honest question in that jar.

Which meant that, at the beginning of class, he reached in and pulled out the only question, put there, eternally, by Kyle Magolski: "What is 69?" Jukes read it aloud, his disgust at the stunt, three years and counting, unmistakable. But he so wanted his mayonnaise/question jar to be taken seriously that he answered anyway.

"Sixty-nine," he began, "is a kind of oral sex. Simultaneous oral sex." He drew a 6 and a 9 on the board as geysers of laughter erupted around the room. I let out a little cough-laugh myself, but, actually, I hadn't known what it meant. Boys shouted it in pep rallies—"Let's go, number sixty-nine!"—but I'd vaguely thought it had to do with 1969, the Summer of Love, etc. "Both partners give and receive pleasure—the vagina, the penis, or the anus," Jukes said to additional hilarity. "But, everyone, be careful. Having this kind of intimacy can lead to STDs, too. Gonorrhea, herpes, and, well, you get the picture."

Question time over, he pushed on with the regular lesson, the implantation of the zygote. I was still wondering how exactly you went from unhooked bra to sixty-nine. Would it feel good? Had Brook ever tried it? Why did she and I never seem to talk about that kind of stuff? Staring at those two numbers nestled luridly together on the board, I was so lost in my thoughts I didn't hear Kyle Magolski slip into his strangely peaceable snoring.

Nor did I notice when Mr. Jukes, without pausing in his lecture, raised his fat teacher's copy of *The Human Body: A User's Manual* above his head. As it smacked down on the floor, Kyle Magolski shot straight up in his seat, his shoulders jerking like a marionette's. But as he woke suddenly up, I seemed suddenly to fall asleep. Or not sleep exactly. I slumped in my desk, my pencil rolled to the floor, my eyes fluttered closed. The tingling lasted longer this time, fourteen or fifteen endless seconds. It grew more intense, like when I was little, learning to swim in the river and I dove deep, the pressure in my head climbing to a whine. I could hear the other kids whispering around me and felt my cheeks burning. I tried to sit up straight. I tried—nothing was happening. I couldn't get my legs or my hands under me to push myself back up. I couldn't even stiffen my back to stop from sliding further down. I felt somehow sucked out of my body, caught in an undertow, kicking and flailing, powerless to get back to the surface.

Then the tingling faded. My eyes fluttered open. Mr. Jukes stood before me, a skeptical, disappointed expression on his face. Because my dad was dead, a lot of the teachers at Arcadia were "rooting for me." I sat up, blinked out of a thicket of worry and shame, the 6 and 9 flitting in and out of view. A few kids tittered. But I was lucky. They really thought I was asleep. And sleeping in a blow-off class might have been considered cool. So I'd gotten away with it. But whatever *it* was terrified me.

FOR REASONS STILL FUZZY to medicine—it's thought, it's fucking thought—my immune system was blasting away at receptors in that mysterious part of the brain where muscle control, emotion, and sleep intersect. Puberty is the common trigger for this catastrophe, and I was dead in the center of that lovely time. Here, then, was another plausible explanation: my period. But the few times I ventured to ask other girls, Brook included, if they'd ever felt anything like my tingling or buzzing, they just shrugged. "Headaches? Sometimes. Who doesn't?" So I shut up about it.

But it made me wary. I began to dread the boys who were always marauding down the hall and, accidentally or not, bumping into girls like me. I flinched in anticipation, started to pull into myself, bracing for the next time it came, even if I could never seem to predict it. I learned to act. If I drooped when someone told a joke, I'd make it seem like I was hanging my head in weary resignation at how dumb it was. With my fluttering eyes, boys always thought I was flirting, though I did my best to make it seem like exasperation. When my face went slack, I'd try to turn it into the dead-eyed, sarcastic expression Brook had recently, witheringly developed. We like to think our personalities are something we mold and hone. We think we build our own fates. But, no, we grow like a tree does when it finds itself pushing against a boulder or a street sign or the hulk of a blasted building; we bend and warp ourselves to the shape of the impediment.

THAT WINTER I MADE varsity volleyball. Through most of middle school, I'd been a gangly mess on the court. Then, in eighth grade, I suddenly became agile and confident. I moved over to middle hitter, grew consistent, even fearsome, with my spikes. And on defense, I was unflinching, reckless. I'd dive for anything.

At the beginning of the season, Coach handed out T-shirts to all the freshmen on the team. "Pain," they read, "Is Just *Weakness* Leaving the Body." If I kept my head down and drove myself hard, I told myself, I could banish this strange thing that had crept over me. Every time Coach shouted, "Hundred and ten percent, ladies!" I'd bite my lip, another squat, another shuttle run, another push-up. I thought I could feel my Weakness departing, slinking off, moving on to some other, more accommodating host.

Varsity volleyball, because we'd been to state nine years in a row, packed the gym. Matches were deafening: the pep band blaring, the cheering squad screaming, "Be aggressive! B-E aggressive!" I bounced on the balls of my feet on the sideline. Poets and artists and musicians are supposed to be our elected conduits of feeling, the ones overwhelmed and transported on our behalves. But sport sets off riots, makes grown men weep in public. And that's just the spectators. The athlete gets it all undiluted and either lets it drive her into frenzy or labors to stay strategically, rigidly sober. For me, the latter was never an option. Stepping onto that court was a pure, liquid high. I glowed with the energy it fed me.

But once we made it to the quarterfinals, the crowds grew louder, more chaotic. The glow smoldered on the edge of the buzzing in my skull. I'd feel the hesitation creep in during warm-up, that tinge of reluctance when I took a first step, when I swung my body up into a spike or a block. Then, when we came to our match against Thessaly Union, some idiot had snuck an air horn in and kept letting off abrupt, shattering blasts in the middle of points. My nerves were jangling like mandolin strings.

In the first game, I was flat-footed, just barely getting under my sets. "Daphne," Coach called out, "look alive!" Briefly I redeemed myself with a tricky little dink that landed right at the feet of Thessaly's front line. The crowd thundered their feet on the bleachers, the energy so frenzied that, somehow, it made me even more sluggish.

In the second game, we were up 22–20, three points from taking the match. The bleachers shook to "We Will Rock You." Then that idiot started blasting his air horn again. My skull began to fizz. Not now, I thought, please, please. The gym fluttered in and out of view. I'd never felt more electric. But I could hardly keep my eyes open.

Coach called a time-out, mercifully. "Irvine, you okay? You need something? Drink? Snack?"

"Don't know." Sweat and confusion were pouring down my face. "Ga-tor-ade?"

"Good, chug some. And get the hell back in the game."

I tried to forget the crowd, ignore the buzzing. But Thessaly pulled to within a point. Their hitter put an off-speed at me, thinking I was just a rookie and would fall for it. I went to the net, visualized my next step, saw myself bending into the squat I'd grown so strong in, launching straight up for the block. Just then, a cold pulse went through me. The tingling flashed down to my toes. My whole body relaxed, like that soul-sighing moment, as a kid, when you finally let yourself pee your pants. And instead of going up for the block, I stayed rooted in place, arms drooped moronically at my sides, like I'd just given up. Thessaly's drive landed just inside the right sideline. "Irvine!" Coach screamed. "What are you *doing* out there?"

He benched me for the rest of the match. We won. Afterward, he pulled me aside, wanted to know if I had anything hurting, if I'd pulled or sprained anything. He told me to check in with the doctor, maybe look into some PT. I said I was fine, insisted on it several times. He wasn't convinced. Neither was I.

Maybe if I'd learned earlier to quarantine myself from other people's emotion, I could've gone on playing. Or I could've pursued the individual sports, the meditative, self-denying ones. My dad had been a champion swimmer at Arcadia, or there was cross-country or track and field. Back in the '80s, there'd been a pole-vaulter with the condition. When he learned he'd made the Olympic team, he was so overcome he flopped over right on the track. In a way, it must have been a relief when, after all of that discipline, he could let himself just tumble down.

But I didn't learn early enough how to control the current in me. When Coach sat me out in our next match, I pretended to be heartbroken. As I did when we lost, ending our chance at a tenth straight trip to state. But, really, I was grateful. I was growing warped, deformed. Anything that caused the buzzing I would try now to simply avoid. Slowly, my branches and trunk began to twist and bind around the condition. And in all of the obscuring foliage, the smiling girl in those yearbook photos began to disappear.

EIGHT

Coming down Haight Street the Saturday after our shambolic make-out at my apartment, I half-hoped Ollie hadn't come.

There on the couch, my jaw had sagged all the way, leaving him to press his tongue into my gaping mouth. "*Ahhhg-ggh*," he'd said, like a patient at the dentist. He'd pulled back, narrowed his eyes. "This is what happened last time, right? After the bar?"

"May-be this is just how they kiss back in In-di-ana."

"Look, you can tell me. I'm not going to jump out the window."

"No, you're too nice for that. You'll just go running out the door." I'd let out a deep breath and scooched away on the couch. "You'd better have another glass of wine. It takes a minute."

I'd educated him, given him the speech, the ancient speech. I even used Dr. Bell's puppet metaphor. When I finished, he was silent. I was silent. An annihilating silence floated in the room. "So, there's baggage here," I finally prompted. "A fucking 747's worth."

He'd asked questions, made an effort. I regaled him with anecdotes, told him about back in the dorms in Bloomington, my suitemates and I drinking berry-flavored beer, gossiping, carrying on. I had this little routine: I put a pillow on the table, and every time I cracked up, *thump*, my forehead went down on the pillow. Of course, everyone laughed even harder, me included, so I just kept thumping down, again and again, while the laughter rained all around me.

"That sounds tough," Ollie had said, his face long. "And complicated."

"No, it's pretty simple. I feel something small, I make funny faces. Something big, I fall down."

He'd squeaked out a sad grin—"Sorry, I can tell you don't like being interrogated"—checked his watch, and apologized: He really had to go, an early wake-up to get on a job. He'd wanted to make weekend plans, a walk in Golden Gate Park. "Sure," I said, "I'll text you. I'll even use my real number this time." But he'd insisted on just meeting there, without any devices intervening. He'd kissed me good-bye on the cheek, like a boy with his spinster aunt. Then he was out the door.

Now, approaching the two stone pillars at the entrance to the park, I tried to prepare for either eventuality. The hollow, empty sag of disappointment—he wasn't there. Or the choking tautness of anticipation, expanding possibility, and desire—he was. Maybe, if I didn't look too hard,

I would simply miss him. But there he was, next to a knot of street kids and their dogs. He spotted me, waved, and I swallowed hard.

Itemize his face: soft, patchy beard; two birthmarks, one on chin, one partly covered by sideburns; delicate cheekbones, smooth, boyish even; thin, pale, slightly chapped lips; wide-winged nose; flaring, almost puckish ears; thick but not overbearing eyebrows; surprisingly long lashes; and his eyes, smoke-colored, reticent, curious, startling . . . Look at anyone's face close enough, and the parts make no sense. Still, the little muscle in the center of my clavicle clenched tighter—I almost launched into a coughing fit as he came near. But that wasn't the problem. The problem was that once I started cataloging, I couldn't stop. My thoughts raced and smeared together:

The easy way he drew me into a hug, "There you are!" his scent weaving with pot smoke from the nearby kids, street dogs with bandanas around their necks, the lofty cypress trees above us feathering the breeze, Ollie tipping back his head, sighing, "Middle of February, we get days like this?" laying it on a little thick, me smiling at him, a tight smile that wanted to broaden, seeing him seeing me in my hiking shorts/stair-climbing shoes/hoodie, like I was ready to help someone move, we passed under Lincoln Ave, and God I loved the park, the city disappeared, the shaggy curve of Hippie Hill, everyone so glad and easy, but distant, just distant enough, laughter and beers cracking open, the deep pulse of a drum circle rising and falling on the breeze, dogs barking, running down tennis balls, happy free dogs, Ollie bending to unlace his work boots, a slightly too long glance at his ass, stuffing his socks into the boots, slinging them over his shoulder, "It's necessary to get some grass between your toes now and then," me needing to make a crack about it, "You'd get a fucking hypodermic in my neighborhood," trying to recover, asking him about the radios he fixed up, telling him I had an engineering degree, "I like problems I can solve," him answering that he just liked to fiddle, liked poking around inside things, laughing, "Sorry, that sounded like a bad come-on, maybe I've been in construction too long," describing the Outer Sunset dives where he drank with his crew, illegal Irish guys mostly, they got up on their stools, unhitched their tool belts, dropped them right on the floor, "No women for miles, me lurking down in your hood is a luxury," and I said, "So you put your name on the chalk-board and wait for some little thing to rack up a game," "Nah, I wait for the tall, leggy ones, ah, shit, sorry . . ." Ollie scratching his head, frustrated, damn it, was I back-footing him into these lines? him confessing he was nervous, me confessing, "Me, too," wanting to say, Our bodies already recognize each other, even if we don't know how to talk yet, instead saying, "What a gorgeous day," so inane, but truly it was, fine-grain California light burnishing everything, the smell of pine and eucalyptus and this man walking next to me, and I thought, Enjoy this, just enjoy this right now, not too much but also not too little, and I said, "I'm enjoying this"—just this could be enough—and he said, "Me, too," and I heard a bird way up somewhere echoing, "Me, too, me, too," everything ringing at the precise same note, sometimes feeling is just a resonance, a pitch too high and pure to be heard, and then I took my own shoes off, both of us laughing about it, just enough, grass slippery waxy sweet between my toes, letting myself laugh a little more as he told stories about the Irish guys, not too much not too little, control it, control it, but Christ did I have to, couldn't I just—we came to Stow Lake, pretty little pond pretty water grasses lilies Japanese bridges, pretty couples out in paddleboats, giggling their way around, sunlight diamonding on the water, grasses tipping back and forth, eerie, too much like *the cattails, the willows, the river sparkling in the noon light*, or maybe the envy I tasted seeing those happy heedless couples was just too bitter, either way my side knotting up—why? I couldn't say, only I needed to get away and Ollie didn't protest, just a curious glance at me, we kept going, a veil of fog slipping over the park, the salty, steely ocean from twenty blocks away, suddenly I shivered and shivered, Ollie offered his jacket, and I said, "A chilly day in paradise doesn't bother a midwesterner like me," shivering inside, we came to another pond, middle-aged men sailing model boats, Ollie wanted to watch, the little boats' wakes sketching quick trembling diagrams on the surface, so gentle, so delicate, but I pulled us away again, unsettled by my own urgency, "Sorry, I want to see the bison," the fog layered and thickened, the flat-topped cypresses looming prehistoric, silence for whole minutes, say something, Daphne, say something, finally we came to the bison pen, leaned on the fence, seeing only their dim bulks in the murk, a foghorn blew across the bay, huge and hollow in its loneliness, and the bison started moving, disappearing further, though one broke off, drifted toward us, we watched it take size and shape until it stopped only twenty feet away, watching us, small skeptical eyes, the bearded monolith of its head, steam rising off its body, dissolving into the fog, Oh, what did *it* feel locked inside all of its improbable flesh? maybe fear sometimes, the impulse to flee, brief dark glimmer in the veins, though even that was hard to imagine, so forbearing, animal stoicism, feed reproduce feed reproduce, no thoughts about feelings, feelings about feelings, thoughts about feelings about feelings about—no, goddammit, enjoy this, just enjoy this, it *is* magical, this creature crossing over to watch us watching it, Ollie leaning into me, me leaning into him, let go, let go just a little, propping myself between Ollie and the fence, warm, an improbable ray of sun through the low gray fog, Ollie's warmth gathering me in, the strain of keeping my pleasure from vaulting too high, tiring, all just so tiring . . .

"We'd better get back," I said. "UV rays through the fog, we'll get burned."

And as we turned away, a sudden, swift arrow struck me, that this was both so much and so little, and I lost a step, just one clumsy step.

"Was that it again?" Ollie asked quietly. "Your thing?" He said he'd tried to do a little research, tried to see what he could learn on his own.

"You did?" I was impressed, touched even. "Well, don't wear out your library card. A lot of it's impenetrable."

"No, I . . . I find it fascinating."

That set me off—"fascinating"—though I knew he didn't

mean anything by it. "When you tell someone, you get two kinds of responses. The first is no one believes you. They think you're faking or just making it up. Or they say, 'Oh, I know, I get *so* emotional. I'm always so *depressed*.' Everyone thinks you're just depressed. Though, Lord knows, it's depressing enough. A lovely little circle: You get sad because of the condition, then the sadness triggers an attack, which makes you even sadder. Fantastic fucking irony."

"It sounds tough," Ollie said again, hesitant. "Really tough."

"The second kind of people, they want to cure you. Have you tried yoga? Meditation? *Prayer*? Or they've got their home remedies. There was this woman, a friend of my mom, she kept telling me to eat these mushrooms. She said she'd cured her sister's cancer by feeding her these certain mushrooms. Everything was goddamn mushrooms with this lady. Now they say, Go gluten-free! Egg-free! Get your fillings pulled so you're mercury-free! At least the people who think you're faking just end up leaving you alone."

"But there is no cure?"

"Listen, don't worry about it. It's my thing, I take care of it."

I sounded so fucking miserable even to myself. We both went silent again, the buzzing was rising, I tasted tears gathering, we came back out into the broad open green, there everyone was still laughing and playing, my legs wanted to run, they wanted to but I didn't trust them, preparing, looking for a good place to land, always preparing to fall, so stupid to think I could do this, the buzzing, control it, stupid, a soft place to land, anywhere to land, no just control it, control it, stupid stupid, can't you just—"Hey," Ollie said, took my hand in his, "you okay over there?" and—

His hand. His bony, scraped, scarred fingers. His warm, rough, callused palm. We stood near a grove of eucalyptus, their ribbony leaves rushing in the breeze, releasing their dense, daydream scent, and I held his hand tight, as tight as I could, and my despair, my tumbling, rushing despair began to leach away.

"I'm o-kay," I said. "I think I'm going to put my shoes back on now."

"Me, too." We sat in the grass, legs partly intertwined. Ollie watched me fumble with my laces as the buzzing receded. Once, twice I failed to tie a knot. "Need help?"

"No, I've got it." But I wasn't ready to leap up yet. "Can we just sit here a while? The smell . . . I love eucalyptus."

"Got nowhere else I want to be."

I lay against him, he lay against me. We watched the fog spin fine lace, then soft wool, over the last of the afternoon sun. "You know what I like about you," Ollie said. "You're always paying attention. People who do that tend to be kind."

"Or cautious."

"Still worried about getting burned?"

"I could lie here all day. But . . ." I was exhausted, from tracking my thoughts so minutely, from how sad and soaring every moment seemed to be. "Yeah, we should go."

We came back out into the scruffy bustle of the Haight.

"So, hey," Ollie said, "I don't really do 'dates,' dinner and a movie and all that, but I really—"

"No movies," I said brusquely. Claustrophobia, the cold taste of steel . . . I pushed the memory down. "Why don't I cook for you again? Come to my place. I'll stuff you silly."

"No, I have an idea." He searched my face. "If you don't mind a surprise."

"Those can be kind of tough."

"I know, but I really want to show you this."

Is this your research, I wanted to say, telling you people like me don't get out much? Instead I said, "Okay." Maybe he was the second type, a curer, and didn't understand yet how useless the effort would be. Still, for now, I wanted to luxuriate in this a little. I put my arm around him, breathed him in.

A cab came down Stanyan, and I flagged it. Ollie kissed me once, on the lips. I girded myself for it—*smoke, cattails*—but there was such a charge built up I fell into him slightly. Maybe he was getting used to it. "Friday," he said. "Seven p.m., 16th Street BART. Meet me there?"

"Assuming the transit cops don't go on another rampage."

"God willing."

As the cab pulled away, my body was humming or maybe shivering again. I turned and looked for him, but he'd already disappeared into the crowd.

NINE

I WAS ON TIME, FOR A CHANGE. I WATCHED THEM COME IN. Miranda looked harried, downtrodden. It was the middle of the semester, when she started to fall apart a little. Teshawn seemed unusually alert, gave me a big hello and a flirtatious smile. I cocked an eyebrow back—Who you looking at, big boy? This cracked him up, enough he had to get down in his desk quick. Bill was a little shell-shocked, polo pit-stained, five o'clock shadow. Someone had been sleeping on the couch or, anyway, not getting his wife's usual attentions. This happened a few times a year. Being so dependent put him in a weak bargaining position. Actually, it was good to see she pushed back on him now and then.

Sherman arrived late and launched into a flustered, tongue-thick apology. We didn't get the whole thing. Right behind him, Russell came in, on crutches. He had a bright red abrasion down his right arm, and his right leg was in a huge wire and plastic cast.

General alarm and eye-fluttering.

"Russell!" I couldn't help exclaiming. "What the hell'd you do?"

He hobbled over to a desk, fit himself into it as best he could, his right leg stiffly, painfully extended, and started to explain. He'd been playing bike polo on one of the caged basketball courts in Dolores Park. "A straight-up, normal match," he told us. "Except this dude kept fucking with me, poking his mallet at my spokes like he wants to flip me. He's dogging me the whole time, and I don't even know who the hell he is. Then it comes to me—the door guy at El Rio, who thinks I was scheming on his boyfriend the other week. I'm trying to stay chill, but"—Russell winced at a pang in his leg—"just as I'm going to shoot, he hip-checks me, slams right into my bike. I see him coming, so I stay up. But now I'm pissed—he's carrying on like I jacked *him*. Before I know what I'm doing, I'm charging him, full bore, out of my fucking mind. Except I don't even get to him. I get that little dizzy spell, that weird fizzing thing, and then I'm gone. The bike goes out from under me, my leg all jammed up in the frame, and I flip over, skid like ten feet. Which, yeah, is why my arm's fucked, too."

Russell sat looking at all of us looking at him in horror. He seemed to not quite credit what had happened. "The other guys," he said, "they said it was like I got struck by lightning. I folded like a pup tent in a fucking hurricane."

We were all consternation and advice: Russell, what were you thinking? You shouldn't even put yourself in that kind of position. And if you do, walk away! Or better yet, sit down for a minute. Protect yourself. Lie down on the court if you have to.

"Lie down?" he said. "I'd look like a total dipshit in front of everyone!"

I'd mostly been sitting out the conversation, but I thought of myself on the volleyball court. "Russell," I said, "you're sick. You've got to understand that."

He had his arms crossed over his chest. The look he gave me tried for "whatever," but I could see the doubt eroding it. "My doctor says I'll just get kind of weak sometimes. What's new, man? That's been happening forever. I should get more sleep or something."

"A decent night's sleep helps," I said, "makes you more even-keeled. But, Russell, it's not going to get better."

"I come here, listen to you people, and all I hear is bitching and moaning. I mean, seriously, who cares about your kid's fucking birthday party?"

Bill muttered something under his breath. Ordinarily, Sherman would've stepped in. He hated any argument. Today, however, he let it go. He wore the same shirt from last week, a now-rumpled blue-and-pink gingham. I caught his eye. He only nodded at me—go ahead.

"Russell, I'm not saying never get on a bike again. But you've got to—"

"I listen to you people saying, 'I can't laugh at a joke. I can't hold my kid. I can't fight with my husband or wife or whoever. I can't look at a beautiful sunset. I can't even drink a few beers and fuck—' "

"Russell," I said, "calm down. Take a breath."

He was starting to droop now. Somehow, though, he kept up his indignation. "I can't listen to all your defeat. It's just fucking sad. You're worried about me hurting myself? Man, I should *kill* myself if I can't do all the things you say."

Glum silence followed. "Remember, everyone," Sherman murmured, "stay open." Eventually, Miranda shared the sob story she'd clearly come today to tell. She was up for tenure, and no way in hell was she getting it. She could barely engage with her students, who were always crying, literally crying, about their grades. Her attacks were getting so frequent and wore her out so much, she hadn't been able to start a paper, let alone publish one, in over three years. So, on top of her nonexistent social and romantic life—dating was a joke—now she was facing losing her job as well. By the time the meeting wrapped up, it had turned into a real mess. Sherman made another plug for the study at Stanford. But we all just wanted to get the hell out.

Outside, my car service was waiting. Russell leaned against the wall of the church, scowling and scratching at his red raw arm. "Waiting for someone?" I said.

"My buddy's coming for me. Running late, I guess."

Russell was, what, nineteen, twenty? I remembered how angry, how wronged I felt back then, to have these absurd limitations clamping down just when I should've been breaking out into my own. There was so little I could say that would reach him. I didn't look like any kind of role model. "Want to share this ride? On me."

"Nah," he said, annoyed, "I'm good." He kept scratching, looked away. And I felt pathetic for pretending this thing wasn't going to crush him in its gears.

After that meeting, he never came back, and, really, I didn't blame him.

BY THE TIME I got home, I was in a mood. I'd gone to group hoping to share a nice little story about my date. Now all of their suffering and recrimination was thudding around inside me, pushing and shoving to get out. I got myself snug on the couch, propped up by cushions and pillows, a couple on the floor, in case I spilled out.

I cued up my video mix. A lot of it was just internet stuff, cute videos of kittens and other baby animals playing, finding their legs, tumbling adorably, heart-meltingly down. But that was just a warm-up. I moved on to old clips of Sally Struthers, saving the children with her quavering voice, starving kids with xylophone ribs, close-ups of them shyly, weakly smiling. Often, at this point, my slurred little yelps of cat-video joy would have dissolved into sloppy tears and headbobbing. But I'd seen these videos too many times. The effect had worn off.

Time for the harder stuff: the clips, so common over the last few years, of people in impossibly remote parts of Pakistan and Yemen and Somalia. Their bombed or burning villages, their dead all around them, they wailed and keened and stumbled into one another with the gale force of their grief.

Their weathered faces contorted, they threw back their heads and screamed. And still I felt nothing, or only the faintest tremors. I kept clicking through the clips, rewinding, skipping ahead, trying to get the worst all at once. And I knew it was coming, the one that always pushed me over the edge: a blurred cell phone video, Tunisia, the fruit vendor who lit himself on fire, the thought of his sizzling hair and charring flesh, as if his rage and longing had caught fire from within, even before he doused himself in gasoline and struck a match—I shored up the pillows under me, prepared myself to click on it.

An alert sounded through my laptop speakers. *Evening! Get my package?*

~~*Whtfucik??!scardshit!!!*~~ I got my fingers back before I hit ENTER. *Yeah got it mom thanks as always.* It arrived once a month: Easy Mac, powdered laundry detergent, toothpaste, homemade brownies or cookies, condoms. My mother had been sending these parcels since I went away to college. "In case you don't feel like going out." Eventually I gave up my protests. I now had an entire cupboard of one-load boxes of Tide.

Honey, sit down for a second if you're not already.

This takes on a fairly literal meaning for people like me.

Um I'm on the couch what's the big surprise?

Well, it's nothing, really . . . Okay, look, I just got home from a date.

My only response, and not just because my fingers weren't quite working: *??????????????????????????????*

Oh, you think your mom's not an eligible bachelorette?

~~*I think dating in your late fifties is like learning to drive in Venice couldn't you have tried this twenty years ago so*~~

my childhood wasn't like walking on eggshells? Mom of course not you're a stone fox I'm just surprised is all

I don't want to get my hopes up. But Alden's wonderful! He took me to that wonderful Italian place in Carmel. Such a gentleman. And he runs his own business!

Alden what a name he sounds like he runs the elks lodge or hangs out with militia men where you'd meet him grocery store or something?

He took out that old stump the mailman keeps backing into. He was very charming and gave me half price.

Hey wow a stump guy que romantique

All right, Daph, enough of your sass.

No mom really it's great news glad for you god I hope he doesn't break your heart going to see him again?

Wednesday. He's taking me to the opera down in Indy. We're having such a blast.

Wait hold on which date is this?

Number four! Sorry, it's been hard keeping it to myself. I know how much you've been thinking about your dad lately.

I didn't know what was weirder, her treating me like a girlfriend, or that I almost reciprocated and told her about Ollie. But that would've been more emotional mileage than I could log in a day. It was easier to evade. *Thanks thanks I really miss him*

Just remember that I'm here and I love you.

Through my laptop, peasant women in Waziristan were still wailing. I signed off with my own *love you*, got up, and paced the apartment, straightening, cleaning, trying to make some space and light and order.

TEN

WORK THAT FRIDAY WAS A MESS. AS THE MEDEVAL shuttle crawled through the main entrance, a crowd of black hoodies, black bandanas, and camouflage pants jeered and cursed us. Animal Liberation Front. Half of them were waving big bolt cutters around. A few wore shirts with a design of an upraised fist next to an upraised paw. "Murderers!" they screamed as we pushed through the gates. "Butchers!" They were hanging a huge banner over the fence as security simultaneously pulled it down—blown-up photos of chimps and pigs with bleeding, festering sores, swastikas printed over the images.

When the driver let me out in front of the lab, I felt the morning damp. "If it rains," I told him, "that'll quiet them down."

"Hey, they don't get it," he said. "Keep up the good fight, Doc." I only had my MA and a CMAR certificate, but I didn't correct him. He called everyone "Doc."

My email was full of the usual security reminders. Lock all entrances, report lost or stolen IDs, do not engage with unauthorized visitors. I skimmed and deleted, got on with my day. An hour later, I looked up and realized only Hidalgo was in with the dogs.

"Where's Staci?"

"Just using the bathroom," Pin said.

"How long has she been in there?"

"Hmm, only a little while maybe."

Byron squinted at us both. "She's been in there all morning." He made a pitter-pat gesture over his chest. "My, oh, my, here we are the experts, but can we truly—I mean, *truly*—do anything for this frail little organ?"

FROM THE LAST STALL in the row, I heard sobbing, hard, gulping, and loud enough to echo off the peach-colored tiles of the women's room. I stood a few steps away, cleared my throat. *Cattails, willows, drifting smoke.* "Staci, how we doing in there?"

"I'm sorry, I just needed to . . . take a minute to . . ." Her voice went vibrato, broke up. This was far from the first time Staci had disappeared into the bathroom.

"Maybe you should take the rest of the day."

"But there's no one to cover me."

Yes, but I would've rather cleaned out the pens myself than dealt with her breakdown. "We'll figure it out."

Her voice steadied, turned brave, wondering at herself: "I'm never like this. Never. It's just . . . I've been all over the place lately. Then those animal rights people screamed at me, and I got to thinking about our dogs, and, and—"

Another racking sob. *Sun-bleached picnic tables, the river.* "Staci, is another twenty minutes in here really going to help? Take the day. We'll see you Monday."

"Oh, God, you're going to fire me."

"Just come in on Monday. We'll talk through everything then."

Staci came out of the stall, red-eyed, pale-lipped. She splashed water on her face, tried to shore up her slack, cried-out expression. "I'm okay," she said. "Really, I am. I'm serious about this job. Please, you know I am."

OVER LUNCH at the company café, Pin stuck up for her. We had an almost parental relationship over Staci. Pin played the indulgent one. I wasn't thrilled about having to be the disciplinarian.

"A smart girl," Pin said. "She will get there. She doesn't like being queen of drama." Six years ago, Pin had come over from one of our Taiwanese partners. She still had a little idiom hiccup now and then.

"Well, when is she going to toughen up? I know how important the tuition program is for her, how expensive vet school is. But how will she even get through if she can't handle a dead animal or two?"

"Yes, but better she begin with compassion. Not everyone has it."

I poked at my salad without comment.

"Some people, when they don't know something is right, they put even more passion in. How they decide. Same for Staci, same for activists. Still, I think it's better."

I shrugged. "Sounds exhausting." Sometimes I felt like I was the only one not allowed to break, and if I did, the whole lab would fall apart.

For the rest of the afternoon, Staci kept wafting apologetic smiles my way. With everyone else, everyone not her boss, she was upbeat, frisky even. Some people enjoyed these wild swings. They crested and troughed, thrilled and wallowed, and came out strangely purified. I probably would have to fire Staci for her sensitivity, her excess. After all, she might go on like this her whole life. Or maybe, with all of her yawning lows and staggering highs, she'd finally just get worn down. Maybe. As I watched her, I kept sipping my coffee, trying to get the bitter tannin of envy off my tongue.

I STOOD OVER Biscuit's pen. A sour musk filled the room—fear, stifled adrenaline. Biscuit was buried in the corner, out of the glare of the overhead fluorescents. I opened his pen. "Come on, boy, time for a walk." He looked at me with rheumy eyes, then followed slowly behind as I led him to the outdoor play area. It was a mellow, golden afternoon. The sun raked through the dust billowing over the foothills. On a ridge, I spotted two figures in windbreakers looking down at me. I waved to them. They didn't wave back.

"Oh, well, I've got you to keep me company."

I let Biscuit nose around, get a taste of California air, all of those outdoor smells. I'd toss him a ball; he'd amble over and very slowly nose it back. I brought him a bone, and once, just once, he gave me a happy little bark. I leaned against the fence and watched him gnaw and slobber with an energy he hadn't shown in weeks. Happy, bored, miserable, loyal—were those even the right words for these animals? Everything we did to our dogs, and still they loved us. Maybe love was just pragmatic. All of those wildfire feelings were just some ancient survival mechanism. Someone seemed willing to keep you alive, and, surprise, guess who you fell for.

The door to the lab swung open, and Hidalgo stood there, his headphones silent around his neck, hat in hands, long hair held back with a rubber band. "Hey, Daphne, everything cool out here? Need any help?"

"Just getting in a little play before quitting time."

"Okay if I ask you about something?"

"Well, I was about to . . . No, of course. Go ahead."

He wanted to work overtime, doubles, nights, anything I could spare. Angela's medical bills. His daughter, I hadn't even known her name. He pulled out his rubber band, flustered a hand through his hair, clearly embarrassed to ask.

The fact was we were already short-staffed. I could've used an extra day tech and two more at night. But the budget, always the budget. And the question of benefits. If Hidalgo worked more hours, we'd have to bump up his health coverage. For a company devoted to healing, Med-Eval was stingy with its coverage.

"We might—*might*—have some shifts opening up," I said, thinking about Staci, the inevitability of letting her go. "No promises, though." I didn't know quite where to start. "Your little girl . . ." I said, "Angela, how is her . . . swallowing?"

He looked at me, as if unsure who exactly was speaking to him. "She's still real skinny," Hidalgo said. "She has to have everything through a straw. If she doesn't get better soon, she's going to miss a bunch of milestones. But kids, they're resilient, right?"

What could I say? Even if you did get through, you still got marked. Some scars barely faded, never mind disappeared. But no one wanted to hear that.

"Whatever you can do," Hidalgo said. "For me. For us. I appreciate it, you know?" He put his hat back on, pulled it down over his eyes. But for an instant I glimpsed such a naked look of worry that my mouth hung open. I stiffened my jaw into something like resolve, but he'd seen, too.

If only we could all stay a mystery to one another.

ELEVEN

I GOT HOME AT SIX, TOOK A QUICK SHOWER, CHANGED into jeans and a warm coat. On my way to the train to meet Ollie, I nearly got past him, my now familiar half-man.

"There she is, the tall, pretty one."

"How's everything, Jeff?"

"Got twenty dollars you can spare for a new pair of shoes?"

"Shoes?" A pair of scuffed, child-size Nikes, still too big, were loosely laced to what he had for feet. "What happened to the surgery?"

"A real success. Never felt better." My eyes drifted again to the needle marks on his arms. You'd think he'd cover them. Instead he kept the sleeves of his hoodie pushed up. He saw me looking, dug in the pocket, and flicked a bright yellow keychain fob onto his lap, not unlike the ones the guys in AA were always nervously chewing on outside the church. "Clean and serene for nine months," Jeff said.

"How about five bucks for a burrito?"

"Make it ten, we got a deal."

"Fine," I said, looking in my wallet and finding nothing smaller anyway. "I recommend El Farolito for sheer value and grease."

"And you have a fine evening, pretty girl. You'd look even prettier with a smile."

A line men never tire of dropping on women, but it still got under my skin. By the time I saw Ollie outside the 16th Street BART, I was feeling self-conscious and shy. Ollie lit up when he saw me; he was ready to kiss me hello. I offered up an awkward half-hug.

"Ready?" he said, trying to read my expression. We went down into the station. At the base of the long escalator, a guy played violin. His eyes bloodshot, the veins leaping out on his neck and arms, he sawed away, moaning, swaying. But there were no strings; he was bowing the bare neck, the scratching and tearing like the inside of a migraine. "It's either madness or performance art," I said.

"I don't know," Ollie said. "I hope he's okay."

Ollie had an old wool blanket stuffed in his backpack. When we got on the train, I asked about it, but he wasn't giving up the surprise. Despite my reservations or maybe because of them, I snuggled closer to him on the musty padded seat. He wanted to know about my week. "Oh, God, my job. You don't want to hear about my job."

But he did, of course. So I told him about Staci's breakdowns and Byron always sniping at me. I told him about the dogs, the ones we had to sacrifice, but we saved lives, after all, it was worth it, God, I hoped it was worth it . . . We were across the bay by the time I'd finished. "Sorry, it's a rare job that's boring and horrifying at once."

"Your company's really called MedEval?"

"I wear a suit of armor to the lab. On bad days, I carry a lance, too."

"The lady doth fend for herself."

"Most of the time," I said as the train pulled into the West Oakland stop. Ollie rose. "Wait," I said, "we're not going to Berkeley? Not even Rockridge?" He put his arm around my waist as we went down to street level. "Don't worry," he said. "It'll be fine." In the twilight, we passed overgrown lots and dilapidated two-flats. The blocks turned industrial. We came to a work yard filled with old road construction materials, girders, broken-up hunks of concrete. I swallowed down a burr of fear. "Not exactly the obituary I was envisioning."

"Come on." Ollie pushed through a loose section of chain link. We picked our way through rusty twists of rebar. The dark shapes of concrete sewer pipes loomed. Above us, fog blurred the lights of the highway overpass to splotches of amber. "Are we going to a cockfight or something?" I said. "What is this?"

The faint jangle of an acoustic guitar floated toward us. I saw several dark figures gathered at the end of one of the concrete tubes. A pale orange light flickered inside it. Ollie whispered hello to two guys smoking cigarettes. We ducked into the tube.

There were at least thirty people inside, early or mid-twenties, some high school kids. They huddled under blankets, rested on pillows, or crouched in place, fitting themselves to the curve of the tube. Ollie unfolded our blanket, positioned himself so his feet were on the bottom, his back against the side. I started to protest again. He put his finger to his lips and drew me down to him. I squirmed.

"Nice," Ollie said, "we're just in time."

A guy with a sparse beard and a wan, hunted expression hunched to the center of the tube and perched on an orange Quikrete bucket. In corduroys and a Pendleton jacket, he hunkered over his guitar, trying to look like he'd just rolled in on a cross-country freight and not, say, his girlfriend's Jetta. He strummed absentmindedly, like we weren't all actually, uncomfortably there to hear him, and began to sing in a ghostly whisper.

> *I am a moonshiner*
> *Seventeen long years*
> *And I spent all my money*
> *On whiskey and beer*

He closed his eyes, as did several others, lost in this little fantasy about how tragic it was to booze and wallow. "Oh, please," I groaned, but Ollie pressed a finger to my lips.

I watched the singer's face. It contorted with the shapes of the lyrics, the ascent of the melody. He smiled, as if at some far off memory, shook his head as if it were fading. He winced, took on a cockeyed expression, arched his eyebrows, like he was riding out some exquisite pain. It seemed so practiced, like he'd worked on all of these looks in the mirror and wore them now for effect.

"Ollie, please. This concrete. My ass is falling asleep."

Why this fucking pipe? I thought. But as the guy played another subdued ballad, it became apparent. In the close, echoing confines, the notes seemed to sound directly in my ears, as if the singer were right next to me, strumming and murmuring. He paused, considered, picked out the intro of a new song. "This one here's about an old friend," he intoned, "now departed for parts unknown."

The song was in a minor key and kept dissolving into the next set of chords, all low-level dread and, the way the guy sang it, resignation. He summoned a familiar landscape: country roads winding past waving fields and grain silos and tumbledown barns, a clear lake with little waves tipping toward shore, white geese settling onto its surface. He sang about a boy, a wild and bored and lost boy, driving through those endless fields. And I couldn't help thinking of that brief year after I got my license, when I knew something was wrong but before my diagnosis, before I knew just how dangerous it was. I'd take out my mom's Sentra and roam the Indiana countryside, sometimes with Brook, mostly alone, my dreams of travel slowly but steadily unraveling across all that flat vacancy. The future stretched vast and featureless, and I felt like some high-flying, mysterious creature slipping off into the towering midwestern sky. The chorus arrived— "If you're going over," the guy sang, "then let me, oh, let me go with you"—and I understood that the boy he sang about was gone, gone gone, yet lingered somewhere, felt but always just out of reach. I thought then of my father, the shimmering shape of his memory, and something rose in me, flooding me, drowning me with—

I went for my phone, opened up the camera, set it to video, Bill's strategy for his son's birthday. Through the screen, I watched the guy play and sing. It pushed him back, pushed him away. I thought of concerts I'd seen on TV, half the audience holding up their phones, looking on from the outside, living their lives in third-person.

"Hey," Ollie whispered. I turned the camera on him, watched his face. Through the screen, he reached out, pulled my hand gently down, "Come on," shifted so I could rest more fully against him, "get comfortable."

I closed my eyes, as if that would insulate me. It only brought it all closer, every tremble in the singer's voice, every tiny squeak of his fingers slipping along the neck of the guitar, my father's rust-red beard, delicately hairy chest, tentative smile, and sad, always averted eyes. The buzzing spread down my face, through my shoulders and arms, down my legs. Under me, I felt Ollie's chest rise and fall. "It's fine," he whispered. "I won't move an inch."

Sorrow passed through me, waves of frustration and guilt and anxiety. In the tremor of the singer's voice, I heard my mother's sobbing. All of that ancient dread moved through me. I couldn't stop myself. I could only let it all wash away.

THE WIND PICKED UP as we walked back to the train, ushering us back across the bay. I let myself rest against Ollie again. "Listen," I said sleepily, wiped out, "I'm not helpless. I'm not some helpless little girl."

The tips of his fingers played with my hair. "You shouldn't have to miss out."

"But, Jesus, when you take me weird places like that, warn me first."

He laughed. "Cheap date, I know. Sorry."

The howling of the train at full speed drowned out any more talking. As it slowed into Embarcadero, our mood had grown solemn, charged with possibility. "So," Ollie said, trying to sound casual, "what now?"

"I'm too tired for anything but home." A long pause hung between us. "I wouldn't mind you walking me, though."

In front of the Grove, we kissed a little. In my exhaustion, I could contain it, just. But I couldn't bear to say good night. "You could come up. I can't promise much, but . . ."

"No, no, that's fine," he stammered. "I'd love to."

We got up to the apartment. He wanted to kiss me in the doorway. I shied away. "We should probably get horizontal if we're doing this." We climbed up to the loft, my nest within a nest. He started to take off his shirt. I put a hand out to slow him, then pulled him down to me instead. He kissed my neck, my collarbone, my hips, my—"Hold on," I mumbled. "Bring down the temperature a little."

"Should I do something different? What should I do?"

"Sorry, it's hard to explain . . ." I'd hoped to put off this conversation as long as possible. We could've stuck with junior-high heavy petting forever, as long as it kept me from putting this on the table. "There's this guy," I began, "in my support group . . ."

"Have you mentioned this before, your support group?"

"Not exactly the best opening line on a date."

"But I wish you could trust me with—"

"Listen, I found this group online four years ago, and my friend Brook made me email. But this guy, Sherman, he wanted to speak on the phone. And I was blown away. The symptoms, the triggers, I'd never talked to anyone like me before. But then Sherman starts asking, What's it like when you hold someone's hand? When you hug them? Goof around, make little jokes? And I realized, even then, he was way sicker than me. He used to be married, but he couldn't kiss his wife or even look at pictures of their wedding without an attack. Sometimes, he had them one after another, on the couch for hours. He used to joke that he was allergic to love. At least he could laugh about it, sort of."

"Jesus, how is he now?"

"What I'm trying to say, there are things he really can't do. A lot of things."

"But he's more"—Ollie searched for the right word— "sensitive, right?"

"Well, almost all of us are a little sensitive. To, you know, that."

"Oh."

A whole history rushed into that syllable. Through high school, I ignored and deflected the advances of boys, too frightened of my body's weird betrayals to want anyone else investigating them. In college, when I finally knew what was wrong, I drank. The nights blurred and rushed around me, my suitemates laughing and shouting as we made our sloppy way to parties, Beta, Sigma Nu, guys with their expectant glances, me trying not to feel more than a gathering velocity, making out on some guy's unmade bed, not even hoping to stay in control. But I could never numb myself enough. The excitement and shame and disgust were too potent. My head would start lolling, and the guy would think I was too wasted to go through with it. Or he wouldn't want me puking in his room. Or he'd just get bored and go off to join his brothers.

One night at Beta, I switched all the way off—the fucker's name was Jay—and lay there, feeling his hands all over my body, his cologne seizing up my nostrils and throat. Then he started tugging off my jeans. I went wild with fear, which froze me even deeper. I tried to kick, tried to flail and hit him, but I was trapped inside myself, knowing it was happening and powerless to stop it. I heard his belt slither from its loops, his zipper coming undone. But some couple stumbled into the room, and Jay swore savagely and disappeared. As did the couple. I lay alone in the dark wanting to flee, to cry, to scream, but unable to do anything, frozen inside my terror and fury. Since, I'd had a handful of boyfriends, a couple in grad school, a couple in San Francisco. All nice guys in their own well-meaning ways. But one thing united them all.

"It's okay to be disappointed," I told Ollie. "This is when they all go running."

He rolled onto his back and blinked up at the ceiling.

"I'm not disappointed. I'm just trying to figure this all out. I mean, it's not as bad as it is with your friend, right?"

"It depends on the, I don't know, intensity of the experience."

"Like, anything up to third base?"

"That's usually a pretty close call."

"But what about—?"

"When I orgasm, if I can even get that far, I just ragdoll completely. One guy thought he killed me. That was an interesting little freak-out."

Ollie furrowed his brow. "What about doing it yourself?"

I had my Rabbit. It had a few modifications, straps to keep it in place. Paraplegics use them—amazing what you can learn on the internet. I couldn't remember the last time I'd pulled that contraption out of the drawer. It just went and went after I switched off, and made me very sore the next day. "Not a frequent occurrence," I said.

"There must be ways other than straight-up sex?"

"To be honest, it's not something I love exploring."

Ollie let out a sigh. "Sorry, I'm not . . . Okay, I *am* disappointed, frustrated, whatever. With the condition, not with you."

"I'll give you a blowjob. I can be fairly dispassionate with those. Actually, I think most girls can."

"Daphne, please, I'm trying to be serious. You having an attack, it could even be kind of hot."

"You'd get some pretty immediate feedback, anyway."

"I might just be into it. No reason not to find out."

"I enjoyed tonight. I want you to know that. At the least."

He turned and wrapped his arm around me. "People make things work," he murmured. "Happens all the time." A few minutes later, he was snoring softly. I lay there, exhausted, staring up at the ceiling, unmoving, everything inside me writhing.

TWELVE

WHEN I WOKE HE WAS GONE. THERE WAS A NOTE ON the kitchen counter in his girlish script: *Didn't want to wake you. You were sleeping hard. Got a call for a job down in Pacifica. Me and the Irish boys building some rich folk a deck.* He'd written down his number. *I thought I'd bring us up to the 20th century. Call me later?*

His smell lingered in the apartment. I had that odd nostalgia again, felt somehow dislodged from the present. All I could do was sit on the couch in the late-morning sun, buoyant, hollow, stretched thin, like I'd floated into too rarified an atmosphere. I had a new boyfriend. I touched the idea carefully, giving myself little hits of pleasure and trepidation, trying to enjoy a few moments of delicately balanced equilibrium.

I WAS NESTLED in the corner with a midafternoon glass of Moscato. The Pit Stop had recently expanded its wine selection and, to my further dismay, taken out the pool table and replaced it with two plush, horseshoe-shaped booths. I sat in one, watching a young guy in a saloonkeeper's vest wash and wipe glasses.

When Brook finally came in, she had on big round sunglasses, threw her handbag into the booth, and, without comment on the improvement/defacement of our bar, signaled the guy in the vest, who was already mixing her Manhattan. "Sorry, lady, sorry." Her voice was raspy, and when she let out a big yawn, I got a blast of Listerine and bourbon. "Got caught up again."

"Jesus, B, have you even slept?"

"In the car back up from San Jose. So, that's, what, an hour and a half?"

"You're just coming from a party *now?*"

"Yeah, they never want it to stop, and they're all like fifteen or whatever."

"Don't you have a contract or a terms of service or something?"

She pushed her sunglasses up on her head. "Christ, what kind of light bulbs are they using in here?" Her pupils were the size of manhole covers. "Some of these pills, they last so long you actually get bored."

"Just because they're high off their asses doesn't mean you have to be, too."

"If you promise them the greatest night of their lives, you

can't just stand around like a hall monitor. Anyway, who do you think gets them the pills?"

"Great, and now you're a drug dealer."

"I took Halloween with me, showed him what he'll be paying for. You have to go full service. But enough about goddamn business. Let's talk about your new fella."

I'd texted Brook a couple of days ago, to bring her up to speed on Ollie, help me sort through everything. I'd come ready to continue that conversation, but now I felt the old reluctance again. I could never talk to her when she was in host mode or fucked up.

"B, I'm really upset right now."

"Nothing sagging that I can see."

It was true. I'd expected her to blow in like this. "Please tell me you're not dating a goddamn client."

"He isn't bad company. And, besides, this one's my exit strategy."

"Wait, how much can you make off one party?"

"Just enough to keep the doors open. That's the point." She explained that she'd been looking for an opportunity like this for a while, a start-up that was going to get big enough to need a full-time events person. Halloween seemed receptive, or anyway she was going to make him receptive. "Is it wrong to want a 401(k), dental coverage, a seat on one of those Google buses?" She signaled the bartender again. "Shit, what's his name? I need someone for Friday."

"I wish I didn't have to worry about you."

"I used to tell the Miller Lite girls, 'Spend your erotic capital while you have it.'"

"You don't believe that horseshit. And an exit strategy is actually using your Berkeley degree for something real."

Brook looked at me blankly. "Remind me what your fella does, works with his hands, just so he can say he does at parties, make all the other guys feel like pussies?"

"Come on . . ." Now, finally, I was starting to wilt. "That's not what he . . ."

"And what do you two do together? Cook fancy meals and go to the movies?"

"You know I can't go to . . ."

"Right, sorry, shit, didn't mean to"—Brook winced—"I *cannot* get a migraine tonight. Do you have anything? Tylenol, Aleve, a shotgun?"

"B, p-lease . . ." I was curling over in the direction of my wine. She reached across the table, gently pushed me back—almost second nature for her.

"Don't worry, take your time, take your time." She checked her phone. "But, fuck, I should get out of here by five." Her cocktail arrived, and she got wrapped up chatting with the bartender about hiring him for some after-party. He looked at me skeptically. "Don't worry about her," Brook said. "We were out all night."

SHERMAN SAT SLUMPED in his desk, pencil between his fingers, methodically crosshatching the paper on which he jotted notes for the meeting. The rest of us milled around the snack table. Sherman usually liked to start right on time.

Finally, everyone just drifted toward their seats. "Why don't we open things up today?" Sherman said without looking up from his slowly blackening page. "Daphne, let's start with you."

I glanced around at the rest of them, feeling ambushed. "Okay, we could talk about . . . visualization techniques." Good. Something bland and almost personal. "I use this image—or the memory of it, I guess—of this river near where I grew up. I don't know, maybe it's the comfort of the familiar or—"

Miranda cut me off. "We talked about visualizations the other week. You weren't here." I suggested running down some of the topics trending on the forums. Miranda sighed. "We can just go online if we want any of that."

Everyone was looking at me expectantly. They wanted me to really talk about myself. "Okay, fine," I said. "I met someone."

Sherman looked up, gave me a thin smile. "That's great, Daphne."

"How long?" Miranda said, a little too urgently.

"A month maybe." Almost exactly that. "We met in a bar. He has his own business. He works in . . . electronics restoration." Christ, what was that? Was I embarrassed by what Ollie did to scrape together a living?

"The kids in this city," Bill said, fidgeting today in a mint green polo, "they build an app, sell it for five hundred mil, can't even fix a leaky faucet."

"What matters is"—Sherman bobbed momentarily,

something roiling around in that shaggy head of his—"that he's supportive."

"Sure," I said, "he's thoughtful about it, sure."

"So he knows about the condition?"

"Yeah, I told him."

"How did *that* go?" Miranda said.

"It's a lot to ask of a stranger." Bill butting in again. "I've known Carianne since high school. She practically saw me grow up with it."

"Does he have a temper?" Miranda said. "I went out with this guy once, handsome but what a temper."

"Trust," Bill said. "Everything Carianne and I have is built on trust."

Across the circle, Teshawn cleared his throat. "Yeah, yeah, trust is nice and all." A grin poked out through the muffling of the drugs. "What I want to know is, have you done it?"

Giggles flitted around the room. Half of their heads slowly bobbed back up. I wet my lips, tried to swallow, looked to Sherman to break in and save me. "We're working on that," I said. "We're going slow. Ollie doesn't mind."

"Oh, man," Teshawn said, "dude is crazy, then."

More giggles. I let myself have an uncertain laugh.

"What I'd be doing," Teshawn said, "I'd be telling my girl, 'You've never seen this kind of crazy shit. But get ready, we're going to get there, *all* the way there.'" It was strange, the somnambulant way he said all of this. You could only just hear his lust and humor squeaking their way out. "What

I'd do, I'd start out on top, nice and slow. 'Cause if I go wild, I might flop all over her. And that's ending a night *real* quick."

It was hard to imagine Teshawn having enough energy to even get on top. He went on detailing his technique. I could tell he was cracking himself up, though he only rolled his head once. I listened with reluctant fascination. The forums had endless threads on sex. I'd scrolled through them a few times, though what was the point when it would just turn into a freak show? But, Jesus, if there were people here who could get it done . . .

"I just lie there," Teshawn was saying, "and she's working on me, and I'm thinking, 'Wait till I come out of this, just wait, we're gonna start all *over* again.'" Another titter went around the circle. There was kinship here, when we confessed our most awkward or excruciating moments. But Teshawn had to be exaggerating. Were these things he did or things he *wished* he could do?

Sherman signaled it was time to wrap up. Everyone else had been enjoying Teshawn's bragging, but Sherman had taken up his pencil again. Nearly the whole page was black, the lead pressed so hard it shone. I lingered to help him with the clearing up.

"Well, that was an interesting meeting."

"Good to hear Teshawn open up like that."

"Sherman," I said, "everything okay?"

He dumped the last of the snack tray into the garbage.

"Were you thinking about Olivia during that conversation?"

Olivia, his ex-wife, who'd left him shortly before he

started our group. She'd told him she needed to be with someone who could keep up with her, share her lifestyle, get through a dinner party without threatening to face-plant in the entrée. She just couldn't let her own life be run by his "allergy."

"It's just that . . ." Sherman teetered on the verge of answering. "Prince Hairy, he's been sick. But what else is new, right?" He took out his phone, swiped through some photos: his lordship in better days, apparently, though the thing still looked the color of raw chicken, all alien eyes and translucent, bat-like ears.

"Adorable," I said. "He doesn't look a day over a hundred."

Sherman kept swiping: Prince Hairy resting on Sherman's belly. Having his eyes stroked back to slits. Batting at a little felt punching bag with the feeblest of paws. "Look at him." Sherman couldn't help another smile. "On his own, he wouldn't last a minute."

THIRTEEN

MONDAY: UP AT 6:15, PRACTICALLY A LUXURY. Throw together an outfit, lollygag my way to the train, into the lab by 8:15, a little bickering from Byron, tune out till he's just a general braying in the background. Mid-morning, put my head down, email, datasets. Afternoons for tending to everyone, but Staci seems steady, Hidalgo quietly stoned, Pin distracted, dogs healthy. Mondays still endless, grueling, but, after the intensity of a weekend with Ollie, almost a relief.

Tuesday: He comes for dinner at the Grove. Start with prosecco or a crisp, dry Sémillon. Sort through the week's produce box, ten different ways to cook kohlrabi, Ollie chopping, me marinating the pork loin or tenderizing the milk-fed veal, listening hungrily while he tells me about whatever prime bit of real estate he and the Irish guys are working on. Eat like beasts, pudding onto the couch. Hour or two of TV, try to get him into *The Grand Design*, but just reminds him of work. Make out for a while, sleepy enough it's luxurious, not wild blind desire, until he has to pull himself away, get the bus home, get up early. Take the cushion he'd been sitting against up to bed, wrap myself around it, fall asleep like a lofted feather gently, gently swinging to the ground.

Wednesday: Our night out. Quiet neighborhood bistro down in Glen Park or Diamond Heights, somewhere out of the way, the regulars middle-aged, comfortable, childless, lives of mild professional setbacks and commendations, Bikram, home brewing, and matching bicycles. Ollie and I finish our tofu-avocado-quinoa bowls, set out for Bernal Hill and the sunset razing the Bay Bridge and downtown, trembling, liquid fire balancing on the Transamerica spire before bedding down in fat peach clouds, everything copper then bronze then every flashing shade of gold. Ollie wraps his arms around me, I sag forward—how can anyone stand *not* to live in California? Flinty April evenings, everyone zipping up hoodies and fleeces, dogs yipping, dog owners calling out in the half-light to half-strangers and strangers alike—"Good to see you! Good to see you! Aw, what is he, French Bulldog?"—Ollie and I tumble down the impossibly sheer hill for a slice of chocolate-walnut at Mission Pie before he has to get the bus home, then he's gone, the taste of his kiss lingering, not knowing what to do with myself, wandering my improbable neighborhood—brunch place, quinceañera dresses, brunch place, vacuum repair shop, Santería candles, needle exchange, brunch place—almost home, staring up at the body shop sign—ERFECT DETAILING—they'd tried to fix it, but the P keeps flickering, ERFECT PERFECT ERFECT PERFECT . . .

Thursday: Catch-up day. Stay late at work, later at the company gym, forty minutes on the stair climber, forty kicking and punching the heavy bag, constant exertion to keep from thinking of him every minute. On the train, Brook texts me—*Shit, slept with Halloween. He wanted a meeting at his place, bunch of people were rolling, so it wasn't not fun, but how shitty exactly should I be feeling today?*— not knowing what she expects me to say, letting it go, probably better just to let it go. By the time I get to the Grove, I'm jelly. I don't fall into bed, I dissolve.

Friday: Midnight, half-asleep, clothes still on in bed thinking about calling Ollie, still thinking about what to text Brook, getting lost in Interior Life instead. Space and light and order ... Maybe I *should* get a Corbusier armchair ... Mentally reshuffle all the furniture, imagine rehanging my vintage national parks prints, read an article telling me drapes are sumptuous but blinds trending ... Get so worked up looking at all the half-ass "Appealing Apartments" on their site that finally I kick off the sheets and start pushing and dragging stuff around—the Noguchi here, the old card catalog I use as an end table there—but when I get out the Nikon to snap a few photos, thinking I might wing them off to Interior Life's editors, the whole apartment looks weirdly abandoned, an exhibit on "21st-Century Spiritual Exhaustion." Fall asleep on the couch, dreaming of *smoke drifting over picnic tables, diamonds glinting on the river ...*

Saturday: Take the N-Judah to the Outer Sunset, Ollie's place, practically all the way out to the beach. Huge, raw space, high ceilings, concrete floors, divided into rooms and almost-rooms by hand-sewn curtains and salvaged drywall. Obvious where Ollie had a hand in it, the work straight clean solid, but he "doesn't fuck with other folks' habitats," so the rest is just comfy chaos. One Saturday a drum kit and guitars set up in the common area, the next some frightening wire/scrap-lumber sculpture being formed into the shape of . . . a head? Ollie's roommates: artists of some kind, musicians of some kind, hazily welcoming stoners, bewildering entrepreneurs. One guy's online business—giveashit.com—delivers . . . shit, to your friends and enemies alike. Cow shit, dog shit, llama shit—he runs down the menu for me, then a couple of weeks later he's gone, moved back to Portugal. ("He wants us to liquidate his inventory," Ollie says and doesn't seem to be joking.) People come, go, no one has an actual lease, all just making a shaggy, improvised life till the landlord wises up to the market. Ollie's room is his workshop: half-rebuilt Victrolas, handsome console radios with their guts pulled out, tackle boxes filled with old fuses and transistors, stacks of dog-eared paperbacks, crates of LP records, and in the middle of it all his mattress; we lie staring up at the silvery gray afternoon filtering through the frosted skylight, kissing in a diffuse, dreamy way, half-undressed, running my fingers along his arms, his legs, through his hair, stay diffuse, detached, pull ever so gently away. Get dressed, drink beers with the roommates on the old, half-sprung couches, everything loose and funny, act like I'm passed out a little, so funny, after a few beers, Ollie pulling me in tight, listening to everyone laughing, not wishing this was my life, just nice to visit now and then, every day could be different, every day new, and you wouldn't need all this order, order, order . . .

Sunday: Alameda flea market. Get there early, always start from the back. Move quick if I see something, no mercy for the old and tentative. A brass table lamp Ollie can rewire for me, a couple of majolica flowerpots, a lot of vintage hand mirrors that might hang nicely on the TV wall. Hunt for a shade to fit the lamp, find a red velvet one like a fez, Ollie, of course, plopping it right over his head. Have to sit cross-legged on the asphalt for a bit—Christ, so adorable—finally getting it together to snap a few photos of him. Grinning on the train with all of our finds. "Hey, aren't you going to miss your group today?" Telling him not to worry, everyone misses a week here and there. (Then skip the next three weeks in a row.) At home, order in sushi or Thai, nuzzle on the couch, kiss on the couch, let him touch me a little on the couch, push his hands gently down when he gets too excited. When I get too excited. Start letting him see my funny faces, he whispers, "It's all right, it's all right," says he likes it, it kind of turns him on. What can he do? How can he make me comfortable? Take his hands in mine, keep them from exploring further, tell him, "Hang in there, okay? Okay?"

And as the weeks rush along let him go further. Let him touch me right up to the brink, right up to the point I can no longer push him away. The buzzing—long to push through, as if the deadening electricity won't come and, after, the nausea, the depletion. Touch his sun-bleached stubble, sharp hip bones, tanned, grooved forearms, left index finger healed crooked after some job site mishap—men are so careless with their beautiful, unwieldy bodies. Tell him, "I'm kind of falling for you. And I don't even mean that as a bad pun." Him not flinching, not laughing either, telling me the same, he means it, truly. His erection against my thigh. "Soon," I tell him. "Soon." Start kissing again, slowly, imagining my river, cattails, willows, trying to retrieve every detail, straining to stay in control.

In the morning, he wakes me, sits on the edge of the bed, kisses me good-bye, dressed already, work boots, jacket, jeans, as I swim up into consciousness, back into a world suffused with his presence, the warm sheets, the ghost of his body printed next to mine, his actual body hovering over me, almost translucent in the honeycomb light, I murmur good-bye, he murmurs good-bye, kisses good-bye . . . dissolves into light. A drowsy, suffused hour to myself before leaving for work, a little space before jump-starting another week. But on the train, on the bus, at my desk, in the company café, with the dogs, lost in blocks of code—even in the deep thickets of work now I feel him close, his care and desire trying to wrap around me. I feel harried, breathless, never a moment to pause and rest, and there is no routine, all moments tumble into one another, everything prelude to seeing him again, everything the resonance of having seen him. And sometimes I pray I could just stop dead in the middle of the street, in the middle of the day, and root myself fast in place.

Then, almost immediately, I want him again.

FOURTEEN

W E WOKE LATE AND DECIDED TO STROLL OUT TO the Richmond, to a dim sum place on Clement that Pin had recommended. The fog had already burned off of a glorious, high-skied morning. Then, on our way up Mission, I saw Jeff looming. I tried to catch his eye, give him a little twinkle to say, I'm walking with this good-looking guy on my arm here, just trying to enjoy the weather and a lazy Sunday, just like anyone—so if you could give me a break today, let me slide past, I'll get you back with a ten when I see you next, okay? Are we okay here? And I saw him raise his tiny hand, a gesture of acknowledgment: Yup, I see you, we're good, hey, we respect each other, would I hassle you on a day like this?

But as we were passing him, Ollie stopped, reached into his jacket pocket, took out a lighter, and bent over to light the cigarette I now saw Jeff had between his lips. He hadn't been signaling me but asking for some flame. I stood there awkwardly. He stared up at us with the crystallized gaze of a Byzantine saint.

"Hey, Jeff," I said, "happy Sunday."

He took an enormous drag, exhaled a Hiroshima of smoke. Slowly, he seemed to recognize our human specificity. "Bud," he whispered at Ollie, "watch out for this one. She speaks her mind."

Ollie gave me a look—Who's this guy? and She does?—but demurred.

"Say, bud, which kind you smoking?"

Ollie dug in his pocket again and pulled out a crumpled pack of American Spirits. He knocked a couple out and handed them to Jeff. Or, anyway, politely deposited them in Jeff's lap. "What, no Luckies?" Jeff drawled. "No Camels?"

"Watch out for this one," I said. "He always asks for more."

In slow motion, Jeff wiggled his feet. "See my new shoes?" The Nikes were gone, replaced by sad, grimy tube socks several sizes too large. "I'm taking donations."

The sight was too depressing, as was the thought of what he'd probably sold those Nikes to buy. "Next time, Jeff," I said and pulled Ollie away. We cut along 16th and into the Castro, where the brunch lines were already backing up and the streetcars grinding cheerily along. "Friend of yours?" Ollie said.

"Perks of your block being 'on the edge.'" I didn't want to think about addicts or the general human wreckage of the city, not this perfect morning. "Since when do you smoke?" I'd never even smelled it on him.

"Good way to sneak a break on the job." He looked sheepish, his hair still bed-tousled. "Sorry, I thought you wouldn't like it."

A gust of affection hit me. I pulled him close, drew his arm around me. "Hell, I might even bum one."

"After lunch"—he kissed my forehead—"I can do delayed gratification."

The dim sum place was bright, loud, hectic. But being the only white people in a huge room of Chinese families made me feel somehow detached from the bustle. Between the unending small dishes, I reached under the table, held Ollie's leg. We stuffed ourselves, paid the bill, reeled out into the early afternoon sun. "Fuck it," Ollie said, stepping into a corner store, "after a meal like that." He came out with two tall cans of Tecate wrapped in paper bags.

"Well, since it's Sunday," I said, happy and loose. We walked and smoked and drank. The warm, the pleasant, the fond—give me all of that and forget the rest. That's what youth missed, the enormous consolation of everything mild and plush. Meanwhile the middle-aged thought they wanted all that old frenzy back, just one last time, and launched into their crises and embarrassing affairs—my mother, dating again, suddenly molding her life around this random stump yanker. But, if it gave her some company, some insulation, I couldn't begrudge her a little care or attention. Floating through my city, cigarette on my lips, my man on my arm, I just couldn't bring myself to worry about her.

"There's somewhere I want to show you," Ollie said as we crossed Geary.

"What, is your singer buddy playing the Chinese brunch circuit now?"

"This is cool. Hardly anyone knows about it."

"Please," I said, "show me."

At Arguello, he took us south for a block, then up a slight hill. We turned onto a cul-de-sac lined with manzanitas and stucco bungalows. A large domed building stood behind high wrought-iron gates, somehow hidden on this brief, pretty street. We left our beers tucked outside the gate and crunched around the gravel path that circled the building. A silver-haired woman knelt near the entryway, planting dark orange marigolds in a narrow flower bed. "What a beautiful day," she said, her gaze placid, her voice ethereal. "Would you like to go inside? Visiting hours until seven."

We went through slab-like oak doors into an echoing marble rotunda. Smaller halls extended off the central room, two more levels stretching above, their chilly air pressing down on us. Over the arches leading into the halls were chiseled "Zephyrus," "Olympias," "Arktos," other Greek words. Everywhere I looked, there were niches cut into the stone—arched, foot-high, fronted with glass doors with last names stenciled on them. Behind the doors sat little groups of objects: an open Bible, a vase of fake flowers, a sheaf of sheet music, a statuette of two men with their arms around each other, a child-size baseball mitt. "What is this?" The temperature dropped another few degrees. "A cemetery?"

"A columbarium!" Ollie tipped his head back to the noon light hazing through the glass dome. "The only place you can be laid to rest in city limits. Not even death can afford to live in San Francisco."

The woman came in, started misting the windows with Windex. "Any questions?"

Each small glass door was an eye staring back at me. "We're fine," I said tightly.

"We were built in 1898, the design by Mr. Bernard Cahill, also a noted cartographer. Each room, as you can see, is named after one of the mythological winds."

I tugged on Ollie's arm, dizzy, cold, the air being pushed out of my lungs.

"How many plots are left?" Ollie said, picking the worst time to be polite.

"Only twenty-five, out of five thousand." The woman put down her Windex and rag and stood admiring. "You're welcome to go upstairs. Just keep walking in a circle if you get lost. You'd be surprised how easy it is to get lost."

My limbs prickled with panic, glimmering on the edge of an attack. "Please," I got out. "Let's go."

"Sorry," Ollie finally said to the woman, "we're a little late for something."

Outside, I could barely catch a breath. I kept going, as far from that place as possible. At the corner, Ollie stopped me. "Hey, what's going on?"

"Why the fuck did we go in there?"

"I thought it'd be . . . You know, all those little doors, it's kind of . . ."

My teeth ached, the taste of steel was so strong. "I need home. Now."

Ollie stopped, turned back to the columbarium. "Shit, our beers."

"Leave them," I growled.

"What is this? What's wrong?"

I was almost running now, all but stumbling down the hill.

"Hey, come on! Wait a second!"

A cab pulled up to the light. I hailed it, threw myself in. "The Mission," I just managed to get out. "18th and Capp." I tried to tell him to wait for Ollie. But all that came out was a slurred jumble of syllables. The driver must have thought I was drunk and gave me a cautious, aggrieved look in the rearview, worried about me puking on his upholstery. I slumped in my seat, unable to turn to see where Ollie was. The cab pulled away. Only the seat belt kept me from sliding to the floor.

OLLIE GOT TO THE GROVE fifteen minutes after I did. He must have rung the buzzer twenty times. But I was on the couch, switched off, unable to cross the room to let him in, shivering inside even as I couldn't on the outside. My phone rang and rang, all the way over in my bag where I'd dropped it by the door. The attacks kept rolling through me. A hard, black cold set in. My thoughts flowed thick and sludgy as tar. When I woke, it was dark. My stomach clawed for food.

On hands and knees, I got myself over to my bag. But my phone was dead, and finding my charger, just then, seemed impossible. All I could do was crawl up to the loft, listen to the muted bleat of traffic on Mission, the dull shouts of junkies and working girls. The image of all those little doors . . . It kept shoving me down to the root of my terror. And, still, I couldn't touch it.

In the drawer of my bedside table, I kept a bottle of prescription pills. Teshawn might have built up a tolerance, but the stuff fucked me up completely, left me, the next day, woozy and disembodied, caught in the worst jet lag imaginable. The doctors and specialists will tell you they don't know exactly how the drug muffles the condition, but it was initially developed as a heavy-duty tranquilizer—it muffles everything. One pill and I'd be sunk for the night, so deep, so numb my brain wouldn't even have a memory of sleep, those hours only a blank, part of my continuous self snipped out, the broken strands forever disconnected.

I shook out a pill. It was sticky with age and clung to the tip of my finger. I hesitated, then put it on my tongue and, wanting to retch, swallowed hard. It began to blossom in my stomach. My head went grainy. I dropped onto the pillow. Sleep closed in, but another darkness came quicker. Parts of me were already going dim, those parts I forever had to police. I started to drift. The bed slipped from underneath me, and I went up like fog into an already gray sky. Panic still sludged through me. Then it all began to drift away. I fell as I rose, expanded as I dissolved. Guilt and shame and terror receded, dark undertones on a black canvas. I might have felt relief or even, momentarily, free.

But the drug had taken over. I didn't feel anything at all.

I WOKE. The bed was wet. I'd wet the bed.

Cold and wet, I hobbled down to the toilet. The toilet seat was icy cold. My bowels released. I sat there, staring at the floor.

I dragged myself and my phone to the couch. I had to email Byron, call in sick. Email in sick. Whatever. Ollie had left voicemails, texts. A dozen, more. I stared at them, all of his worry. I couldn't. Couldn't call him, ask for his help. Not in this state.

Lunch—oatmeal, a few sips of tea—threw it up. Hunched over the toilet, everything came up. Wrapped myself in an old comforter on the couch, the TV just a smear of color and sound. Slept, woke, slept. Rest from the pills, no rest at all.

Five-thirty the next morning, I came around. Soaked in sweat but half-whole. I showered, thought I might go to work. No. The woman in the mirror, frazzled, cadaverous, shook her head no. Another email: I'd be out for the week. Hauled myself back up to bed. Another pill on the end of my finger, choked it down. Went back down.

OLLIE CAME TO THE GROVE, rang the buzzer again and again. I couldn't answer. It was impossible, a delusion that it could've worked. A few more weeks, he would've known, too. He wasn't dealing with someone who just had quirks or a weird hangup. Each bad attack had a memory attached, some absurd, some almost funny, some so heavy they crushed me all on their own. I had broken dreams of him, his old radios, tangles of wiring all around him. When I woke, I picked up my phone, opened my contacts. My finger hovered over the little portrait I'd taken of him, red fez lampshade over his eyes, framing his goofy smile . . . No, impossible. I tossed the phone away, rolled onto my back, in case I switched off. But the pills worked. No tears, no regret, no longing. The ghost of his photo hung before me. Then it dissolved.

THAT SUNDAY I WENT to group. Because I hadn't left the apartment in a week? Or I wanted easy sympathy? They were the only people I'd let see me like this? I don't know. I got into a black car in front of the Grove, I got out in front of the church. The pills took me. Autopilot. The AA guys were out front. The action figure held the door for me. "Right on time," he greeted me, "right on time." I couldn't even mumble thanks.

The reek of cleaning vinegar down the dim corridor, Sherman's smile as I came in, brighter than it'd been in weeks. "Great to see you back, Daphne!" There was general chatter, everyone talking about their weeks—dropped plates, embarrassing stumbles—until Sherman started up on the Stanford study again. He had a fading yellow bruise on his temple he kept reaching up to touch. Corner of the kitchen table? Counter? My mind dully marched through possibilities. It had hurt. I saw that it had hurt. But . . . floor? Doorknob? Doorframe?

Sherman wanted to know: Anyone participated in clinical trials before? Sparse murmurs of assent around the room. "Yeah, yeah," I heard myself murmur. Anyone like to share their experience? I stared at the ceiling, counted holes in the acoustic tile.

"Daphne, want to tell us about yours?" He gave me such a hopeful look. "The studies aren't so bad, right?"

"Hmm."

"Go ahead, Daphne. Stay open here."

Oh, God, that. If only he hadn't said that.

"Try it," I heard myself say, the words on autopilot, too. "Be my guest." Now I was staring at Sherman's bruise. "If you really need the cash, knock yourself out."

"The money seems fair," Miranda said. "And, in the end, it's helping all of us."

"Don't expect miracles," I said. "Miracles are not coming anywhere near us."

"Okay, then," she went on, "since we're listening to an expert opinion here."

"Are we talking about curing cancer? Heart disease? Baldness, for Christ's sake? Why would they bother? Why work on some freak thing hardly anyone knows about? Nothing in it for them. Money? Fame? Recognition? Nope."

"But Dr. Francis," Sherman said, "he studied with your Dr. Bell."

And if only he hadn't mentioned Dr. Bell, who put me through so many tests and overnights when none of them added up to a damn thing. "These guys are scientists, not healers," I said. "They'd cut open our skulls and start poking around if they could. You ever try to sleep with thirty electrodes taped to your head? Try that and tell me it's worth seventy-five bucks a night."

"It's one-twenty now," Sherman mumbled.

"Okay, great, one-twenty. Worth it"—I turned my dead gaze to Miranda—"if you're about to get canned."

People fidgeted in their desks. They glanced back and forth between Sherman and me. Didn't matter. Truth was better than empty promises and cheer. "I'm just trying to save you the trip down to Palo Alto. Might as well spend the time on the couch where it's safer." I shrugged. "Sorry, I'm just staying open here."

Sherman rushed through the rest of the meeting. I could've stayed afterward, explained myself, told him what had happened, told him it was the pills talking, only the pills. But I didn't. I slipped out as soon as we finished.

At home, I stood staring into the mirror. I thought of the singer, practicing all his looks. I grimaced. I smiled. Maybe I could catch a glimmer, an echo of each feeling. Frowned, startled, pouted, jeered at myself. No, there was nothing. Not even an echo.

FIFTEEN

A T WORK EVERYONE WAS CIRCUMSPECT. I'D COME
back after an unexplained week away looking like
an invalid: puffy, slack, bloodshot eyes. Had Byron told
them? He probably had his suspicions about why I'd been
out. His squint was even more knowing. On Tuesday a
memo came across my desk: He'd written up Hidalgo, a
dress code violation, Hidalgo's Giants cap of all things.
It'd gone up the ladder, come back down with a query
from the bosses. I shredded it. Just then Byron passed by
in a three-piece suit and a garish paisley tie, like the model
employee. With the muffling of the pills, my response to
him was bland, impersonal, and I saw him more clearly:
a man so afraid of being ignored or passed over that he'd
turned himself into the group's villain just to get some,
any, kind of recognition. Still, my tolerance for the drug
must have been building—I could've grabbed him by that
tie, fed *it* into the shredder.

I KEPT TO MY OFFICE, caught up on email. My mother tried to chat me a couple of times, but I was telegraphic in my replies, and she either took the hint or got busy with her own work. On Friday I called Staci into my office. She perched on the edge of her chair, alert, penitent. I'd put off this conversation too long. "Reviews aren't till the end of the year," I began monotonically. "But we should talk now about your position and whether—"

She broke into her old pitch, how she'd always wanted to be a vet but her parents never had the money for school, and when she saw this job, she knew it was perfect for her. And she wanted to help our dogs. They did such important work. They helped us so much, they needed someone to help them, too. As she went on, it started raining heavily. I listened to it pattering the skylight, thought about how rain was good for the Central Valley farmers, wondered what I had coming in my produce box that week. "I can toughen up," Staci was saying, "and I just want you to know how grateful I am. This opportunity means so, so much to me." I told myself, She can either do the job or she can't. And I'd all but promised Hidalgo the overtime. But if I did fire her now, I'd have to feel *something* later. Resentment, guilt. Christ, just send her packing, be done with it.

"Reliability," I said, "that's what this lab needs. More importantly"—she wasn't the only one who could play on feelings—"that's what the dogs need. Someone who steps up every day. Ask yourself if that's you. If it isn't, maybe it's time to start—"

A muffled clang sounded from somewhere in the building. The slightest tingle in my skull—I dropped my pen. Otherwise, it was so aberrant, I wasn't sure what I'd heard. "Hold on," I said, got up, and poked my head into the main room. Pin had her earbuds in.

"What was that?" I asked Byron.

He let out an annoyed grunt. "Some fresh disaster, I'm sure."

Then all of the dogs started howling at once. There was another loud clang and several muted shouts. I went to the glass and looked for Hidalgo. He was pressed against the far wall. I rapped on the glass and caught his eye. He pointed to the door to the outside play area, then ducked out of sight. The door hung crookedly from its frame, its top hinge popped loose. Then I saw, moving between the pens, three figures, two in black hoodies, one in a dark green raincoat. "Pin, Byron," I said. "Get security here, now."

I ran to the air shower, yanked it open, hit the button. The vents kicked on. Without a Tyvek suit on, they stung. But I didn't think of that, or how much I hated that cramped, chill space. The inner door released. I shoved out into the din of howling dogs. "Security will be here in one minute," I heard myself say in a hard, clipped voice. "You've got exactly one minute to get out of my lab."

The two hoodies squatted at the end of the third row of pens. They both had fence cutters and were snipping at one of the cages, which was already half-open. Raincoat stood a few steps back, a huge bolt cutter dangling from his right hand. The other two had ski masks on. Raincoat only had a camouflage bandana over his mouth and chin. In his eyes, there was a disbelieving, terrified shine.

"You've got forty seconds." I'd gone so still, so dead, I was almost outside myself. "Thirty-five." It wasn't the pills—they'd burned off with the jolt of seeing the intruders—but something deeper, the fight reflex kicking on, closing down anger, fear, everything. Or maybe it was all of my practice, my constant tamping down. Either way, there was only one second, the next, the next. "Thirty." One of the hoodies looked up, glared at me, grabbed a hand-cart, and threw it over. Part of their strategy was to wreck as much property as possible, but he wanted to rattle me as well. "Good, very good," I said. "Already going to jail, might as well up the charges."

"You defend the corporation's filthy profits?"

"Even if you get one of those dogs out, how far you think you're going to get? They're all chipped," I lied. "We'll find them, and you, in twenty minutes."

Raincoat started delivering a nervous speech—"You don't have to be the oppressor!" he bawled at me—but the barking threw him off. His jeans were soaked and muddy, sweat stood out on his forehead. Any moment he might break and run, or start swinging those bolt cutters.

I narrowed my thoughts, no time for the willows, the river. The barking was catastrophic. Staci had come in behind me. "Get out!" she screamed. "Just get the hell out!" I advanced, my gaze locked on Raincoat. He was eighteen, nineteen, way too young. The hoodies were bending back the wire of the cage, about to pull out the dog. "Please, lady," Raincoat said, "stay back, okay?"

"Don't go any further with this," I said. "You're about to mess up big-time."

He gripped his bolt cutter tighter. I could picture him bringing it down on my skull. But if I could get him to run, the others might follow. "Shut up!" Raincoat said, straining against his uncertainty. "This place is Auschwitz!"

"You think we do this because we like torturing dogs?"

"I don't care why you *think* you're doing it."

Lord knows I fantasized enough about setting all our dogs free. And not doing anything here wouldn't have cost me my job. Our security team would catch hell, but I wasn't required to face these people down. It wasn't a question of protecting company property either, though I winced when one of the hoodies grabbed a device interface—six grand worth of electronics—and slammed it against the wall. The dog they were going for cowered in the back of its cage, yelping so loud it wrenched my guts.

"Run out that door right now, you might get off light, a slap on the wrist." Jesus, where the hell was security? "Run up into the hills, you might just get away."

"You motherfuckers! Get out!" Staci's fury was towering, but I didn't want to push Raincoat over the edge. I motioned for her to calm down. Mercifully, she did.

"You're upsetting the animals," I told him. "That's all you're doing right now. Listen, I get it." I gestured at the cages. He couldn't help following. He seemed almost transfixed. "This sucks. It sucks that we have to do this. But there's a reason."

"Don't listen to her!" Hoodie One turned over a bin of dry food, scattering pellets everywhere. "She's a fucking corporate tool!" Hoodie Two was half inside the cage, reaching for the dog.

My eyelids fluttered, my own trance fading. With a brutal effort, I shoved everything down. "Get out of here right now, you might not wind up in jail tonight. You could still disappear. But in ten seconds, my security people get here." I kept my eyes fixed on Raincoat. "Look at that dog, he's so frightened he can barely move. Come on!" I shouted, struggling to hold it all down. "Get out now, wake up in your own beds tomorrow. You'll still feel like you *did* something."

Raincoat's face crumbled. "Guys, come on."

"I've been to jail before!" Hoodie One shouted. "Who gives a shit?"

"Guys, I can't. I can't." A tremor got into Raincoat's voice. "My scholarship. If I get in trouble again, they'll take away my scholarship."

"Chris, just shut up and start cutting."

Raincoat looked close to tears. "Dave, you can't get another charge. They'll give you, Jesus, I can't remember what they'll give you. Just come on, this is crazy." He was backing away. "Guys, please," he said, "let's go already."

Hoodie Two suddenly backed out of the cage and hurled his fence cutters at the wall. His right cheek was covered in blood. He'd cut himself on the wire. Nothing like a tiny injury to make you truly dumb with rage.

"Go!" Staci shouted. "Get out!"

"Just get out." I heard my voice go weary. "Just leave."

They could do no more now than wreak a little extra havoc. They tried to tip over a shelving unit, but it was bolted to the wall. As they went out, both hoodies gave me the finger. Then they were gone. I heard the rattle of them going through the hole they'd cut in the fence, then it was just rain spattering on the concrete outside and the thrum of the overhead fluorescents. I closed my eyes, put out a hand to steady myself. Someone touched my shoulder.

"Jesus," Staci said. "I can't believe you did that. I—"

"Check on the dogs. Check and see they're okay."

"*Putas*," Hidalgo muttered, reappearing. "*Hijos de puta*." He paced back and forth, worked up, or maybe embarrassed that, in the moment, he hadn't done anything. Or, no, he hadn't been scared, just calculating. He didn't get paid to put himself in harm's way, not on his benefits plan.

"It's fine," I said. "Just start picking up. Back to work." I grabbed a bag of treats and went down the aisles, dodging pieces of shattered glass and plastic. The dogs' tails were stiff and upright, batting noisily against their pens. I came to Biscuit's pen. He was curled in the far corner, trembling. I opened the pen, reached in, then refrained from petting him. I took out his bowl, dropped in a fistful of treats.

SECURITY ONLY CAUGHT ONE of the activists—Raincoat. I didn't want to know anything more about it, didn't want to see the kid or hear his story. The Animal Liberation people always shook us up, but this . . . I told Staci to take the afternoon off; I didn't need her crying in the bathroom. But she insisted on staying to help clean up. I started an inventory of what had been broken, kept my head down. The trembling started to creep in. Head down, head down.

It was pouring as I waited on the Caltrain platform. The train came late, no seats in any car, the heater full blast, people packed into the aisles. I felt their fraying patience shoving in, gritted my teeth, tried to let my mechanical self take over. At 16th Street, I waited in the dreary, sodden line for the escalator, mechanical as a clock grinding through its gears. But when I hit street level, I found myself not pointed toward the safety of home and more pills but raising a hand for a cab. Then I was riding through the city, out to the avenues, watching the drawn faces of commuters slogging their way home.

When Ollie opened his door, I registered his surprise, then my eyes fluttered closed. "Hey," he said. "It's you. You're here. Why haven't you—"

He'd just been able to catch me. My strings had been cut. I hung there in his arms, the only thing moving the tears streaming down my cheeks.

SIXTEEN

THAT NIGHT, I TOLD HIM.

We lay on his mattress, surrounded by old radio parts. It took more than an hour for the last of the attacks to wash through me. We lay apart, neither of us quite willing to touch. He was confused and angry with me. I couldn't blame him. But, as it was, I'd barely been able to talk about the break-in. Now he wanted to know what had happened at the columbarium. "You just freaked the fuck out. Where have you been? Shit, I don't even know what I did. Why haven't you even called?"

"What, never had a girl go crazy on you?"

"I'm definitely not taking that for an answer."

"It'd take all night to explain."

"Well."

I shivered. The memory froze me as hard as oak. I didn't know if my tongue could even get it out. I tried to start, once, twice. "O-kay," I began again, "you ever go to dumb movies when you were a kid? Just to make fun of them?

Ollie gave me a doubtful look, still worried I was evading.

"My friend Brook, she had all the irony. But I was just . . . susceptible."

Truly, I loved every movie we saw. The huge, beautiful faces of the actors, the seismic bass of the soundtrack, the vividness and velocity of the lives flung up on screen—even the lousiest, corniest stuff grabbed me, held me tight. Brook was always snorting and coughing out her hard, sharp laugh. But I could never get that distance. In the moments when the story, no matter how worn and predictable, began to yearn toward its climax, when you knew someone was going to die or sacrifice themselves or do something truly, foolishly noble, I couldn't keep my heart from gonging in my chest.

Plus, in the dark, no one could see me: my sagging jaw and fluttering eyes. God, sometimes it was like my eyelids weighed a ton. This was junior year. Despite everything I'd tried to avoid—stress, arguments, competition, flirting—my weird little moments had grown more frequent. Kids started to pull faces back at me in the halls. I hid myself under droopy bangs, brown lipstick, ribbed Henleys, and chunky Docs, mimicking Brook's style. And when I had to be seen, in speech class or gym, I'd rattle off my notes or listlessly shoot hoops, all my concentration spent on trying to ward it off. I had my methods then, crude as they were. Counting back from a hundred, that kind of thing. But at the movies, finally, I could surrender.

That afternoon, Brook and I had been out with Samantha and Tina. They were more Brook's friends than mine. They smoked, cut classes, wore Joe Camel sweatshirts and baggy jeans. Tina had even dated Kyle Magolski. In other words, Brook was busy shrugging off the Sunday-school sweetheart her Evangelical parents still expected her to be, and Samantha and Tina were part of the campaign. At least they never mentioned my funny faces.

Brook insisted on some period drama. It was set in the 1930s, a dusty cattle ranch down by the border. The lead was tall and dark with a perfect, floppy haircut such the height of '90s fashion he might as well have been wearing a beeper. His love interest was a beautiful Mexican girl he first glimpsed while breaking wild horses for the stern widower father who kept her locked away. I remember that the theater smelled of burnt nacho cheese, and that, three rows in front of us, two farm boys wearing Colts caps, in this movie because they thought it was one girls liked, kept turning around and ogling us. And still, despite their leers, the actors' cardboard cutout performances, the hopelessly out-of-date plot, the love interest's ridiculous fake accent, and Brook's running commentary on it all—despite every distraction, I watched that movie like I was living it.

Near the end, there was a scene straight out of the old black-and-white movies my mom loved so much: the lead mewling ballads under the beautiful Mexican girl's balcony, trying to convince her to forgive him and just maybe succeeding through the force of his syrupy passion. "Oh, God," Brook groaned, tossing a fistful of popcorn at the screen. But the look that passed between the two lovers, the earnest twinkle in the lead's eyes as he hit the high note, the swooning sigh from the girl . . . What rose up in me was pure—pure laughter, unrestrained, all joy and dumb, innocent longing. Everyone turned to look—my perplexed friends, those boys, several annoyed adults—and knowing I shouldn't be laughing made it rush up even harder, my stomach leaping like on the Vortex at Six Flags, an enormous bloom of giddy pleasure I just couldn't hold back.

The buzzing started, even stronger than what I'd felt reading in bed or playing volleyball. My whole skull fizzed as the laughter plumed. When my body dropped away, I pitched forward. I was at the end of the row and tumbled into the aisle, my forehead glancing a seat back, my right shoulder landing hard on the floor, right cheek coming to rest abruptly on the hard carpet.

"From that mo-ment on," I told Ollie, "I re-mem-ber everything."

That gritty, musty industrial carpet, the caramel taste of RC Cola still on my lips, greasy popcorn finger marks on my white Lee jeans . . . And underneath and between the seats: furred-over Raisinettes and Starbursts and the mismatched socks, one brown, one argyle, of the woman across the aisle. Time moved in slow, lazy motion, and my senses scrupulously recorded it all.

Brook shrieked—my stunt probably looked, at first, hilarious—and Tina and Samantha followed suit. For a moment, I wanted to join in, wanted it all to be funny. But the laughter, the actual sounds anyway, wouldn't come. I told myself, Okay, get off the floor. Get up. Get up already.

And nothing, absolutely nothing, was happening. I could only lie there, staring at the argyle sock. I blinked. I could do that at least, blink.

Then things got still. I could hear the movie's dialogue, but other, unfamiliar voices were now whispering above me. Someone—Brook maybe—took me by the shoulders and shook me, thinking she could wake me up. But, as I'd come to find, being manhandled during an attack only made it worse. Someone rolled me onto my back. My body was so completely limp that a bolt of panic shot through me. My eyes fell closed. I couldn't open them again. Another flurry of whispers. They merged with the distant but ultra-clear sound of rain, the movie soundtrack playing some culminating, cathartic storm. For an absurd instant, I wondered what I was missing.

Then the movie went silent—someone had cut it off—and I heard Brook whisper, "Daphne, what the *fuck* are you doing? This is way too much. Come on, already." Someone, Samantha, it sounded like, tittered nervously. Someone else tentatively pinched my arm. I wanted to cry out in pain or annoyance but couldn't even part my lips. It seemed as if everyone in the theater had gathered over me and that the weight of their sudden attention was pressing down, keeping me pinned to the floor.

"Lady, *please*," Brook said. "Seriously, what is this?"

Two thick, sweaty fingers pressed against my neck, and an unfamiliar male voice said, "Jesus, we should call an ambulance, huh?"

The whispers quieted. The house lights came on; I could

see them through my eyelids. No one was touching me anymore. For that, at least, I was glad. The floor was hard against my back. I wanted to squirm into a more comfortable position, wanted to tell everyone I was okay, I was fine, I was just . . . But even if I could've explained, I didn't know what I'd say, couldn't seem to chain any words together. With each passing minute, I felt both more flustered and more sluggish. The laughter, the embarrassment—in front of my friends, in front of those boys—the fear, the suffocating proximity of all the confused people above me . . . I didn't know about rolling attacks then, each one building on the other, weight upon weight.

A woman spoke. The theater manager maybe. She had a southern Indiana twang and sounded pissed. "What's going on here? Christ, y'all been drinking." I thought I was going to be poked or pinched again, but the woman held back. "Y'all drunk, ain't ya?"

"No, ma'am," Brook said in a very adult voice. "We haven't been. She just . . ." Brook tried to describe what had happened. But she was drowned out by someone asking for a refund, someone else bitching about teenagers ruining every movie. It seemed they'd forgotten about me. And I was growing less aware of them. When I first went down, my heart had been hammering. Now my breathing and pulse guttered. I felt listless, near sleep—the exhaustion of multiple attacks. Briefly, I bobbed back up. All of their body heat had drawn back. Two male voices were telling everyone to clear a path.

A large, warm hand took mine, held two fingers against the inside of my wrist. I vaguely felt a blood pressure cuff around my arm, growing tighter with each pump before a soft, almost pretty release of air. A hand touched the center of my chest, the palm flat, pressed hard several times, then stopped. Lips touched mine, breathed into my mouth. I tasted something like salami, felt the burn of stubble. "Okay, Bob, the salts," a man said. Five seconds later, an ammoniac vapor hit my nostrils. My brain exploded, a thousand flashbulbs bursting. I wanted to scream, *You idiots, you fucking idiots, what the fuck are you doing?* But they did all the tests. Not as well as they might have, but they did them. What none of us knew then: the deeper my panic, the deeper the paralysis.

"Okay, Bob?" the man said. "Let's get the gurney?"

"I want to go with her," Brook said.

"Miss," the man said, "I'm not sure it would be appropriate."

Brook didn't answer. No one did.

"Can someone call her folks, tell them to come to St. Mary's?" the other EMT said. "It's . . ." He paused for a moment, then reeled off the address.

"I'll do it," Brook said, her voice trembling. "I'll call her mom."

People shuffled apart, making way. There were hands underneath me. I was lifted into the air, deposited onto the gurney. They tightened the straps, pulling them so they bit into my arms and legs. They wheeled me up the sloping aisle and out into the lobby—I heard the distant rumble of movies playing on other screens—out the double doors, and into the parking lot, where the humid August air suddenly clung to my skin. Before I could think to somehow protest, they'd slotted me into the back of the ambulance. Then my panic became ravenous.

Neither of the EMTs rode in back with me. I smelled only the stink of my own sweat as my mind lurched, stumbled, flailed to sort all of this out. Yet, somehow, it cohered. It wasn't a dream. As the ambulance moved through the streets, all of the weird things that had happened over the last couple of years—my lapses and spells and "growing pains"—began to twine together. An entire hidden history unspooled underneath me as we accelerated, decelerated, turned, accelerated again.

We stopped. The rear doors opened. They pulled the gurney out. It began to roll again, one wheel squeaking now. Automatic doors parted with a whoosh. We slid into a sterile, chilly cavern of air. I heard elevator doors open. But only when I felt us descending, not ascending, did I guess where we were headed. Then I was senseless with terror.

The elevator opened again. The density of the air had changed, a basement level. One of the EMTs started whistling the chorus of some pop song.

"Beers at Billy's after we get off?" the other said.

"Come on, I can't be there *every* time you hit on that bartender." The whistler squawked like a chicken. "You goddamn pussy."

"Wrong beast, dumbass."

"You're the wrong beast."

We knocked through two sets of swinging doors. The temperature plunged, and the smell hit in layers: bad taco meat, the boys' locker room, a sharp, chemical lemon, the frogs we dissected in bio. The light was so bright that, even through my closed eyelids, I wanted to flinch. A deep hum vibrated the air. A high-pitched, aggrieved voice said, "Shit, not you two again."

"Same bat channel." The whistler whistled the old *Batman* theme.

"Can't you and Robin come back when I'm not slammed?"

"Key-rist, are these all the wreck on 465?"

"These *were* the wreck, yes."

"Okay, Dr. Grammar, where'd you want this one?"

"She's young. What happened?"

"I don't know, cardiac maybe. Her friends looked druggie. Anyway, isn't that your job?"

"Write out the sheet, put her in twelve. I'll sign when I'm done with these."

They moved me only a short distance. A latch clicked. Rollers trundled on a track. My arms were arranged over my chest, one hand over the other. Something that felt like an Ace bandage was tied around my wrists. One of the men pushed my feet together, lifted me by the legs while the other took my shoulders. The firm padding of the gurney disappeared, replaced a moment later by frigid, stinging metal. Someone took hold of my big toe. I felt another pinch.

The rollers trundled again. It was suddenly cold and so dark behind my eyelids I didn't even see shapes or the ghosts of colors. I lay there, trying to blink, failing to blink, trying, trying to snap myself out of it.

Time passed. I seemed to be falling, bottoming out through

all the layers of my terror. Then came murk, a bog of dark, turbulent sensation: sorrow, regret, guilt, all churning. I'd done something wrong; this was punishment. I remembered all of my petty exasperation with my mother, thought of her crying alone in our house while the wind yowled off the river. The dark and cold—I'd somehow fallen out of the world, stranded myself somewhere between bright, moving life and the blankness of the other side. One moment it was excruciating—my skin adhering to metal—the next an eerie stillness settled over me. I felt the humming in my bones. But, gradually, both it and the smells dissipated, and only the stillness remained. A long, slow, thin shiver went through me as everything took on an icy, hard clarity: While I waited in line for the coroner, I was either going to suffocate in that drawer or freeze to death.

As each second passed, cloudiness seeped in. My head began to silt away. My body went thick. Indifference lodged in my stomach. My skin, down to the muscle, went as hard and thick as bark. Time got cloudy, the passing seconds fogged together. Time went hard and still.

Then something prickled. Beneath the bottom, past the stillness, another thin shiver.

It began to spread, a million tiny pricks of pain, like numbness receding from a foot that's fallen asleep. It went on forever, agonizing. But, after a time, I could open my eyes again. Was I imagining it? The darkness didn't change—open them, close them, open them—but the muscles in my brow had perked up. My legs were as heavy as telephone poles. Yet, it seemed, I could twitch them.

Flinging everything into one exhausting effort, I

shrugged my right arm off my chest, brushed the tips of my fingers against the cold steel and, knowing it was still real, panicked again. My arm and hand fell limp.

Then, after an endless span in which I kept fighting but not understanding what I fought, I let myself go still again. Gaining confidence, I tried to kick at the metal panels. But there was barely room to move, and anyway my kicks were too feeble to make enough noise. Outside, I could hear voices, metallic and muted through the steel. No one had heard me. I waited. The darkness thrummed. My tongue was coming back.

When I tried to clear my throat, my mouth was so dry I almost choked. The first sound from my lips was a pathetic, slurred whimper. Then, swallowing, gritting my teeth, working up my saliva, I spoke once into the darkness. Not more than a slurred syllable. It came back, a tiny, hollow echo, but it spurred me on. I had to gather all my strength.

The coroner on duty later said *he* nearly had a heart attack when it happened. He was working alone, had just turned on the radio, when he heard another voice, muffled but still distinct, speak from seemingly out of nowhere.

"Ex-cuse me," that voice said. "P-lease. Could you help me? I'm not dead. I'm in here. Help, I don't think I'm dead in here."

OLLIE LAY LISTENING, watching me, not taking his eyes from mine as I mumbled my way to the end. "Ah, Jesus," he said solemnly. "One person shouldn't have to . . ."

"That columbarium," I said. "Too familiar. All those little doors."

"I should have warned you."

"How could you? I don't talk about that day. I don't even think about it."

"You can. We'll figure it out."

"Is that what you always say?"

"Look," he began, and the sparkle in his eye drew inward, like the silvery twist trapped in a marble. He was about to make a declaration. I put out a hand to stay him, reached for my phone. No way my tongue could get it out. And my fingers were still clumsy as I typed. A moment later, his phone dinged with a text. " 'Ollie, I really, really lice you,' " he read aloud.

I sent another. " 'Fucking autocorrect.' " He put his phone down, pinned me again with that silvery gaze. Then the smile squeaked out. "Daphne, I think I lice you, too."

As best I could I rolled my eyes.

SEVENTEEN

Top drawer: His tighty whities, bleached V-necks, and slightly crusty socks.

Second drawer: My work tights, day-of-the-week panties, faded "There's More Than Corn in Indiana" T-shirt, two unopened, expired boxes of condoms shoved in back.

Third drawer: his work hoodie, his "dress" hoodie, his track/house pants, a shirt that read "Oscar Grant: The Movement for Justice."

Fourth drawer: his spackle-spattered jeans, my vacuum-sealed bags of going out/modestly revealing outfits, backup pajamas for when Brook used to spend the night.

Bookcase: my art and design books, his Merle Haggard, Replacements, and Ramones LPs, *Whole Earth Catalogs*, and heavily highlighted philosophy books, from which I'd patiently removed all the dirty yellow "Used" stickers.

East wall: flat-screen TV concealed and revealed—cleverly, I'd add—by my vintage pull-down classroom map of California. My display of hand mirrors working perfectly by the door. His (ugh) Budweiser poster of a dog playing pool he insisted he could not live without. His (much better) immaculately restored console hi-fi, which lent the apartment an intriguing '70s rumpus-room feel I'd not previously considered.

South wall: I'd stenciled, right on the wall, the outline of a fireplace and hearth and inside of it arranged a clutch of bleached driftwood to bring out its Goldsworthy-like qualities. On the old card-catalog side table, his slightly shaggy bonsai tree—"Steve," he called it—next to a Rhys chair that maybe wanted a partner, a little conversation nook in progress or evocatively unfinished, I wasn't yet sure.

West wall: I'd stretched to buy in the Grove for its waist-to-ceiling windows, the promise of watching the sun melt over the neighborhood and Twin Peaks, the evening laying its soft blanket of fog over the city. But now, every time I looked out at all of that widescreen beauty, the question beckoned: drapes or blinds, drapes or blinds, drapes or . . .

Kitchen area: No changes other than the occasional six-pack of Tecate in the fridge. When Ollie moved into the Grove, he didn't bring a single pot or dish or piece of cutlery. He and his roommates had owned all of that collectively, and it and they had dispersed when, mid-May, their landlord sold the place out from under them with less than a week's notice. Ollie had talked about finding his own place, maybe even on a real lease. But on his scraped-together earnings, he would've had to live in Oakland or Daly City or worse. I couldn't have him that far away. So now I had him close, very close, and I liked the sudden bustle of life together, the choreography around the sink and chopping board as we made long, elaborate meals, fitting ourselves together on the couch, me wearing his dress hoodie around the apartment even when I wasn't chilly, just to wrap his presence around me. And there was the new casualness of touch, him brushing a crumb off my chin, me playing with his hair in the drowsy morning, his body glancing mine as we followed our separate but parallel paths through the day.

Closet: The nightmare was locked away. His old CDs and mixtapes jammed into milk crates, boxes and boxes of fuses and resistors and capacitors, at least forty envelopes of loose snapshots—family, life on the commune, travels in the drizzly Northwest. His mud-caked work boots, his Carhartt jacket hanging right in the middle of my pressed, plastic-sheathed coats, making them smell like a construction site. In fact, the air in the entire apartment seemed to have changed. Even after Ollie started using my shampoo and all of his clothes had gone through my washer with my detergent, it felt different, ionized in some peculiar way. I held my hand up to my nose and drew a breath, and I couldn't be sure, but I swore I could smell him on my skin.

WHEN I CAME HOME from work, I'd often find him on the couch, fiddling with some old radio part while watching the news: Crowds packed the Wisconsin statehouse. Judges were choking one another. The exultation in Egypt had given way to trials, paranoia, more beatings. Everywhere, there seemed to be mobs in the streets, dirty plumes of smoke, scattered, charred car parts, body parts, and the women, always the women, coming out of their homes to wail and scream, to suffer before the cameras—everything in the world coming undone, and Ollie inhaled it all. And if I succeeded in changing the channel, he'd pace the apartment with my phone, reading aloud the latest horror story. I'd keep murmuring in agreement, then, finally, pull him down to the couch.

"What?" he said. "Aren't you interested?"

"Seven billion people in the world, I'm working on my own little corner."

"We're talking *historic* change. We can't just perch up here and ignore it."

"Haven't we just had ten years on why we should stay the hell out of other people's business?"

"And if the revolution goes worldwide?" he asked in all sincerity.

"Remember three years ago, election night, everyone partying in the streets? He said one word—'hope'—to us, and we all went insane. Admit it," I said, grinning, antagonizing him with a little too much glee. "Politics is *all* emotion—hating the other side, valorizing your own, propping up your own identity. I'm right, I'm righteous, I *care*. No one can stand to admit they're as compromised and clueless as everyone else. People decide something *feels* right, then they warp all their thinking around that."

Ollie got up and started pacing again. "You can't rationalize disengagement. That's how we get the Third Reich, Rwanda, the fucking icecaps melting." I watched him warily as he went on about the people's voice, the end of tyrants and strongmen. "Don't you wish you could get over there? Cairo, Tunisia, Syria?" He wandered back to me, a big, expectant smile on his face. "Don't you wish you could *see* it?"

"You're about as much revolution as I can take right now. Here," I said, reaching for him again, "come back down here, my little Molotov cocktail." With a laugh, an eye roll, and a sarcastic but eager wrinkle of his brow, he flopped back down on the couch. "Wait," I said, "hold on." I got up, grabbed my camera. "Do that again."

"What?"

"That look you just had on your face. Just hold that a minute." He sat on the edge of the cushion, looking at me with vexation. I fired off a few shots. "Okay, come on, relax a little." He slouched and sat on his hands. "Not like that. Stretch out, put your hands behind your head."

He grimaced into a new position. "Okay, make like this is the happiest, most relaxed you've ever been." He broke into a big crackerjack smile. "Now you look like Jack Nicholson putting his head through the door. Stand up." I adjusted a few settings on the Nikon. "Now fall down on the couch. Just like before." He did a stiff, perfunctory flop. "Okay, but more casual. And more energized. Both at the same time." He did it a few more times. I got off some decent shots. "If only we had a dog for you to pet," I said. "But then there'd be hair all over everything. Jesus, those tours are such manicured bullshit. I swear they bring in professionals. Here, one of you and me."

I put the camera on timer, then positioned myself next to

him on the couch, straightened my shirt, ruffled my hair. I'd only half-done my makeup that day, but Interior Life liked their shots "authentic." The camera started beeping down the last few seconds. I did a little hop off the couch—"Hey!" Ollie cried—and bounced the two of us into each other, so it'd look like we'd been frolicking all afternoon. But when I checked the photo, my huge, open-mouthed grin looked a little insane and he just seemed irked.

"This is for that website you're always looking at?"

"Let's do one where we're just next to each other. Sit up straight, okay? They sometimes like these weird, ramrod-straight *American Gothic* poses."

When we finished, he was mopey and put out. But a few shots were good enough to send off that afternoon. Him looking fed up and vacant and me stifling a smile somehow came off as chic.

"ONE LAST THING, EVERYONE," Sherman said as we were extracting ourselves from our desks. It was my first time back at group. They all seemed to have, more or less, forgiven me; our worst selves often came to these meetings. Sherman seemed quieter, and there was a reluctant crimp to his mouth as he ended the meeting. "About that study I mentioned . . ." The rest trailed off into a mumble.

"What about it?" I said, loud enough for the rest of them to pay attention.

"Canceled," Sherman said offhandedly. "Low enrollment."

There was a ripple of acknowledgment around the room, but no one seemed surprised. The rest of them raided the cookies one last time and shuffled out into the July evening. Sherman and I stacked chairs in silence. "I'm really sorry," I finally offered.

"Like you said, probably pointless anyway."

"But it's Stanford. And Bell probably thought pretty highly of the guy running it. Not that I ever met this protégé. But he didn't trust many people with his work." Sherman hefted up a last chair and stood rubbing his jaw. I saw another bruise under a couple of weeks of beard. "What'd you do to your chin there?"

Sherman rattled out a desiccated laugh. "Let's just say it's time for a new coffee table. 'Skin heals, wood doesn't.' Olivia used to say that."

"How's Prince Hairy?" Maybe I should've let him go on about his ex-wife. But I wasn't sure if I had the strength to get him off the floor by myself.

"The Prince has been puking on everything."

"The royals do have all of those adorable ailments."

"Maybe it's time for him to find a new kingdom." Sherman took the snack tray and dumped the whole thing in the garbage. "You didn't want any of that, did you?"

"No, Ollie and I are roasting quails tonight." My phone vibrated, a text saying my car service was outside. "Need any more help? I can hang out for a bit."

"Janitorial staff gets the rest. These rooms don't come free."

"Want a ride home, then?"

In the back of the car, I could smell the sweat coming off him. His pre-rumpled Oxford had a few extra rumples, and his brogues hadn't been shined in weeks. "We need to make a stop for my friend," I told the driver. Sherman's address was further out than I thought, almost as far as Ollie's old place, out where the fog veiled everything and the city dissolved into ocean, sand, and sky. Sherman told the driver to stop in front of a faded pink stucco two-story.

"Want some company? The quails can wait."

"Apology accepted," he said.

"And it'd be nice to meet His Highness."

"You're kind. But I'll keep the cat puke to myself. See you next week maybe."

"No, I'll be there," I said. "Next week. Definitely."

I watched Sherman drag himself up his front steps. Until next Sunday's meeting, he could work from home. He could order in groceries and cat food, get his laundry picked up, dropped off. Obscure movies, craft beer, high-end toiletries, organically grown weed, gift-wrapped llama shit—anything he could dream of ever needing he could call up online and never have to go out. I watched him check his mail and disappear inside. Back home safe.

Trapped but safe.

EIGHTEEN

OVER THE NEXT FEW DAYS, MY CONSCIENCE KEPT poking me. Maybe the Stanford study getting canceled had been my fault—my antipathy for researchers and clinics had spread to the whole group. Maybe I'd infected them with my scorn.

After the movie theater, there was no more pretending. Until then, I thought I'd been hiding my little slips so well, even if my mother had been after me for months: "Are you eating? Lunch? Every day? Eat more fruit. Get more iron in your diet. Daphne, sit up. You're practically falling asleep at the dinner table. No more staying up all night. You think I don't see the light under the door?" Neither of us understood then. Her finely honed concern, my somersaulting adolescent exasperation—of course I was fluttering and slumping. I'd been holding myself so delicately, just getting through the day left me frazzled. Still, I acted as if she were persecuting me, a cover for my own bewilderment.

After the movie theater, I expected my mother to freak out. And when she got the call from the hospital, when she burst into the recovery room to find me wrapped in a blanket and sipping orange juice from a paper cup, she did. She plastered me with kisses, clobbered me with hugs. Then she screamed at the various administrators who came to us with their apologies and litigation-anxious assurances. She wanted the two EMTs fired and the coroner as well. Not that I minded her outrage; Lord knows I couldn't express my own. But what came later unnerved me: the eerie, freighted resignation she carried through our endless appointments with specialists and therapists—as if she'd always known some catastrophe would visit us.

Our family GP only knew how to kid around and treat me like I was still eight. He asked me all of the same questions everyone at the hospital had, ordered some blood work with the halfhearted suggestion that we might look out for anemia, then asked my mom to step out. "Okay," he said when we were alone, "you know how these work?" He handed me a small plastic stick about the size of a toothbrush.

"I'm not pregnant."

"Don't worry, we won't mention this to her just yet."

"But I haven't even . . ."

I wasn't going to cry, not in front of this man who used to give me lollipops when I bawled after vaccinations. That test and all the others came back negative. But they set in motion a series of visits to gynecologists and questions about flow and cramps and discharge that all ran together into one long humiliation. Then came the child development people, the psychologists and psychiatrists, two neurologists, CAT scans, MRIs. Every time some new possibility was raised—palsy, epilepsy—a dull panic pulsed through me, made me weak and leaden. But several months passed without answers, and I grew inured to the constant speculation about my body. It was mid-August, two weeks from the first day of my senior year. I'd spent the summer in doctors' offices and on the couch at home, watching movies and playing Nintendo, stretched out in my dad's old spot, the cushions still worn to the shape of his body. Sometimes Brook came over to veg, or we'd ooze around the neighborhood, pitching stones at stop signs, hot and bored and apprehensive. My mother would just stare at me, as if trying to memorize my face, then smile so sweetly I'd almost eye-flutter from impatience and dread. We were all waiting for the big, awful news: cancer or some other body-rotting disease.

The third neurologist—an Indian neuropsychiatrist at IU-Purdue—didn't order any scans, thank God. He talked to me for an hour and a half, about school, sports, my plans and ambitions. He had me describe, several times, my spells and when I had them, nodding the whole time and taking notes like he was interviewing me for a job or something. At the end, he took my mom aside. He was referring us to a colleague, a researcher with a lab down on IU's main campus in Bloomington. "A brilliant man," the neuropsychiatrist said. "Leagues ahead of everyone in this field. Truly, leagues. However, please, do not judge him on his personality."

MOM DROVE US DOWN to Bloomington on the Saturday before the first day of classes at Arcadia. We found the address, a cinder-block building that looked like some maintenance way station. The waiting room was filled with dusty institutional furniture, one armchair still wrapped in yellowed plastic. I'd gotten used to idly flipping through *Time* or *National Geographic*. Here there were only stacks of blandly designed periodicals with titles that started with *The Journal of* and ended with strings of words I could barely decipher.

Off the waiting room, there was a locked door. Mom knocked, called out hello. Several minutes later, a skinny guy with wiry, dark hair poked his head out, drawled, "Ten minutes, you're early," and closed the door again. A grad student, who looked about as stoned as Kyle Magolski after lunch hour. When we went through to the exam room, he pointed to a folding chair, "The mother, there," gave her a long, appraising look, then turned to me. "So, you're the one those second-raters at St. Mary's put in the freezer."

And, of course, this was no grad student but the miraculous Dr. August Bell. He didn't look older than twenty-five—thirty-eight, it turned out—and his dry, red eyes and high, hollow cheeks came not from pot but from all the sleep he skipped. His baggy khakis bloomed around his thighs like riding pants, and his name tag was pinned, upside down, to the untucked hem of his shirt. There appeared to be a fleck of salsa on his glasses.

"Well, this isn't church," he said to me, his voice pitched between disdain and conspiratorial collusion. "We're not servile and mute. We *speak*, don't we?"

Haltingly, I tried to explain the last few years. Mom cut in, but Dr. Bell would only give her a wan, abstracted smile and turn back to me. "Keep going," he said, "keep going. This *is* interesting, don't we agree?" After a time, however, his attention seemed to wander. He dug through stacks of paper, put on a pot of coffee, finally wiped off his glasses. "Describe the episodes," he said brusquely when I trailed off. "More detail."

I came to the movie theater, the EMTs, the morgue. He seemed no more moved by this than any of the rest but made me describe at length—"detail, please, detail"—the actual moment of my attack. "Yes, very common," he said, circling the room like a ringmaster about to blithely bait a tooth-less lion, "an utterly common trigger." I went on, not under-standing. He circled and circled, seeming annoyed. Then he stopped, looked me straight in the eye, and said, "Did you hear Princess Di was on the radio?"

"What?" Princess Diana, I thought, had been dead for months.

"Oh, yes," he said, "and on the dashboard and the steer-ing wheel and the . . ."

Was it funny? Or was I just taken aback by him telling an actual joke? Either way, I slumped over in my chair, and with one quick step Dr. Bell took me by the shoulders and propped me back up. "So, now we see!" He grinned wolfishly, batted his lashes at my mother. "Common—the first major episode triggered by laughter—utterly common."

But when we asked him to explain, begged him even, he just turned us out of the office, saying he wouldn't make a diagnosis until he knew more, more detail—oh, why didn't anyone ever know themselves well enough to give him proper *detail*?

When we came back a week later, he took blood samples and made me spit and pee in plastic cups, samples for his research. And he did other, more bizarre things: Startle me by clapping loudly right next to my ear. Make me look at upsetting photos—car accidents, fly-covered corpses—or watch scenes from violent, chaotic movies. Sometimes he shone a light in my face with what looked like a tanning reflector—I never understood that one. I wondered what my mother would make of it all, but Dr. Bell kept her in the waiting room. He was solicitous, always bringing her cups of scalding black coffee and asking about her work at Arcadia's town hall. But, after that first session, he'd banished her from his exam room. "No distractions," he told me.

When he gave us the diagnosis, then, I already had a vague idea what was coming. I'd seen a pattern forming. But my mother was incredulous.

"Her emotions? It's her *emotions* doing this?"

Dr. Bell dug in his khakis, came out with a starlight mint, began sucking. "It's the, yes, correct . . ." He clattered the mint around his teeth. "Intense emotional activity in the brain intrudes on the . . ." He made a pair of legs with his two fingers, walked them along in the air. ". . . much in the way REM sleep triggers muscle atonia. Sudden loss of muscle tone." The legs crumpled into a fist. "But during wakefulness. Naturally."

"But she usually doesn't fall over," my mother said. "She just makes these faces."

"More severe episodes will follow. The movie theater was merely the first."

"I don't understand . . . Every teenager has crazy emotions."

"Correct. The condition typically onsets with puberty."

"So it goes away afterward?"

Now Dr. Bell was happily crunching on his mint. "Um, no. Implausible."

"Well, let's talk about the treatment. About the cure."

"No need to worry about that. Let me show you." He spun on his heel and disappeared into the adjacent room.

My mother turned to me, sick with worry. "Whatever it is," she said, "honey, we'll fix it. I'll move heaven and earth, heaven and earth."

Dr. Bell came in carrying a plastic model of a brain, bobbling it between his fingers like a basketball. Then he knocked it on the edge of a countertop and split it into its two halves. "Ah," he said, "look here!" He fingered a bean-shaped piece, color-coded blue. "The hypothalamus. Yours"—he touched a finger to a point on my skull—"has depleted neurons along the lateral area, hence no hypocretin, or orexin if you prefer that dubious terminology. Now, as to whether the abnormality is produced by lesions on the brain or is simply genetic or perhaps—"

"Daphne's father," Mom said. "He used to have little spells, like hers."

Dr. Bell cocked his head, considering. "Good. Yes, that's good."

"So the treatment, it's fairly straightforward? Jesus, if only Don could have—"

"Treatment?" Dr. Bell said.

"That's what we're talking about, isn't it?"

He smiled at her, seemed to search, for a change, for the right tone. He failed utterly. "Let's see, how many excitatory neuropeptide hormones can *you* synthesize?"

My mother regarded him with gathering hatred. "That's what you're working on here, right?" she said. "You're working on . . . whatever you just said."

Dr. Bell gave his mint a final crunch. "Eli Lilly may own half this state. But I won't be yoked to big pharma like a mule. This is a research facility. Quite simply."

"Then what, for fuck's sake, are we here for?" Mom said.

He looked at her helplessly. "I'm sorry, I didn't mean to offend. I understand that I can be a little—"

"Offend me all you like. All I care about is her."

"Well, yes, I can help. Keep bringing her, every week."

My mother slung her arms around my neck and pulled me close. "If only Don were here," she whispered. And then to me: "You're just like him. Jesus, you've always been just like him."

FOR THE NEXT EIGHT MONTHS, she and I made the weekly drive down through Indianapolis to Bloomington, where Dr. Bell would take me through round after round of tests. He might have been solicitous with my mother, but he was never particularly tender with me. Once I complained that my weird little moments had made me quit volleyball, that girls at Arcadia had gone on to play for Penn and Stanford, and now I never would. Dr. Bell scoffed. "Get a scholarship on academic merits, then. Good Lord, if I have to hear any more about the plight of student athletes . . ."

Senior year was no joy. Samantha and Tina had blabbed about the movie theater all over school. I couldn't bear all of the wide-eyed glances in the hall, so I became a ghost, flitting from class to class, never seen. An injury lawyer took up my case—all brisk, dollar-sign optimism at first—then dropped us when he learned about my diagnosis. Other than Brook and Mom, I probably saw more of Dr. Bell than anyone. "You're lucky you found me," he'd say. "There isn't anyone else east of the Mississippi who knows a thing about you."

The condition seemed in a holding pattern, growing neither worse nor better. Or at least, spending all my free time on the couch with bad TV, there wasn't much to stimulate or upend me. I neglected the dusty stack of books on my bedside table and idly flipped through magazines and catalogs instead. Movies, of course, I avoided completely. Even trailers on TV were too harrowing, too ruthlessly tuned to wring some immediate response out of the openhearted viewer. Once, I asked Dr. Bell flat-out, "What am I supposed to do about all of this?"

"Nothing," he said. "There's nothing you can do."

But something in his voice seemed to suggest possibilities. On another visit I asked again. "So what can I do about this thing?"

"Get plenty of rest. Eat your vegetables. Salute the flag."

"So what can I do about this?"

He put down his clipboard, noisily unwrapped a mint, and with a sigh said, "What do I do when I'm frustrated?"

"What do *you* do?"

"Good. Her auditory synapses seem unaffected."

"Don't make fun of me."

"What, you can't answer a simple question?"

"Fine. What do you, oh wise doctor, do when you're frustrated?"

"What does anyone do? It's unproductive, all this fretting. It impedes my work. I can't control how these bureaucrats fund anything."

"But you can't just ignore it all," I said. "Emotions have to go somewhere."

"Manure. Pop-psychology manure. The Greeks thought feelings blew in on the winds. Do you believe that, too?"

"You haven't answered my question. Your question, whatever."

For a moment, he seemed uncommonly reflective. "The elevated train in Chicago, I grew up in an apartment tower two blocks away, and at night I could look out and see the train throwing off sparks. Whenever I'm stuck on the campus bus and some Cro-Magnon farm boy who shouldn't even be in a university environment keeps bumping me with his backpack full of books he won't even read, to keep from utter despair, I put it all back together in my head: the rumble coming up through my feet, the green light inside the train, the people staring out into the dark, those beautiful blue-white sparks coming down with the snow on a winter night." He blinked at me, took off his glasses, seemed embarrassed. "I don't know, something like that."

It didn't take me long to land on the river, the cattails, and the willows. Though I hardly went down there, the riverside park was the prettiest spot in Arcadia. Close enough, I figured, to the things most people saw when they closed their eyes and summoned up some serene, meaningless view.

"And what about depression?" I asked on another occasion. "What about that?"

All that time at home on the couch, all of those gawkers in the hallway, the nights when I woke out of nightmares, unable to move, still trapped in that morgue drawer—I wasn't even sure if depression was the right word. But Mom was already struggling with my medical bills, forget about weekly trips to a therapist.

"Please don't say you want me to prescribe you something," Dr. Bell said. "You're not beaten that easily, are you? Depression is just a survival mechanism. Ego reinforcement. There's a little voice in you that says, 'No one has ever suffered like this. No one. I'm special. I've received some special punishment. No one can *ever* understand what it's like to be me.' You see, our overweening sense of individual destiny keeps us from erasing ourselves. It's a purpose-built, evolutionary mechanism. Because the sole specimen really isn't of consequence, but species survival, of course, is of the utmost."

"Well, thanks. That's exactly the comfort and reassurance I was looking for."

"Here." He took another mint from his pocket. "Something to make you feel better. Or do you want some candy from our overlords at Eli Lilly?"

I doubt he cared enough to think about it, but his goading helped. All of those drills and squats and push-ups in volleyball, "Pain Is Just *Weakness* Leaving the Body"—even after a whole summer drowsing on the couch, I was still that girl stubbornly grinding away. No, I wouldn't be beaten. That year I graduated sixth in my class. Brook was salutatorian. After Rob Schaple, the valedictorian, finished his corny exhortation to "live out all your secret dreams," she got up on the podium, a hot pink wig under her cap, and said there was more than corn in Indiana, yup, there were racists and homophobes and teachers who couldn't find Berkeley on a map and once she got out there she was getting the Golden State tattooed on her right butt cheek and never, ever coming back. I wanted to laugh so hard I nearly slipped out of my chair onstage, the first time my visualization—river, cattails, willows, drifting white smoke—really saved me.

That summer, Brook left for an internship at an alternative weekly in Oakland, and I found myself alone with my magazines and Nintendo and my mother always hovering. The days slouched by. My thoughts turned grim and circular. At night, I woke with the taste of stainless steel and chilled flesh in my mouth. The spot where my dad had always sat on the couch loomed like a lifetime sentence.

Then, in the fall, I enrolled at IU. Mom was terrified, but she trusted Dr. Bell to look after me more than she trusted herself. It seemed he and I were making headway; any day now we would beat the condition. Meanwhile, I began my little pillow routine—thump, thump, to my suite-mates' laughter—and tried to bury myself in Late Victorian Fiction and Biological Mechanisms. But I was so scattered from watching my body and my thoughts that the textbooks barely yielded to my scrutiny. Thinking I might try something "marketable," I'd also signed up for Intro to Com-Sci. By the end of the semester, I was hooked. Deep in a C++ or Java exercise, my chattering brain just shut the hell up. Between that, drinking, and all the new faces who knew nothing about the movie theater, college was all-consuming, the distraction I so desperately needed.

Late that spring, The Gothic and Female Sexuality, in which I was flailing to keep up, got interrupted by a crowd of students pushing out into the hallway. The professor went to investigate, and a few of us followed. I pushed my way to the window at the end of the hallway, the eighth floor of Ballantine. Three floors above, a girl, a sophomore, had used a chair to break the plate glass. Most of her body was blocked from view by the building, but I could see her legs, clad in dark jeans, splayed out unnaturally, a starburst of shattered glass around her.

It could be done. That tiny, bewildered voice crying inside me could be silenced. I'd already died once. It would only take a little effort to do it again.

NINETEEN

NATO STARTED BOMBING LIBYA. OLLIE AND I WENT to a beatboxing concert in the basement of a shop that sold antique typewriters. Greeks were protesting in the streets, and the entire world economy was again on the verge of collapse. We checked out an art opening in a Hunters Point warehouse, guys in saggy jeans doing live graffiti while a fierce-looking girl twirled on a ribbon of silk hanging from the ceiling. A Norwegian guy killed seventy kids and blew up a chunk of central Oslo. We went to a kombucha festival and a lecture by a guy who claimed to have cured his own blindness. The president of Egypt sat in a cage in court, and London was exploding with riots. Going to dinner, we got swept up in a parade, ramshackle floats bumping house music, everyone in feather boas and zebra-stripe vests, some crazy pre–Burning Man thing pulsing with perversity and possibility. A bloody, chaotic battle in Tripoli overthrew Gaddafi. We met Brook for a drink.

In the Pit Stop, she sat across the booth from us, sipping her Manhattan. How had I not seen her in almost three and a half months? "Jesus," she said, "you went to a *parade*?"

"Yeah, somehow"—I pulled on Ollie's arm, smiled—"and I maybe even enjoyed it."

He and Brook worked their way through ten minutes of what do you do and where are you from. And why had I hardly mentioned one to the other? Brook's phone kept vibrating with texts. She kept breaking off to check them. Well, that was why.

"You two have known each other basically forever, right?" Ollie asked her.

"Longer than," Brook said.

"Despite having zero in common," I said.

"Well, you both grew up in a place you kind of hated," Ollie put in after an awkward silence. "And you both made it out here."

"Then again," I said, "us midwesterners have a hard time adjusting to paradise."

"God damn it"—Brook's phone went off again—"this guy is going to be the death of me. After Halloween, I'm taking the rest of my life off."

"Her 'full-service' client," I explained. She gave me a look. Neither of us addressed it.

"So, tell me, Brook," Ollie said, stepping gallantly back in, "how did you find your Miller Lite girls? I mean, is there an agency?"

"When you pay forty bucks an hour, they come to you. The trick is keeping them on schedule and halfway sober."

"Forty bucks an hour? I'm in the wrong line of work!" I felt him laboring to keep things going. "How do you think I'd look in a crop top?"

"Now this fucking cocktail waitress is trying to fucking cancel on me." Brook started furiously typing a response. Without looking up, she said, "At least promotions was honest. Drunk guys get to flirt with sexy girls, then they buy stuff. Straightforward."

"Spend your erotic capital while you have it," I said.

"Parades," Brook murmured. "At least you two have *something* to do together."

Now I gave her a look.

"Got to love La Mission," Ollie said uncertainly, "always happening."

Brook glowered at her phone, clattered it down on the table, fixed Ollie with a stare. "The first thing you need to know is that Daphne's brave as fuck. If I were her, I probably wouldn't even cross the street let alone go to a parade."

"Jesus, B, it's not that bad."

"And the second thing, young Ollie, is that if you break her heart, I'm going to hunt you down and kill you."

"Brook, go easy." I was touched, confused, dismayed; she was already gathering her things to go. I'd been downing a whiskey soda. An ice cube slipped out of my mouth.

"Oh?" Ollie said, still trying. "And how exactly would you kill me? Death by Miller Lite? Jose Cuervo?"

"I don't know yet." Brook was pulling on her coat with one hand and texting with the other. "But I'm about to practice on this fucking waitress." And then she was gone, and all I could do was stare at the ice cube on the table, melting in its own water.

ALL THOSE TEXTS Brook was sending, fewer and fewer were coming my way. My chat window, on the other hand, was filling up with Alden.

Alden taking my mother wine tasting, Alden pruning the sumacs overgrowing the backyard, Alden getting them both season passes to the Indianapolis Opera. My mother had only ever liked Billy Joel and the *Miss Saigon* soundtrack. Now Alden had her listening to Verdi and Puccini. She used to drink Bacardi Breezers and Taster's Choice. Now she went on about Frascati and Illy espresso. There were times when I actually wanted to talk on the phone, just to confirm it was the same woman. Alden, Alden, Alden. She hardly mentioned my dad.

I remembered my father the way you saw things through water, blurred and wavering, almost taking shape, then fluttering back to the depths. Everyone always talked about his athletic glory; he'd set every swim team record at Arcadia. "Such a strong swimmer," everyone said. The little I'd known him, he'd been sedentary and beer-bellied. Yet even in repose he was kinetic, picking up a *Field and Stream*, whipping through the pages, putting it down with a sigh, roaming through channels on the TV, turning it off with a grunt, turning it back on, whittling a fishing lure with shavings cascading down his shirt, reaching for another magazine—until suddenly he launched himself from the couch with a *chunk* of the reclining lever. Then he'd trundle around the house, which suddenly came alive, floorboards squeaking, pictures rattling on the walls.

"You're just like him," Mom told me after the diagnosis. "I noticed. His little fainting spells, I just thought he was tired from work." As if days at the town hall, where he and my mother had met, her in Payroll, him in Sewer and Water, were so taxing.

Once I got into trouble. I'd gotten a new set of markers for my fifth birthday, and I scrawled a house, a car, a tree, a smiling family all over my bedroom wall. Dad had just paid a couple of grand to have the house painted. He was livid. Yet it upset him to spank me. He drew his hand back and . . . His head lolled. His jaw went slack. He could only manage the weakest, glancing blow on my butt, and I watched in confusion and queasy relief as he stumbled backward, slurring under his breath, reeled into the living room, and dropped back down on the couch.

For a man like him, the swimmer, to die at thirty-seven of a heart attack—maybe if he *had* gotten off the couch now and then. Mom was always letting him "rest up." Whenever I was bouncing off the walls, "Daph, let your father rest up now." The funeral had been a haze of solemn, stunned adults, though I did remember getting a new dress and never being allowed to wear it again. She must have known something was wrong when she married him. She couldn't have believed his "spells" were just from long days at the office. Or maybe she hadn't always been so vigilant, so attuned to frailty. In old photos, she's a different woman, all flared trousers, bead necklaces, and smoldering looks at the camera. A heart attack—some shocks just keep on reverberating. Since that day, she must have told herself: prepare.

When you insulate yourself against disaster, you're always waiting for it to arrive.

TWENTY

S UMMER, REAL SUMMER, DIDN'T ARRIVE UNTIL SEP-
tember. Then every day, eighty-five, ninety, the skies a
pale, pure blue, the parks thronging with people in various
states of undress and elation, the bars up and down 16th and
Valencia and 24th pumping out desire and sweat, everyone
out, searching, scrambling to gather up all the bliss the city
promised—finally, in September, it felt like the San Francisco we all need to imagine.

The homeless, too, were out in force, selling old paperbacks, VHS tapes, and scrounged trinkets on blankets on the
sidewalk, the junkies scoring in broad daylight, nodding out
against my building in the hazy afternoon sun. The guy with
the stringless violin played his excruciating concertos down
in the BART. And Jeff was still on his corner. He'd give me a
bleary smile as I rushed by on my way to work, drawl, "Hey,
pretty girl." But as often he didn't even notice me, his eyes
milky with curdled ecstasy.

Ollie had been glued to the TV—the hordes on Wall Street picketing and milling—and to my phone, reading hastily constructed websites with pages and pages of unformatted text, endless speeches and the minutes of "general assemblies." He paced, waiting for updates or groaning at the snide pronouncements of some perfectly coiffed CNN anchor. "As if you'd even understand their agenda, you perma-tanned pod lady!"

"Why don't you get your own phone?" I said.

"Sorry, Daph, I'm just . . ." Then he'd go off on another rant at the TV. He started talking about buying a ticket to New York. "Listen, let's just *go*."

"It's on every hour of the day. What else is there to see? Or do you just want to go live in a tent and antagonize some cops?"

"It's making the movement visible! And if the cops let themselves get used as private security for the kleptocracy, then, yes. God yes!"

I told him that if the protestors really wanted change, they should call their senator, raise money, donate, go out canvassing. They talked about real democracy, but no one wanted to slog through legal challenges, legislation, lobbying, fielding candidates, campaigning. "Too much hard work. All of the drums and chanting and meetings and speeches"—I grabbed my phone from him, tossed it on the couch, took his hands in mine and wrestled with him, letting myself brush up against a little attack—"they're just to make people *feel* like something's happening."

"Jesus Christ, don't tell me you voted for the fucking 'Maverick.'"

"I voted for the guy I thought could do the job." We were on the couch now, poking and tickling each other. "Simple as—Ah! Don't make me laugh!"

I was being coy. That night in 2008, I'd wanted to be out in the street with that beautiful mess of people hugging strangers and climbing on top of cars to pop champagne. From my window, I'd watched a Muni bus get stranded and abandoned in the middle of a block of revelers, a whole city paralyzed by its joy.

"I know you don't like activists," Ollie said. "But maybe those animal rights guys have a point. Global capitalism only works if you keep everyone else in a cage."

He'd been getting a little personal lately. Someone had been stencil-spraying SAN FRANCISCO: SANCTUARY OF THE RICH on every corner in the Mission, and Ollie had started saying "Okay, back to the sanctuary" whenever we'd head home to the Grove.

"Yeah, but you know what a caged animal does?" I snapped and bit at his fingers, getting a little sloppy with my aim. Then we were kissing. I played with the condition, let my eyelids and jaw go, brought them back, let myself ragdoll a little in his arms. We'd been going further over the last few weeks. He'd let me get him off, then I'd go over on my back, let him tease me with his fingers and tongue. Once, the outfit I was wearing got peppered with the sawdust he always brought home on his clothes, and I said, "Blow it off," and he did, and I quivered and shimmered with pleasure. But when I felt myself teetering on the precipice, a breath away from tumbling over, the buzzing raced up, too, and I pulled away. A couple of times, I went limp when I really wasn't, closed my eyes, splayed out my arms. Maybe I fooled him. Maybe it made him feel better. I'd let him fuss with my hair, run his fingers along my body. And maybe I *was* content just to lie there, cocooned by his presence.

But then I couldn't stand to be cooped up inside. We roamed the neighborhood in the sultry evenings, climbed Bernal Hill, sweating and panting.

"I must be getting old," I said. "I feel like puking after that."

We stood on the ridge, caught our breaths looking out over our gently thrumming city. "Speaking of which," Ollie huffed, "not too late to do something for your birthday."

Oh, Jesus, my thirtieth. I did not want to think about my thirtieth.

"Let's rent out a space," he said. "Sound system, couple of kegs. Blow the whole thing out. Or a surprise party? We could throw you a surprise party!"

"Ollie . . ."

"What, no points for at least attempting a joke?"

The evening sun spun threads of honey over downtown and the bay, draping everything with nostalgia, echoes of a life I almost could've lived here in this golden peninsula on the edge of the world. "Okay," I said.

"Okay what?"

"Plan it. Just don't tell me what's coming."

THAT MONDAY, HIDALGO knocked on my door. I knew what he needed to talk about. I apologized for not getting back to him about overtime, mumbled something about the schedule being on the back burner since the break-in.

"I know you been real busy." Hidalgo took his hat off, looked at me with eyes reeling with worry. "Sorry to be asking. It's just . . ." They'd found out why Angela was sick, a bad mold allergy, which meant they could finally stop taking her to the doctor. But he'd paid to have his building retested—didn't trust his cheap-ass landlord—and found spores everywhere. They had to move, and with how expensive rents had gotten . . . "I'll work whatever they need. Or maybe, you know, they need someone to clean at night? Whatever they got, whatever."

I heard myself discoursing on MedEval's earnings reports, they'd had some shortfalls, they needed everyone to tighten their belts. This man was practically begging me, and here we both were saying "they, they, they." Not "you," not "I." The taste in my mouth was so awful I kept gulping my coffee just to get it out.

When I finished, he murmured, "Thanks anyway," pulled his hat back on, turned up his heavy metal, and was about to slip his headphones back on.

"The music," I said, "how can you stand it?"

"*Qué?*" I'd taken him by surprise.

"It's so angry. How can you listen to it all day? Doesn't it make you so angry?"

"The music?" he said. "Man, I can fall asleep to the music."

"Jesus, you can?"

"It's everything else keeps me awake."

"Right." I took up my coffee again and swallowed hard, and the space between what I could do and what he needed grew and grew. All of the sacrifices you had to make to raise a sick kid, all of the pain of being powerless to change anything—I thought of my mother, wanted to help, had no idea how I could. "Thanks for coming in to talk."

"*De nada*," he said and closed the door behind him.

TWENTY-ONE

WE WERE GOING TO ANOTHER CONCERT AT THE Tubes. Yet another perfect, temperate evening, and I wanted to drink beer and hear some music, erase myself for an hour or two. After ignoring music most of my life, it turned out I didn't just like but actually required it.

"Hey," Ollie said, as the BART howled up from under the bay into the evening sun over the Oakland dockyards, its skeletal cranes throwing long, geometric shadows.

"Hey, what?"

He gave me a pinched, foggy look, like I was going to have to pry it out of him. "I was thinking maybe . . . we could make a stop downtown. Before we go to the show. But only if you think you'd . . ." More hesitation. "There's supposed to be, well, kind of a rally. I just wanted to take a look. A quick look. Very quick."

"A march? I really don't know if I . . ."

I surprised myself by considering it, and Ollie leapt into

that gap. "We've got time. The music won't start till eight or nine. We won't have anything to do. Anyway, we'd probably only catch the end. The march was supposed to start an hour ago."

Our flirty, antagonistic debates over the last few weeks must've been working on me. I wanted to see it. Or at least stand on the edge for a minute and peer in. "You set me up." I poked him playfully in the ribs. "I didn't think you had it in you."

We got off at 12th Street/Oakland. The platform was all but deserted. Up above, we could hear the muffled bark of an amplified voice and the dull, rhythmic echoing of drums in the distance. "Shit, they already started," Ollie said. "Maybe we can catch up."

He practically bounded up the escalator. Above us, the drums and megaphone seemed to be trailing off, an army already gone to battle. But as we emerged into the close, concrete heat of the East Bay, all around us, enclosing even the top of the escalator, were marchers. They hadn't moved down Broadway but only paused to listen to a speech. "There!" Ollie said, pointing to the far side of the street, where a man on a small platform hunched over a microphone, his voice echoing and splintering off the downtown buildings, as if he were everywhere:

"Everyone's been asking, *Why* are you marching? Well, I say, Why aren't *you*? We can't just speak our minds on Facebook, in newspapers, magazines. We've got to *show up*. And here we are, America! Wall Street wants us to just *shut up*. They're hoping and praying we get *tired*, that we're just gonna *give up*. Then they can get back to robbing the ninety-nine percent, to robbing the planet, polluting the Gulf of Mexico, writing themselves blank checks we're *all* gonna have to cash, robbing from *tomorrow* to get paid *today*. So, now we're out here. We're marching to say this is *our* country. This is *our* world. And this street—this street you're standing on right now, this street laid down with our taxes, swept up and kept up by people like us, with businesses run by people like us, with music and poetry and justice made by people just like us—well, that means this is *our* street! Oakland, you feel me? Whose streets?!" the speaker cried out.

And on cue the crowd roared back. "*Our* streets!"

"Whose streets?!"

"*Our* streets!"

It went on like that, the call and response. Ollie offered his shoulder for me to lean on, but I shrugged him off. I was just far enough outside all of this. "Our streets," I said crisply, remembering volleyball, the wild pulse of the crowd, feet thundering on the bleachers, songs and cheers cannonading around the gym, the bright, untamable energy, life-eating routine being burned away, everyone yearning together for the same thing, public emotion so much more annihilating than private. "Whose streets?!" I yelped, caught up. "*Our* streets!"

Ollie had crept up a few paces. He was chanting so loudly, so percussively, he was going hoarse. People kept turning around to look at us; I didn't know whether to be proud or embarrassed. Not wanting to lose him, I stepped forward, too. Just then, a newly arrived group pushed in between us.

"Ollie . . ." He looked back at me, his eyes dialing back into focus, groped for the sleeve of my jacket, tried to pull me toward him. The voice on the platform rose: "We got these CEOs in our crosshairs! Let's pull the trigger, y'all!" The crowd convulsed. *"Whose streets?! Our streets!!"*

"Shit, Ollie . . ." Bodies pressed in from all sides. No one could move with more than tiny, shuffling steps, but we were all being shoved forward. I tried to hang on to him. "Ollie, please, I need to get . . ." My voice was buried under a sudden eruption of drums and whistles.

We held tight to each other's clothes. The march kept jerking forward, then coming to an abrupt halt, then forward again. Finally, Ollie pulled me through a knot of kids in black hoodies. "You okay?" I shook my head. "Over there." He pointed to the doorway of a nearby office building. "We'll duck in there, let everyone pass." The drums and chants battered in from every direction. "Excuse me," Ollie said, as we edged toward the doorway. "Sorry, sorry." I'd been bearing down, trying to stay calm. But, god-fucking-dammit, he picked the shittiest times to be polite.

Another amplified voice joined the one sounding out the chants, louder, deeper but leaden, monotone. The first voice crackled back, jabbed and wheeled; the second kept droning, "If you do not disperse . . . without proper permits . . . following the designated route . . ." The crowd started chanting, "Fuck the police! Fuck the police!"

I glanced behind me, saw two cops in riot gear and masks, close enough to catch the looks in their eyes. One was icy, implacable, the other puzzled, as if caught in some too vivid dream. His partner raised a black metal tube and angled it toward the sky. The puzzled cop looked over at him, raised his own, flinched as it flared orange and yellow. For a moment I thought: fireworks. Then two soft, hollow pops sounded. Fifty yards ahead of us, a sulfur yellow cloud billowed, a loud cry went up—then someone rammed into me and everything blurred into lurching slow motion . . .

The crowd buckling, splitting tectonically, everyone scattering all at once, tugging T-shirts up over their noses and mouths, boys in black hoodies kneeling, emptying water bottles into bandanas, tying them on, soft smooth intent faces disappearing into the thickening smoke, two girls with red backpacks with white crosses hacking coughing digging at their eyes, another hollow pop, a second cloud, vile burning taste, eyes all around me white with wildness—*willows, willows, willows*—a kid with a white mask pushed up on his forehead gagging, a woman with tears and mucus all down her face, a guy with long black hair staggering toward me in camouflage—the army, I thought, they've sent in the army—clasping his bloody forehead, staring at his bloody hand, reeling off into a clump of black bandanas hurling bottles at the police, the yellow smoke momentarily blowing away from me, finding myself in a little pocket of calm, maybe able to walk right out of this, Jesus, a miracle, turning back to tell Ollie, to pull us away from all of this, and finding him gone.

The chaos went still. I stood in the center of it, a hard knot in my stomach. It occurred to me, then, to feel surprise, fear, even rage: Of course he'd brought me here. Better to endanger me than miss this, all to prove his holy righteous-ness; the second type, the curers, the crusaders, were all the same. Instead I just stood there, staring blankly as another group of protestors rushed my way.

Someone crashed headlong into me. I stumbled, regained my footing—collided with a guy running full sprint. I man-aged to throw out my arms to catch myself. Then I was curled in a ball on the gritty street, voices and people all around me. I squeezed my eyes closed, heard shouts and cries, grunts of confusion, scattered footfalls. Someone knelt over me, touched my shoulder, a woman's voice: "Honey, you okay? Honey, talk to me. We'll get the medics over. We'll . . ." She was brushed away in the chaos. Pebbles and grit scattered against my face. Another waft of gas hit my nostrils. *A raft in the middle of the current,* I thought, *a man on the raft, waving.* "Shit, look out!" someone shouted. Then I heard a crunch, a boot coming down on my little finger and ring finger, and every corner of my brain flashed blank, phosphor white.

Seconds or minutes later, I heard someone calling me. Everything echoed. I concentrated, trying to ignore my throbbing fingers. Somehow I'd been rolled over, the sun warm on the back of my neck. Someone was touching me again. I knew the touch.

"Thank God, thank God"—Ollie's voice tight with panic—"I'm sorry, I didn't know where . . ." He caught his breath. "Are you okay? Christ, are you? Please, just—"

I put out a hand and touched his leg. Another flurry of

footsteps padded around us. He knelt over me, making his body a shelter for mine. "I'm sorry, I'm sorry." His breath rushed in my ear. "Sorry, sorry, sorry."

I pushed myself up to my knees. We both knelt there, watching the crowd scatter toward the south. "This cop," Ollie explained, "he grabbed me, put a zip strip around my wrists. I got rounded up in this containment area or something. But they cut us loose . . . Fuck, fuck, fuck. If I'd known they were going to use fucking gas . . ." He was hyperventilating. "Daphne, are you . . . ?"

"Train," I said between coughs, my eyes and nose still streaming.

On the ride back, he held me tight. Or tried to—he was trembling. I was steady. "Your fingers," he said. "What happened?" They were turning purple, swelling. But now all I could feel was the knot in my stomach, tightening.

MY PINKIE WAS BROKEN but not my ring finger. A resident at UCSF Mission Bay set it and wrapped a splint with foam. I touched it experimentally. The pain made me suck a sharp breath. But after a cab dropped us at the Grove, the first thing I did was pull Ollie up to the loft. I started battering him with kisses. "Easy, easy," he said, bewildered. I kicked off my jeans, pulled off my shirt and underwear. "What about your fingers? They said you should take a pain—"

I got on top. My jaw drooped. I put my hands on his

chest to stay upright. I felt it building, flopped onto my back, slurred, "Now." He was inside me, kept glancing down at my fingers. "Keep going, keep go—" My eyes closed.

"Daphne?" I heard him say through gritted teeth. "Daphne?" The orgasm crept up, and the buzzing—both peaking at once, shuddering through my body. My fingers went, my arms, my legs. I sank into the bed. And then my whole body shook. It shook without shaking, clenched while going slack, cried out by falling silent.

TWENTY-TWO

"WE SHOULD TALK ABOUT IT," HE KEPT TELLING ME. "We should at least *talk* about it. You're mad at me. Admit it. It was completely my fault we were even there."

But I didn't blame him for his curiosity. I'd been curious, too. And it wasn't up to him to know my limits, especially when I'd been testing them myself. How could I explain? It had just been a moment, a few seconds in the middle of the chaos, but I couldn't pick it all apart. I might easily have been furious with him, or at myself for taking such a dumb risk. I might have been afraid, thrilled, or cripplingly disappointed that I really couldn't do all of the things he and I wanted me to. It was even possible that I felt, in the moment, a sick sense of vindication.

"Come on," he said. "Let it all out. I can take it. Isn't it better just to let it all out?"

"Christ, don't you think I've heard that before?"

"Daph . . ." He was quickly beside me, a supportive arm around my waist.

I had to laugh, dry and hard. "First you want me to be angry, then you worry about me being angry?"

"It was my fault. Come on, just tell me."

But there was nothing *to* let out. At the march I hadn't switched off. I'd only been knocked over, then instinctually curled up. I couldn't even say that, in the moment, fight-or-flight had made me preternaturally calm. Or at least I wouldn't have called it calm. Honestly, it would've been easier if I could tell Ollie I was furious with him.

Instead all I felt, then and now, was the knot.

MIRANDA HAD BEEN putting together her tenure file and was all gloom and doom. Bill had sunk into low-grade resentment of everything: Missing his son's soccer tournaments because the kids were too cute in their uniforms. Having to always get rides to work from his wife, feeling embarrassed in front of the guys at the office. Having to miss his weekly golf game after spraining his wrist listening to little Danny tell a knock-knock joke. Teshawn was on a stricter regimen than ever. He spent whole meetings staring through us. Occasionally, he'd talk about wanting to go out, see friends, meet girls, instead of working all day, dragging his frozen ass home, taking a pill, sleeping till work again. With bland indifference, he told us his foreman had threatened to suspend him. A couple of weeks back, he was so out of it he nearly drove a forklift off the loading bay.

And Sherman was more bruised and scraped every time I saw him. He came in one Sunday sporting a scabbing-over gash above his right eyebrow. "Probably shouldn't pick at it," I told him as we stacked desks.

He reached up, worried it with his fingernail. "It's worst when I'm switched off. I want to itch like crazy. You ever get that?"

"Never have. Shit, maybe I cracked a rib, though." I touched my side, the knot, showed him my splinted fingers. "Maybe it's from the same spill," I speculated.

"It's torture," Sherman said. "I can't stand it."

"You ever feel like you're full all the time?" I went on. "So full it almost feels like you're hollow? Shit, maybe I should go up on the roof, scream it out."

"Primal scream. We should all try that some time."

"We'd have to put foam mats everywhere. Or we could rent those big sumo suits. You can go ass over teakettle in those."

He tapped his belly. "Some of us might not need them."

"Listen, Sherman, please, don't take this personally . . ."

"I'm okay about my weight. Really." He sized me up. "Or should I be sitting down for this?"

"It won't be a surprise. The group, I need to take another break. A longer one."

"They find a helpmate, then they just drop out. You wouldn't be the first."

"The study . . . I don't want to ruin anything else in here."

"Well . . ." Sherman said.

We stood there, two specialists in internal weather, unable or maybe just unwilling to ask what squalls and tempests were in the other, what doldrums.

"If you ever want to get out of the fog belt," I said, "I'm a pretty good cook. We'd love to have you over."

"One of these days." Sherman looked down at the floor, but I'd seen his eyes flutter. "Nice to hear you say that word."

"Which one?"

"We."

My phone buzzed; my car had arrived. "Want a ride?"

He scratched violently at his scar, mussing up his hair. It made him look boyish, lost. "Thanks, but I'm going to take a stroll. Enjoy the last of summer."

"Give me January rain any day. Wash all the drunks and idiots off the street."

"Daphne, don't take this personally."

"Do your worst."

"Cynicism is not going to save your life."

"I know. But maybe I can get a stay of execution." My phone buzzed again.

"See you around, Daphne."

"Stay safe." I said it as honestly as I could. "Stay open."

"Sure. You, too."

I reached out and took his hand. I probably did have the tongue to say everything I wanted to then: He was right to hold out for a cure, Olivia never deserved him, I hoped I'd never come back here. Instead, I just squeezed his hand harder. My bandaged fingers throbbed. I think I felt him squeezing back. It was so faint I couldn't be sure.

"HEY," OLLIE SAID AT DINNER, "are you on birth control?"

I put down my forkful of pork belly and broccolini and gave him a quizzical look.

"It's just . . . We didn't use protection that one night."

"That's because I was trying to get pregnant."

He went as white as overcooked salmon.

"What," I said, "no points for attempted jokes? Don't worry, I got Plan B. Wow, long time since anyone's worried about me being pregnant."

Ollie wore an introspective look. "Is that . . . Do you want that at some point?"

I sawed at a tough bit of pork and clammed up. Before, I'd never wanted to even chance saddling someone else with the condition, or with the worry I'd feel every day over such a child. Since I'd met Ollie something had shifted, but I wasn't sure I wanted to vocalize it yet. I swallowed my bite and felt my too full, too empty stomach contract.

"Just because I'm thirty," I said, "doesn't mean we have to talk about breeding."

"Does your mom have it?" Ollie asked. "I could see why you'd want to be cautious." Well, never say he wasn't perceptive.

"Seems like my dad did. No one can be sure, but proba-bly, yeah."

"You don't talk about him much."

"More broccolini?"

"Whenever you're ready. I'd love to hear about him."

I wouldn't have minded talking about my father. But every time I bumped against my memory of him, all I saw were those blurred, fluttering images. "You don't have to be the perfect boyfriend tonight," I said. "Just load the dishwasher."

"Sure you don't want to go out and celebrate?" Ollie said. "The Pit Stop might be quiet. Just a couple of quiet drinks?"

After the march, I hadn't felt like doing anything for my birthday. He'd seemed disappointed but hadn't pushed me. Instead, we'd had this evening, dinner in and an expensive bottle of prosecco, which I was now removing from the fridge.

"Don't worry," I said, "this is enough. This is all I want."

ON FRIDAY, STACI STOPPED me in the hallway, asked if I had a minute to talk, an apologetic smile trembling on her face. Lord, what now? I suggested we go down to the company café, which was dead in the late afternoon. If she was going to make a scene, better there. But she asked to meet in the break room, at five-thirty. She wanted to ask my advice but left without saying about what.

Maybe she was reconsidering vet school. She'd finally gotten a sense of her limitations and wanted to pursue something realistic. Maybe she was going to quit and wanted a reference. When I went in to the pens for the day's last check on the dogs, she was nowhere to be seen. Christ. Biscuit looked up at me with his beagle's frown. "I know how you feel," I said. He put out his tongue, licked a pellet of food. He was looking sturdier, marginally. Maybe now was the time to go back in, see if we could do something for him, if we could save him.

At five-thirty, I shut down my computer, gathered my things, checked my reflection in the black monitor, half-expecting to see myself frazzled and pinched. Instead, I looked uncommonly composed. As I went out, Pin and Byron weren't at their desks. I went down to the break room. As soon as I was through the door, a racket broke out. My chin dipped to my chest—*willows, cattails*—but I got out of it quick.

When they finished with the noisemakers and "Happy Birthday," there was a cake. Two big candles, 3 and 0, and, in icing, the letters *ALF* with an *X* through them. "Okay, who knew?"

Staci put up a mock-timid hand, glanced around as if someone else were going to claim credit. "Well, HR mentioned the date, and I *might* have volunteered to bake."

She cut slices, handed them around, said this was a thank-you from all of them. Whatever her intentions—not getting fired—the mood was festive. Even Byron seemed caught up, or at least the cake agreed with him. He'd had two pieces before anyone else had finished their first. Hidalgo also had a surprise, a bottle of mescal. "My cousin in Oaxaca, he makes it."

"Hidalgo, you shouldn't have. Really."

He shrugged and grinned tentatively. "Man, I should've done more when those dudes broke in. But you came correct. I just, I couldn't—"

"Serious-looking stuff." I held up the bottle.

"Sorry, no worm."

"How about we all take a taste?" I said. "Just don't tell the boss."

I poured everyone a half-inch of the pale golden stuff. We had it out of coffee mugs. Almost on cue, we all wrinkled our faces, exhaled sharply. Everyone laughed, and I let myself do the same, briefly. A nice moment; I should've been enjoying it. But I hung back and found myself next to Byron.

"Someone once said, 'No one will love you unless you succeed by thirty.'" Byron gestured around us. "All of this at such a tender age."

What could I say? For much of my life, I'd been convinced I'd never make thirty. "Well," I told him, "we've got quite the team."

He reached for another piece of cake, wrapped it in a napkin. "Something to take home for the girls. They do tire of mice and rat."

Usually, we all groaned when Byron started talking about his beetles. They were some rare variety that, in his bid to be as off-putting as possible, he kept as pets. Once a week, he went over to MedEval's mouse lab for a fresh bag of sacrifices to feed them.

"Are they really flesh-eating?" I said.

"You should see their mandibles. Nothing to cuddle up with at night."

"Do they have names?"

Byron claimed to be a strict, rational speciesist. He saw the dogs clinically, insisted on their being merely a research tool. Were he running the lab, he'd sacrifice any dog as soon as it took a turn. *He*, at least, referred to them only by their numbers.

"Of course not," he said. "But they're cared for. You should see them come clamoring at dinnertime."

"Is it love or just symbiosis?"

He squinted, trying to read me. It occurred to me that the months and months of sniping and criticizing might have been his idea of begrudging respect. And maybe I, in turn, could appreciate him for not being a pushover or a soft sell, his esteem meaning more for being so stingily given.

"Is there a difference?" he said.

I raised my mug. "If only every relationship were so straightforward."

Two minutes later, I turned back, and there he was wearing a stocking cap, a ridiculous orange thing with the Giants logo on it. "What?" Byron said. "Can't I be gangster, too?" Across the room, Hidalgo was eyeing him with skepticism bordering on disgust. There was no goddamn end to it. I poured myself another shot of mescal. It felt good going down but lit a fire in my gut. I pressed at the knot and felt it, burning.

TWENTY-THREE

Saturday evening, as I was taking my bath, the buzzer went. It startled me, and I slipped a couple of inches down in the tub before I got myself back. I wasn't expecting a package, and Ollie was working late on a drywall job in Tiburon. The buzzer went again. I sloshed out of the water, threw on a robe. Maybe he'd left his keys behind. He was always doing that. But the voice that crackled hoarsely through the speaker . . . Brook.

"Hey, I need to come up." A scratching sound, a burst of static and breath. "Actually, I need you to come help me up."

I found her sitting on the front step in a black sheath dress and a familiar man's sport coat, her stiletto heels kicked off on the sidewalk, her mascara smudged into a raccoon mask, and a small puddle of vomit before her. "Yeah, I know," she said before I could ask. "But can we please get upstairs first?"

I had to sling her arm over my shoulder. On the third-floor landing, she dropped one of her stilettos. It fell all the way to the bottom of the stairwell. She let the other one go as well. "Leave them," she said. "I renounce them."

I got us into the apartment, into the bathroom, where she finished puking, made a few swipes at cleaning herself up. She stripped out of her dress. I went to the bottom dresser drawer. But I couldn't bring myself to unseal her customary pajamas and pulled out a shirt and leggings instead. She splayed out on the couch with a blanket over her, looking like a wax statue. I squeezed into the other end, her feet in my lap.

"Is this the perils of knowing all the bartenders in town? Or are we witnessing the effects of something more exotic here?"

"I'm guessing you haven't heard of head cleaner. The stuff you use to clean old VHS players. Shit, why do rich people do the most low-rent drugs?"

She'd been at a party at Halloween's place. Everyone had passed out around five in the morning. She'd woken up twelve hours later with her head thumping and her dress and bra hanging from the ceiling fan. Halloween's friends were passed out in the living room. He was still snoring on the bathroom floor when she left at six.

"Wait," I said, "it's almost eight. I thought he lived, like, four blocks from here."

"The walk took longer than expected."

"B, I'm so pissed at you right now." But my face wasn't drooping, my eyes not even fluttering.

"I'm really, really sorry I missed your birthday."

"Whatever. No big deal."

"It's a huge deal. Don't tell me it isn't."

I let too long go by without answering.

"Did you even care that I wasn't there?" The question mangled up her face.

"One of these drugs is going to kill you."

"Don't worry, I'm a professional."

"That's very clear to me."

"You're going to have to tell me what the fuck that means."

I hesitated—and then I didn't. "It means I'm sick of you throwing all your partying and fucking in my face."

"Excuse me, you're the one fucked up about sex."

"For good goddamn reason."

"*Fuck.* Even when I come to you like this, you're self-involved. Can you just help for once?"

"With what? Huffing VHS cleaner? Fucking some rich dickhead just to land a job?" I should've been sinking into the couch at this point. My words should've been garbled. But there it was again, the knot. "I can't worry about you this much."

"What the hell happened to us?" Brook croaked, tears about to burst.

"Most friendships go this way. Especially with me."

"Don't lean on that. Just don't."

"Well, I can't lean on you."

Brook lay there fuming at me. I could've pulled things back. We both could have. But, really, was it worth the effort? After a few minutes, Brook groaned herself off the couch. She was too wasted to leave but grabbed her dress from the bathroom floor and started changing out of my clothes. "Keep them," I said. And then I let her go, watched her wobble out the door and attempt the first flight of stairs. When she was gone, I dropped back down on the couch. But I didn't switch off, not even close. I put a palm on the spot where she'd lain, the warmth of her body. I should've told Ollie. But by the time he got home, I was too knotted up to talk.

ON SUNDAY I WOKE RAVENOUS. Brunch, strong coffee—that would unravel it. There was a new place at Dolores and 15th. I gave Ollie a nudge. He rolled over, buried his head in the pillow. A harder nudge. He yawned, fussed with his hair. "What's the big rush again?"

"If we don't get there early, there'll be a line out the goddamn door."

"Isn't that the point of brunch, see and be seen? The comfortable classes showing off with twenty-dollar egg dishes?"

"Oh, Christ, can we not do the Marxist analysis of breakfast right now?"

Finally, we got out the door, turned the corner, and there was Jeff. Or his wheelchair anyway. I glanced over and saw him sprawled, as much as he could sprawl, on the sidewalk, stubby legs jutting out where he slumped against the wall, his chin on his chest, moaning or maybe mewling, a meager, pathetic sound. "Excuse me," I muttered and stepped around him. I couldn't. Everything that'd been building these last weeks—I just couldn't. When I looked back Ollie was kneeling over him, trying to get him to sit up. A police cruiser rolled through the intersection. Ollie ran into the street, flagged it down. The cop got out with an annoyed hitch of his belt. He crouched next to Jeff, then went over to his cruiser and got on the radio. Ollie saw me standing up the block, exchanged a few more concerned words with the cop, then finally caught up.

"We'd better hurry, or we're not going to get fed before two."

He looked at me like he didn't even see me. "But the ambulance isn't here yet."

"Come on, the cops are on it. The system works. Everything's okay in the world."

He glanced back uncertainly. When we set off again, he trailed a few steps behind. Brunch was packed, but we got stools at the bar. Ollie was quiet, pushed his food around his plate. I thumbed through Interior Life, tried to enjoy my Gruyère-prosciutto-cippolini tartine. We walked back to the Grove. Jeff and his wheelchair were gone. I thought about pointing out that the cops wouldn't have stopped to check on him either. Some guy nodding out on the street—hardly a rare sight. But now wasn't the time. We went up to the apartment.

"More coffee?"

Ollie was at the window, staring off over the rooftops.

"Hey," I said, "espresso or drip?"

"I'm going out."

"Where?"

"I don't know, Alameda. The flea market."

"Okay," I said cautiously, "text me later. We can order sushi in. On me, okay?"

He grunted okay. Then he was gone. The apartment vibrated with quiet. I switched everything on. TV, radio, computer, phone, everything.

TWENTY-FOUR

A<small>LL THAT WEEK, HE CAME HOME AFTER ELEVEN. I</small> was already in bed. He said his job was still going late. I murmured good night, rolled over, tried to fall asleep. He slipped under the covers, lay there a while, then went down and sat on the couch in the dark. I could almost feel him pulsing with uncertainty and fear. The whole place stank of it.

P<small>IN AND I WERE SCRUBBING IN.</small> Not that she needed anyone assisting; for her, this was routine. But I'd insisted on being there.

"Yes?" Pin said, eyeing me curiously. "Everything is okay?"

"Point where you need me."

Biscuit was splayed on the operating table, tender belly exposed, a patch of fur shaved. The sight of blood never much bothered me, and under anesthetic Biscuit wouldn't feel a thing. Still, seeing the dogs so vulnerable . . . I started the suction. Pin drew a line with her scalpel, dark red welling up across Biscuit's downy white chest.

The defibrillator appeared first, that little stainless steel fob that could shock a heart back into rhythm, that saved so many lives. I'd half-hoped to see blackness or fluid around the device, proof of an infection or some mistake on our part, which might now be corrected. But all the pink flesh around the ICD looked normal, healthy. Pin cut deeper, following the two wire leads.

And there it was—the heart. I'd forgotten how tiny a dog's was, how hypnotic its beating. Somehow circumstance had put me here at this company, helping build devices to regulate the pulsing of this dumb, precious muscle. What had I felt the few other times I'd sat in on a surgery? Despair, disgust, awe?

"Hmm," Pin said, exploring around the ICD connections, touching the organ with a casualness that ordinarily would've made me flutter. "No, this is fine. Everything is fine. The problem is not here." She looked up at me. "Well?"

I knew what I should've said then. It was time, and he was already under. "Nothing else we can do?" I labored to sound analytical, practical. "A different course of antibiotics? Maybe there's an infection we're not seeing."

"Hmm," Pin said again, hearing something else in my voice. "Yes, okay, a short course. We can always try."

THAT EVENING I GOT OFF at 16th Street and came up into a dream. Mission was closed. The parade was silent. They wore black. Black suits, black skirts fringed with black lace, broad-brimmed black hats. Their faces were white with deep holes of coal black eyes, their expressions blank and unmoving. Some carried candles. Some danced along in vague, looping steps. Everywhere I looked, the skeletal faces stared back. I stood rooted. I had to hold up my phone like a shield, watch them through the screen. They passed on. The dream dissolved. The whole street was empty and still.

When I came through the door, he was on the couch again, sitting there in the half-dark, staring at the blank TV screen. I mumbled hello, went straight to the fridge for a bottle of Riesling. I heard him get up, come tentatively toward me. When I turned to him, his face had gone cubist. Each of its facets—sorrow, confusion, accusation, gut-sick pain—stood out at once. I quickly turned back to the open fridge, its humming light.

"I'm not upset," he said behind me.

"But you're disappointed." I reached for a glass, filled it with an improbably steady hand, sipped. "Look, I know what you're going to say—I saw him lying there, and I stepped over him. I stepped right over him."

"Disappointed . . . ?" Ollie said, as if he'd never encountered the word.

"He was high out of his mind. There was nothing we could do."

"He's your friend!" Ollie's voice leapt up like he was

being strangled. "You stepped right over him and went on to your brunch!"

"I said that already. Look, be upset. Go for it."

"I'm not upset!"

"You don't have to try so hard, Ollie. Really. You can't save everyone."

He stalked back and forth in front of the window, his fists balled up, trying to pull it all back inside him. "He's not everyone. You see him practically every day."

"He's just some junkie who lies to make me feel guilty and give him money. You can't stop for every fucked-up case in this city."

"Look who's talking! A month ago you were in the exact same—" His face crumpled into another shape: regret. "Daphne, I'm sorry, it's just—"

"I can't get involved in every tragic life story." *The willows*. "I can't be this person you want me to be. You can't fix me."

"You think I'm that fucking obvious?"

"If you're sticking around for some other Daphne to show up—"

"This is your narrative? Please, stop."

"The condition isn't separate from me," I said. "It *is* me."

"Don't, don't . . ." Ollie turned in a tight circle, fists beating against his thighs, his whole body trembling. Then he stopped, looked at me straight on, his rage and pain and anguish all slotted together—the face I knew so intimately, every facet now joined against me. "It's not an excuse!" he shouted. "The goddamn condition is not an excuse!"

The buzzing, there it finally was. He went on: Was I ever going to stop pretending to be hardhearted, pretending I didn't give a shit, hiding behind some bullshit tragic persona? He paced and beat his fists and told me how exhausting it was, how completely fucking exhausting, my gentle Ollie, finally losing it there in front of me, the whole room shuddering with everything coming off him, shuddering through me, the buzzing under every thought, about to boil, tremble over, overflow, flood me completely . . .

"The willows shaking their heads," I whispered. "The cattails."

"Fuck, Daphne, are you even fucking listening?"

I crossed my arms over my chest and looked away. "The yellow grass."

"What? What's that?"

"The picnic tables."

"Look, you don't *need* to make excuses." Even in his fury and bewilderment, he was trying to be kind. "Please, I'm trying to tell you. I never want you to—"

"The river, the raft, the raft."

"What the *fuck* are you even saying right now?"

Clattering my wineglass into the sink, I crossed the room, slumped on the couch, put a pillow behind my head, stiffened in anticipation. I could already feel it trembling down my spine. "A man waving from the lip of a raft," I whispered. "A man waving to me." *A man standing on the edge of a raft, a man crumpling.* My strings were pulled so tight I felt I could barely talk, yet the words came out, so even and measured they terrified me. "Calm down," I told

Ollie. "If you can't calm down, I need you to leave." I lay there, praying to be taken away from this, praying to be frozen hard as wood. "Please, leave. Just leave."

He didn't answer, just kept stalking around the apartment in thrumming silence, gone subterranean, though I could feel everything churning inside him, his pacing circles going wider and wider—I knew he wanted to leave; God, he was ready to be free of all of this—as if trying to fling himself out of my orbit. Or maybe he thought he was waiting for me to come out of an episode. I didn't speak either, just closed my eyes until, finally, I heard the door slam behind him. On hands and knees, I crawled to the bathroom. With my clothes on, I pulled myself into the empty bath, the only place I couldn't fall.

HE DIDN'T RETURN THAT NIGHT. He called four times, texted that he'd left his key in the apartment—he'd stormed out without it—but didn't plead to come home. I didn't reply. I went to work, let the hours pass. At the gym I climbed endless stairs, one weary step after another, until I stepped off the top of the escalator at 16th Street, up from the underground into the late evening fog, and floated past the stringless violinist screeching away, the men sleeping in storefront entries and burning their brains out on front stoops, the ends of all those tiny glass pipes flickering in the gloom.

I'd prepared for this, I told myself. I'd known it was coming. So I only took half-pills. I thought I didn't need more than that; the numbness came from inside. The knot was not string but wood, deep in the heartwood. At the lab I could barely hold on to the numbers and print-outs and people passing before me. I closed my office door, dozed in my chair, the office clamor, whirring hard drives, and ceaseless barking all churning under my fractured thoughts.

When I texted him back, it hardly felt real. *Come get your stuff I'll pack it up for you.* I pressed SEND. The words went off into the air, into the atmosphere, meaningless, weightless, wisps of electrons. I got boxes from the produce market, filled them with his things. My apartment smelled like carrots and bananas.

When he arrived, I had to buzz him in. I left the door open, got myself on the couch. He came in. "It's all ready for you," I said in a hollow voice.

He looked at his stuff, his face drawn, jaw held stiff, an expression somewhere between reluctance and defiance. "This is really how you want this to go?"

"It is." My words just floated away. "It has to be."

"You know I can't fight with you," he said. "But Daphne, I—"

"Please. Just get this over with."

It took him three trips to take most of it down. I couldn't help getting up and going to the window. I told myself I could watch from a distance. One of his old roommates was helping him load an ancient Volvo station wagon but didn't come up for anything. He must have thought Ollie and I were going to talk it through. Ollie came in for the last box, his dusty old records. I stayed at the window. "This is it," he said to my back. "Everything."

"Okay."

"It smells like fruit in here," he said, trying to prolong the moment.

"You'd better go quick."

I watched as he hefted the last box out of the front entry to the building. He tripped on the front step and scattered his old records across the sidewalk. Then he knelt there, a full two minutes. Even from four stories up, I could see his shoulders shaking.

After his friend's Volvo pulled away in a rumble of exhaust, the apartment clanged with silence. I took off my clothes, left them on the bathroom floor, got into the bath, turned the hot tap on. When it was nearly full, I left the tap running, just a thread of water to keep it scalding. I leaned back, stretched out, got as low as I could. *Pale white smoke dissolving, noon light.*

Steam rose from the bath, shimmered into mist. My feet blanched white. I let my legs go. They slowly rose. The tips of my toes poked above the water, blanched white. *Picnic tables. Yellow, patchy grass running down to the river.* My little finger and ring finger throbbed. The bandage around the splint loosened, floated to the surface. *Willows shaking their heads.* Fluttering, I watched the steam sway and eddy, curtain and snake. The world turned gauzy, sifted away, the water at my collarbone, rising up my—

I let go, just caved in, let the buzzing surge forward, a huge, tumbling wave. My image slid forward yet again—*cattails, dissolving smoke, the willows, the willows, the*—but my anger tore right through. And right behind it, a trough of sorrow, like slipping off into open air, the hollow jolt of freefall. My jaw went slack. My head lolled. Water gurgled in my ear. The spike of fear—I didn't try to stop it. My arms floated up.

Cattails and pale white smoke and sun bleached picnic tables.

I let the joy in: Ollie laughing. Ollie tumbling down in bed, wrapping his arms around me, staring at me with his sly, boyish grin, quiet and intent in the half-light of morning. Love? Of course. But love is quicksilver. It quickens us in sudden, unexpected moments, then glimmers away. It just wasn't heavy enough for me then.

Pain—that was the unbearable weight, the thing that would sink me forever. The pain I saw every day: the ravaged faces of the mad and the addicted, the cautious, haunted faces in group, the thinly hidden worries of my coworkers, the loyal suffering of the dogs. Ollie kneeling on the sidewalk, his shoulders shaking. And, finally, my own pain, fifteen stifled years—all of it buzzing, electric-cold, snapping with current, every muscle about to go.

The water was halfway up my neck. The barest friction kept me from slipping further. Under the stream from the hot tap, I heard a high whine—the singing of my own blood. I let it reverberate with my panic. A trickle of soapy water slipped between my lips. My body tried to make me gag. I wouldn't. I wouldn't let it.

The image rose unbidden, stubborn. *Picnic tables, yellowing grass, white smoke, cattails, willows, the glinting river. And on the river, a raft. A raft lashed to four blue bar-*

rels, a man, a shirtless man . . . My chest burned. The steam swirled, made tiny, swirling lanterns. I thought of my mother finding me this way, floating in tepid bathwater. She'd known this was coming. She'd been right all along. For a wide, luxurious moment, I found the inevitability comforting.

Then the burning in my chest chewed up those thoughts. *The man waving, his arm drooping, shirtless, pale, his whole body slumping.* My eyes closed, but I could still see the tiny lanterns. They drew me up into a flood of light. The water slid down my nose and throat and into my lungs. The light bloomed all around me.

But the image only grew clearer. *Pale white smoke drifting. Picnic tables, initials carved in the wood, KC ♥ JA. The grass running down to the water, yellow, patchy, cattails bobbing, the big willows making their slow whishing sound, shaking their shaggy heads.* I wavered over the line of consciousness. The light pulsed forward, *the haze of noon sun, a crudely made raft, sheet metal lashed to old blue rain barrels.* The bathwater gurgled and whined in my ears. The water in my throat and lungs made me retch. Only a feeble hiccup, but some tiny, mechanical part of me was working, pushing up against the weight. I saw the figure *standing on the edge of the raft, waving, shirtless, pale, waving, trying to call out, trying—*

The slow shiver, my body coming back—oh, God, my chest was going to explode. My fingers prickled and stung from the electricity shooting through me. I reached for the sides of the tub, hardly enough strength to pull myself an inch above the water. *Shirtless, pale, waving to me, try-*

ing to call out to me. Then, with one huge pull, I hauled myself over the side. The bathwater flooded out, sluiced across the floor. I hung there, half in, half out, coughing up water, heaving in air that made me cough even harder. I fell over the side of the tub, dropped hard to the tile floor. The bathwater pooled around me, the trickle from the hot tap steadily filling the tub, spilling over me. The light receded, drew up into the ceiling, telescoped to an impossible height. The man in the light drew away. I reached for him and couldn't reach him.

TWENTY-FIVE

ALARM, SNOOZE. ALARM, SNOOZE. ALARM, snooze ... Shower if I can be bothered, oatmeal if I can stomach it. Out on the street, dodge the hypodermics, the human shit, the human wreckage. BART to Milbrae to Caltrain, the 8:16, the 8:39, the 9:02, whatever, don't care if I'm late, stare into the armpits of commuters hanging off the grips like apes. Company shuttle, coffee, email, data, dogs, reports, skip lunch, bitter chalk of the drug on my tongue, coffee, skip gym, back on the train, cold leftovers, wine, TV, radio, white noise, rearrange the apartment, fill the spaces left by his books, records, clothes, pill, sleep, pill, sleep, strip the days down, stay low, stay numb, let the drug take over, get through, always got through before.

But I fell. I kept on falling.

Late in the day, when the drug wore off, I'd think of the fight, go down on my knees, on my ass. I dropped a glass of wine. I stumbled, glanced my forehead against the kitchen counter. An awful welt came up. At work they stared but didn't ask. Thanksgiving came, went. Pin and Staci hung Christmas decorations, a holiday party. I hung back, sipped hot apple cider, only tasted chalk. A plastic Santa on the microwave blinked red. Blinked off. Blinked on. Blinked—I reached out, touched it, made sure it was really there.

Get used to it, a shadow world. Get used to falling. Fall so many times, get up so many times, just automatic. Just the dim, gray present, down, up, down, up, a little harder, a little darker every time. Alarm, snooze, get up. Fall, get up, fall. Repeat.

DID HE CALL? I don't know. First I blocked his number, then I deleted it, thought that would help. One afternoon at work an email from his address popped into my inbox. "Hello Just Need 2 Share This With U." I immediately opened it. Stupid. I thought about writing, to say his account had been hacked. But he almost never checked his email. Anyway, the effort it would take . . . And I still needed to check on the dogs. Then a chat window opened. Fuck.

What time's your flight arriving? Need to coordinate schedules with Alden.

Don't know yet

Think Ollie wants to go caroling with us?

I'd made the mistake, weeks ago, of saying he might come. I'd made the mistake of telling her about him at all. ~~Mom please don't freak out~~ we broke up

The cursor sat there, blinking. A moment later my phone rang. I silenced it.

At work can't talk besides old news really don't worry
How old?

Couple weeks not really keeping track ~~three weeks three days~~

Daph, Jesus, you *tell* your mother these things.

I know please it's fine

What about Brook? Maybe you can fly with her?

I don't know what she's doing ~~god don't start asking about Brook~~

Oh, Daph, if I could reach through this screen and give you a hug. You're sure it's over? Maybe Ollie could still come? If he can't afford a ticket, just let me know.

Fuck this is driving me insane just stay out of my shit for one fucking second how do you think I'm dealing with this without you treating me like some terminal patient don't goddamn offer plane tickets or carol singing or any of this shit because I'm going to goddamn explode if I have to type another single fucking sentence My finger went for the DELETE key. Then I realized, through my narcotic fog, that I'd pushed RETURN.

The cursor in the window sat blinking.

Mom?
Hey Mom?

Mom seriously I'm sorry I didn't mean to I just accidentally

I sat listening to the far-off barking. Five, then ten minutes went by. The cursor kept blinking. Blinked off. Blinked on. Blinked off.

THAT MONDAY, MY YEARLY REVIEW. All I could hope for: a pat on the back for handling the break-in, and that they wouldn't bring up my somnambulistic last few weeks.

When they came in, two VPs and our HR woman, they all had big grins on. They were thrilled. I'd kept the budget. Above all I'd kept the budget. They only wanted to talk about some staff reorganization. Well, sorry, Staci, I thought. I did my best for you.

They needed to ensure standards were being upheld. They knew how widespread it was, especially in San Francisco. But certain lifestyles, they said, just didn't mesh with company philosophy. It took me a moment to get it. Hidalgo and his pot smoking.

"It's exhausting work," I said. "Long hours, high stress." I was trying to sound indignant. The pills made it all come out monotone. "If it gets them through a shift, why should I stop them?" I wasn't going to come right out and confirm that Hidalgo smoked. "Anyway, it's not even against the law."

They appreciated my loyalty to my team. Truly, they did. I could see them practically winking at me. By my voice, they probably figured I didn't give a shit.

"I have to cut the techs some slack," I went on. "The job is just too awful."

Of course, of course. They had sympathy for "everyone in the trenches." But they had to draw the line when certain gang-related clothing was worn. Baggy T-shirts and paraphernalia associated with certain sports teams. Certain colors.

Oh, Jesus, the Giants cap. "Hidalgo isn't in a gang," I said, still too dry and flat. "He's a dad. He already works two jobs. He wouldn't even have time for a gang."

Nevertheless, he was cautioned about the dress code.

"That's because I threw Byron's write-up away. Hidalgo never even saw it." Blunted as it was, I could feel my fury stirring. If not for the pills, I might have thrown up an almighty fuss. Instead, it all passed over me like a chill, damp breeze. "He's my best tech." Still too bland. "I need Hidalgo. I need five more like him."

They certainly did appreciate my loyalty to my team. But I needn't worry. They'd be taking on additional hires in the new year. Especially with Ms. Finn cutting back.

"Staci?" I said. "You're letting Staci go as well?"

No, no, Staci was going part-time while she started coursework at UC Davis. A rising star, very passionate. They were so happy to keep her in the MedEval family.

Of course the young white woman wasn't getting the ax. Or maybe Staci had been cleverer than I thought. She'd buttered me up first, then started on the higher-ups. As for the final decision on Hidalgo, they'd leave that up to whoever was running the lab. And choosing the additional hires, naturally. *Whoever* was running the lab, they said again, still grinning. They wanted to bring me back to hardware. Actually, they wanted me to *run* hardware.

"Oh," I said.

They went through the responsibilities and perks. They discussed the salary—*that* penetrated my haze—enough to pay down my mortgage a few years early. I'd start as soon as February, as soon as they'd secured my replacement. I'd done a fine job with the dogs, they said, but they were betting I'd be glad to get back to my roots. After all, they knew the lab could wear you down.

"Jesus, yes," I said. "But, look—"

They wanted my recommendation: an internal hire or bring in candidates? They started drafting the job posting right there, asked me to list my duties and qualifications. I was still too fogged over to process any of it. Later, I understood. Byron. They were finally going to promote Byron. Byron was going to get the lab, and after that, forget overtime, Hidalgo would be gone.

I SHUT MYSELF in my office. When I came out, the night shift was in. Most of the dogs were already asleep, just shapes in the half-light, though I recognized little Oscar by the yip he gave me as I came past. We had one of the new pacemakers in him. His energy hadn't gone down one bit. I passed Biscuit. He was tucked back in his cage, but I knew he wasn't asleep. I could feel his watchfulness.

Talking with the night-shift guys, weariness draped itself over me. The lab was the thing we all hated to remind ourselves we did. My turn now to slip back into the general population, to see those dogs as only output data, points on a graph, numbers. "Looks like that hurt," one of the guys said, gesturing at the welt on my forehead.

"Merry Christmas," I said, brushing my bangs back over it. "Have a good one."

I was anxious to get out of my clean suit and far, far from here. Then I paused, brought myself up short. I went back to Biscuit's cage, touched the bars of his cage, felt a vibration. I undid his lock. "Come on, boy." Staci had given him a bath that morning, but his fur was matted and lusterless. The outline of his ribs showed. The antibiotics hadn't helped. If anything, opening him up again had made things worse.

He followed me out onto the play area, into a clear evening with a soft breeze tickling down from the hills. He went over on his back, in slow motion, and rubbed against the grass. Somewhere up from the depths, pleasure. But after a minute, he just lay panting.

I went back inside, into the surgery room, unlocked a small cabinet, took down a vial and a syringe. *The cattails waving, white smoke.* Back outside I called, "Here, boy," and emptied a whole pouch of treats on the grass. He ate only one. I gave him a rawhide bone. He did his best with it. I let him inspect a gopher hole. Delaying, still delaying.

Finally, I knelt next to him in the grass. I stroked his belly. His eyes went white. I felt the beat of his heart. "Biscuit," I said softly. He rolled over, hearing a command, and offered his jugular, as he'd been trained to do almost since birth. I took out the syringe and, with the flat of my left hand, pressed gently on his side, held him still.

When it was over, I stayed kneeling in the dirt, I don't know how long.

ON THE TRAIN, I checked my phone. An email from Interior Life: "Congratulations!" A mass mailing, more spam . . . No, it was from one of their editors. In overly familiar language, she praised the unity of my design, my careful juxtaposition of textures, the overall aesthetic of me and my "absolutely adorable partner." She wanted a full apartment tour and was assigning a photographer. There were elaborate instructions on how to prepare. They were eager to get "Daphne and Ollie's Cozy Mission Roost" up on the site.

I deleted the email, closed my eyes, and waited for my stop.

TWENTY-SIX

LATE THAT FRIDAY, I TOOK A CAR FROM THE LAB
straight to the airport, shuffled through the long lines,
and boarded a red-eye that was already juddering and lurching before we hit the Sierras. I wanted to sleep, reached into
my backpack—realized I'd forgotten my pills. By the time
we crossed the fat ribbon of the Mississippi shining dully in
the moonlight, I was only half-narcotized and tasting metal
and dread. The wheels bounced down in Indy. I stayed in my
seat while everyone filed off. Not switched off. I just couldn't
face her yet.

In arrivals, she stood next to a broad, tall man in a
pressed white shirt, khakis, and glasses with a brown tint.
She spotted me, gave a flustered wave. When we got close,
she suddenly closed the distance and wrapped me in a hard,
tight hug. She wore a long white sweater and black leggings,
and even her snow boots were surprisingly fashionable. Her

hair looked freshly dyed, a not unflattering auburn. Alden looked on at us, grinning.

"Daphne," he said, engulfing my hand in his, "real privilege to meet you." He smelled like Old Spice and the loam on pulled-up roots. "Welcome home, all the way from Frisco!"

"Yeah, hi." I blinked heavily. "Sorry, I'm . . ."

"Alden's truck is in the garage," my mother said. "He knows I hate highway driving."

"It's a four-door," he said in a big, cheery wheeze. "In case you're worried about having to roll around in back!" He offered to take my bag. We came out into the bland, bright Indianapolis morning. The snow was a foot thick and crusted over with ice. The glare made me wince. "Some day!" Alden said. "*Bella giornata!*"

"As busy as Alden's been," my mother said, "he still finds time to practice his Italian."

"Big snows like we're getting, trees can't take the weight. You hate to see them come down. Profound creatures. Even with a stump, you feel a certain presence."

My mom beamed at him, the tree philosopher in chinos and pervert glasses.

"Okay! Here were are," Alden said, "VIP parking!"

He swung my suitcase up into the bed of a huge red Chevy pickup. We wound out of the airport, my mother and her beau commenting on the traffic and the new Cracker Barrel that had opened in the year and a half I'd been away. When we got home, I abruptly excused myself, went to my old room, dropped onto my old twin bed. Three hours later I woke, leaden, achy, skin and mouth dry, the last of the pills crawling around my bloodstream. I would've fallen back to sleep, if not for a distant banging. I pulled on a faded T-shirt: "Arcadia Volleyball: Pain Is Just *Weakness* Leaving the Body."

I went into the kitchen, following the banging. Years ago, my mom had painted one wall with chalkboard paint. When I was a kid, it was fun making drawings on it, little illustrated versions of the grocery list. But, in high school, if I didn't leave a message to say where I was any given evening, she started calling around looking for me. In all my trips home, the notes and doodles had been the same ones that had been there since I left for college. Now, a big swath had been wiped clear, everything but the cut-in-half words on the very edges, to make room for a large, intricate drawing: the floor plan of a house, this house. It was labeled, in a script not my mother's, "The Villa."

I went into the living room. The old burgundy couch, with its butt-worn corduroy upholstery and duct-taped reclining lever, was gone. In its place sat a dark leather Chesterfield covered by a sheet. The wood paneling that had clad the entire room had been stripped to bare plaster, and in the far corner, all of our family photos were lined up against the baseboard. Baby photos, shots of me on the court making a bump, an old family portrait: My mother in a flowery dress with a lace collar. Me at two or three, a big, gap-toothed smile at the trick—a penny stuck to his shiny forehead—the photographer had used to crack me up. And my father in a flannel shirt, with his red-brown beard, his hair parted, and his eyes slightly averted.

The banging started up again. Something cracked and splintered. I went back through the kitchen, opened the door to the garage.

"Mom, what are you doing? What is all this?"

She wore yellow work gloves and safety goggles, held a rubber mallet in one hand, a nail puller in the other. Before her were several old wooden boxes. "Wine crates, from Italy. Alden found them. Sorry the house is a mess, but, hey, no more cheesy paneling." Her voice was tight, cautious. She was hurt, angry, but wouldn't take me to task. Instead she went back to the crates and pried a nail from one with a quick, high creak. "Reclaimed wood. I thought you'd approve."

"Right. For 'the Villa.'"

She held the mallet out to me. "Here, get your blood moving."

"I'm going back to bed."

"You just got up."

"I'm not feeling well."

"Listen, if you want to talk about Ollie . . ." I heard both alarm and muted triumph in her voice. Those who worry secretly rejoice when given real occasion for it.

"Sleep is better."

She sighed. "Fine, I need you bright-eyed and bushy-tailed for dinner tonight."

"Is he moving in here? Is that what's going on?"

"We'll get to that later, Daph. One thing at a time." She got the nail puller under another nail, more expertly than I expected, and squealed it up. "Maybe I'll even get on that decorating website you like."

THAT EVENING, ALDEN CAME to collect us. He was driving a different truck, this one dark blue, "Stanowski A-1 Stump Grinding: No Job Too Big!" painted on the side.

"Sorry, folks! Last-minute job. Should've run home and changed, but didn't want to keep the ladies waiting!" Now he wore a denim shirt with his name embroidered on the pocket. Before we set off, my mother wanted to show him what she'd done with the crates. He entered the garage like a foreman, hitching up his khakis, getting the lay of everything. "Look at all that beautiful wood." He picked up a slat. "'*Prodotto del Lazio*,'" he read aloud in his twang. "You like what your mom and I are doing with the place?"

"Love it," I said with broad, flat enthusiasm.

He smelled like sawdust, like Ollie coming home from a building site.

"Okay!" Alden said. "Who's hungry for some *autentico* Italian?"

We drove down to Indy, to Carmel, the up-market part of a down-market city, to a restaurant named, with the exclamation point, Grazie! "Best meal in town," Alden said, more than once. "The chef trained back in the old country."

The hostess recognized Alden and gave us a table in the back. Garlands and baubles hung all around the dining room. The bar had little snowmen and reindeer lined up next to ceramic figurines of gondoliers. A blond teenage girl presented us with oversized menus printed on pebbled faux-parchment, a holiday menu. "I was set on spaghetti carbonara," Alden said, "but seeing how it's a special occasion"—he chuckled—"and my ex is gonna scorch the bird tomorrow . . ." He read aloud the courses with the gravity of someone reciting an epic poem. "Moist, sumptuous, hand-basted turkey," he intoned. "Creamy garlic mashed potatoes with the skins left on, *generously* buttered carrots."

A dry giggle squeaked out of me. My mother gave me a cautionary look.

"How's the food here normally?" I said to Alden. "How *autentico* is it?"

"*Si, bella, multi autentico.*"

"You must be Italian."

"Nah, mutt. Good old American mutt. But I do pursue *la dolce vita.*"

My mother and Alden talked about a performance of *La traviata* they'd just seen. They were weirdly formal and polite, as if concerned about easing me into this new arrangement. My mother kept glancing at me, trying to read my expression, measuring my response to Alden. Whatever she wanted from me, I was too achy to ruminate on it. My mouth was so dry I'd had three glasses of wine before the first course arrived. Alden tried asking me about "Frisco," my work, my apartment. I could barely summon the energy to answer. My mother kept quiet, her lips pursed in something like a smile.

After the antipasti, Alden started telling me about a last-minute trip he'd taken to Rome, years ago. "I was feeling kinda impulsive," he said. "Kinda crazy. But it was a great trip. A great, great trip . . ." He glanced down bashfully, seemed unsure about going on. But I didn't contribute anything, and he pushed ahead.

It was just after his divorce was finalized, he said. He'd put his number one chipper guy in charge and just bought a ticket and shown up without even any reservations. He'd wandered around in the rain for a few days, looking at the things he'd remembered from way back in middle school history: the Coliseum, the Pantheon, the Circus Maximus. He asked for filter coffee to go at bars and garlic bread at restaurants, not knowing any better, fumbling his way through. To me, it sounded dreary and lonely. But Alden's eyes were sparkling. He got into a rhythm, saying "*Roma*" for "Rome," pronouncing it with upswinging emphasis: "*Roma!*" Through the entrées, he went on with his story, a *generously* buttered carrot stuck on his fork. He kept lifting it off the plate, but it never quite made his mouth.

At the Capuchin Crypt, he said, he'd gawked at all the bones and skulls and felt a little ill—life lasted about five seconds and then you were just a pile of dust somewhere. The next morning, at the Vatican, he hired a young German guy, a history student, to show him around. (They had a great time and still kept in touch to this day!) At the end of a long, overwhelming day, exhausted and exhilarated from staring up at the Sistine Chapel ceiling, Alden continued on his own to St. Peter's Basilica. Seeing the gossamer light floating down into the nave, though he hadn't had religion for years and had grown up Baptist, not Catholic, he was moved to pray.

First, he asked God to guide him. He thanked Him for the success he'd had in life, asked that he might build the fleet back up again, keep growing the business and help out his guys and their families. He prayed for his two stepsons to do well in school and at hockey, get into good colleges. He prayed for peace, our troops overseas, for his dear departed mother. Finally, he found himself praying for his ex-wife.

He told God that he, Alden, had done wrong, too. He'd rushed into the marriage when he'd known deep down it wasn't over with her and her old boss. Kneeling there before the bones of St. Peter, he prayed that she be watched over, that she might eventually find lasting love, because, God knew, there hadn't been much between them the last two years, not since he found Ray Lantz's BlackBerry on the bedside table.

Then he cried. Yes, he wept like a baby right there in the basilica. "It all came out," Alden said. "I don't know why I thought to make that trip in the first place. I could've gone anywhere. But it saved my life. Jesus, it did. Ah, *Roma*!" He made a flourish with his fork, and finally, perfectly, the carrot dropped off the fork and onto his plate, spattering gravy all over his monogrammed denim shirt.

I hacked out a dry, violent laugh.

"Honey," my mother said.

"I'm sorry, but . . ." Another laugh was shoving its way out. My head drooped toward the table. "This is all so"— I waved my hand around my head—so obvious it didn't require words. Alden was dabbing at himself with a napkin. Seeing the befuddled expression on his face, I gave myself over to the laughter, just let go completely. Every time I looked at him in that jacket and shirt with his embroidered name peeping out, the force of the hilarity took me over. I started to slide out of my chair.

My mother reached over, tried to hold me up. Alden had gone very dark in the face. "Excuse her," she said. "You're seeing her unique way of dealing with a breakup."

"Listen to me going on like that." Alden went an even deeper shade. "Your mom did tell me about your loss. I guess I just wanted to say . . . Ah, shoot, I don't know what I was trying to say."

I slipped out of my mother's grasp, got up from the table, stumbled to the bathroom. The patrons of Grazie! turned to look, though here was a situation—home, the holidays—where I might easily be excused for being stumbling drunk. Swooping Italian ballads echoed off the tiles. I sat on the toilet, propped against the stall, and let the laughter tremble out of me. If not for the last bit of deadness from the pills, I would've been on the floor. When I went back out into the dining room, my mother was squeezing a napkin hard between her fingers, her lips pressed into a pale, thin pink.

WE DROVE BACK in near-silence. Alden dropped my mother and me at home. She went to her room. I lay on my bed, stared at the ceiling, the little fluorescent stars still stuck to the plaster, the ones I used to imagine dotting the skies above

Wessex. God, two and a half more days at home . . . I gave up. I texted Brook.

A terse reply came back. *Yeah, okay, going crazy here too.*

Half an hour later, she picked me up in her parents' old Ford Explorer. She wore a puffy coat, jeans, and an old pink pair of Converse. We drove to What Ales You, Arcadia's attempt at a brewpub. As we came in, a couple of guys at the bar turned to check us out. "Ignore the locals," Brook muttered. The bartender, after touting the virtues of their Hoppy Ending IPA, served me a glass of white and Brook a Manhattan. In the corner, we stared out of the tall windows at lonely downtown and the few swaddled souls hunching by. "What now?" Brook finally said.

"I was planning on drinking enough to sleep through Christmas."

"Ollie's not here. I'm guessing you would've brought him if you could."

"Yeah, that's over. It was coming. No way it wasn't coming."

"I should have called. You should have called me." She rubbed at her eyes. I didn't know which of us looked more ragged. "It was nice, seeing you out with him."

"Back to reality."

"I'd say tell me what happened, but I'm guessing you don't want to talk about it."

"Brook, listen, I . . ." It wasn't Ollie I needed to tell her about. "Look, something else happened. I nearly, in the bath, I almost . . ."

"Evening, ladies!"

I turned to see one of the guys at the bar sauntering toward us. Then I realized who it was: Kyle Magolski. Once of the camouflage pants and helmet hair, now with his locks shorn and gelled at sharp angles and the prongs of a tribal tattoo curling down his bicep. He was bringing us a second round. "Daphne Irvine," he said, addressing me but darting his eyes at Brook. "Health Ed. Second period. My partner in pissing off old man Jukes." He set down the drinks like a lord bestowing his patronage. "You two back at it, huh?"

"Kyle . . ." I looked over at Brook. She was swiping at her eyes again, and for the first time I saw that she'd been crying. "This isn't the best time."

"What up?" Kyle said, jutting his chin at Brook and giving her a once-over. "Golden State girl's in town once again. Should've said you'd be out. I would've brought something you'd like."

Brook gave me a desperate, drowning look. Kyle gestured toward his friend at the bar, who wore wire-frame glasses and a blue and white leather Colts jacket. "My boy Daniel works down at Eli Lilly. And maybe he makes some of those pill shipments just a *little* lighter. Plenty of drinks back at the crib if you want to sample, resupply some of those parties of yours."

"Just tell me what you have, already," Brook said.

Before Kyle could answer, I cut in. "Any downers? Oxy, Percocet, anything?"

Brook looked at me, surprised.

"Maybe, maybe." Kyle sucked his tooth and said to

Brook, "Your friend don't mess around. I thought she was, like, an all-star."

"Forget the drinks," I said. "Let's go already."

We put on our coats and went out to the parking lot. Kyle's friend followed, mumbled, "What up?" and looked disappointed that Kyle was getting Brook. Kyle drove a low-slung Honda with powdered black rims and, on the back bumper, a decal the same design as his arm tattoo. Brook pulled out behind him. We threaded through the quiet streets and onto a lane of run-down bungalows. He pulled up to a house with a snow-covered weight bench on the porch. Brook started to turn in to the driveway.

And then she was speeding off down the road.

"What?" I said. "No, what are you doing?"

She had it up around sixty on the snow-narrowed roads, her right hand clamped to the top of the wheel, her left pushing through her hair. "You didn't really want that Oxy, did you?"

"We can go back," I said. "Let's go back."

"If I turn back, grab the wheel and steer us into the next telephone pole."

The streets were all named for trees—Maple, Oak, Sumac, Laurel—and felt spookily quaint and orderly: two cars in every driveway, mailboxes shaped like barns and windmills and footballs, the icy sheen of every lawn shuddering and cascading with the reflections of the lights hung from every gutter, in every picture window tired or laughing or contented faces frozen in the blue flash of TVs. My hometown. Being here hurt in a way I couldn't specify or locate—an ache, an echo across a chasm.

"B, that thing I need to tell you . . ." I told her—about the bath, about nearly drowning. I kept losing my tongue and having to start up again.

"Did you mean to do it?" Brook said.

"I don't know. I've been taking baths for years."

"Yeah, but, lady . . ." She had trouble speaking herself.

"It just happened." I tried to soft-pedal it. "Things slipped out of my control. I was probably only in danger for a minute."

Brook made a guttural sound in her throat. She put both hands on the wheel and swung the car around. We shot off with a skitter of gravel and road salt against the undercarriage. When we hit the outskirts of Arcadia, Brook finally slowed down. We passed the mini-mall, the laser tag place, the Piggly Wiggly. Then Brook pulled into an empty lot. "Get out," she said.

"No way, it's freezing. Where are we, anyway?"

"You know where."

Brook turned off the car, hopped down to the asphalt, and went around to the back of the Explorer. I looked out at the darkened building before us. The marquee spelled out, with letters missing, the titles of movies from two or three summers ago. The big frames for posters were empty. I squeezed my eyes shut.

Brook knocked at my window, holding a snow shovel. She opened my door. "Come on."

"Jesus, B-rook, you b-rought me here?"

Dragging the metal shovel blade against the asphalt, she marched toward the theater. "Let's go!" she called back.

I slid out of the car. "What, we're going to clear their sidewalk for them?"

Brook pointed at one of the doors. "You get first shot."

As we approached, so did my own reflection in the dark glass. I could just see past it into the guts of the theater, the dim swoop of the curved concession stand, the people-size cardboard cutouts. I shivered, but it wasn't from the winter night.

"No way," I said.

"You worried someone's going to come by? It's Christmas Eve."

"Private prop-erty . . ." I mumbled.

"They're going to tear it down anyway. Go on. Do it."

I swung the shovel back limply, and only tapped the blade against the glass.

"Pathetic. Again."

I swung harder. The blade clanged against the metal part of the door, rattled through my teeth. I fixed on my reflection, swung the shovel over my head, let out a shout that slurred into a moan. That day, my arms crossed over my chest, a tag on my toe . . . The shovel, instead of slamming into the glass, clattered feebly to the pavement.

"You missed. Again."

This time the blade struck the glass full-on, the blow ringing up through my whole body. Something came loose. Since that day, I'd twisted and twined and bound myself up inside to avoid death, the knot there for years, so dense it'd taken me this long to find a loop to pick at. I swung and swung at my dark reflection, wild, clumsy, missed the door completely, struck the sidewalk. Finally, I went down on my knees, clattering the shovel to the ground. Brook picked it up. I heard the glass crunch and splinter, felt it fracture with each of her swings, the glass shivering down on the asphalt. I knelt there, eyes fluttering, listening to the crystalline sound.

WE PULLED INTO my mom's driveway. "If the cops show up," Brook said. "I'm sending them here. Merry Christmas."

"You never told me," I said, "how did Halloween go?"

She braced her hands on the wheel. "His whole company went under three weeks after the party. Lucky I'm only out six grand. I wasn't breaking those windows just for you."

I was about to remind her she shouldn't have gotten involved with him in the first place. Instead, I reached out, touched the crown of her head. "Wait, you've got glass in your . . ." I picked the sliver out, remembered those middle school sleepovers, laughing as dye streaked the sink, when we went around like twins, our hair the same obnoxious colors.

"What are you doing for New Year's?" Brook said. "If I know you, you're getting back to the city as soon as possible."

"B, I'm not sure I can handle one of your parties."

"Nope. Just me and you."

"Aren't you working?"

"My love to your mom. Get home safe."

"What, to the front door?"

"Lady, if you got any funnier, I don't think *I* could take it."

Standing in the driveway, I watched Brook pull away. Then I stood in the cold night and examined my breath rising. I couldn't go in. All of those nights lying awake, listening to my mother weep, the house still hummed with them. I paced and stamped to keep warm. Finally, I went through the garage and into the kitchen. Without turning on the light, I fumbled for the keys to her Focus, slipped them off their hook.

Six months—that's all the driving I'd gotten in before my diagnosis, those lonely drives out in the country, when already I didn't trust myself in town. Now I couldn't even figure out how to adjust the seat. And when I took my foot off the brake to roll quietly out of the garage, the car didn't go anywhere. I pressed the gas. The motor revved noisily up. The parking brake. Only my mother, in a table-flat town, would leave the parking brake on. The roads were slushy. I went slowly, thought I was on another of those old, aimless drives. By the time I got on I-37, I knew where I was going. I put my foot down.

EVEN WITH ALL of the one-way streets in Bloomington, I didn't have to look at my phone to find the place. I didn't want to look at it. It would be filled with messages from my mother, asking where the hell I was.

The little cinder-block house was even smaller than I remembered, dwarfed by the other campus buildings. I parked, got out, thought maybe I'd just peer in the window or something. Then I saw a light shining from one of the inner rooms. I hesitated, wrapped my fist in the sleeve of my coat, hammered on the door. Too quiet. I bared my knuckles, knocked so hard they stung. A moment later, another light came on. The door opened.

His hair was gray at the sides and frazzled. No salsa on his glasses, but his strained eyes stared at me through smudges and thumbprints.

"Dr. Bell," I began. "I . . ."

He looked left and right, as if suspicious of an ambush. "What is it? What do you want?" Then his eyes flashed recognition. "Ah, it's Daphne Irvine."

"Right, yes. I was just driving by. And I . . ."

"It's cold. Come in. You want tea?" It was two-thirty on what was now Christmas morning. Neither of us commented on this. I followed him inside, sucked right back into his orbit. "Or is it coffee?"

"No, tea is great, thank you," I said. "Herbal if you have it."

"Of course. You should avoid caffeine anyway."

"Oh?" Was this some new research I hadn't heard about? The old, brittle hope leapt up. "Would that help with the—?"

"We should all avoid caffeine. Were it up to me, it'd be Schedule IV."

The familiar waiting room had changed. The tottering stacks of journals now lined handsomely veneered bookshelves. The institutional furniture was gone, replaced with Knoll catalog stuff. On the walls were framed portrait photos of three doctors, one of which showed Dr. Bell looking stiff and truculent. And there was a plaque, done in oak and bronze or some convincing facsimile: "Indiana University Center for Addiction Research." Dr. Bell gestured for me to sit. He came back a minute later with two steaming white and red mugs. The tea bags were an upscale brand.

"They've provided us," he said, "with some very efficient beverage-making devices. You spend the money how you can." His expression soured for a moment, then cleared. "So, what is it, then? What have you come to talk about?"

On the drive down, I'd fantasized about screaming at him, without expecting to actually get the chance to do so. Now, seeing him here alone, his graying hair and sad little potbelly . . . "I've been working with one of your colleagues," I lied. "Dr. Francis. On a study at Stanford."

"Francis? Haven't spoken to him in years. I'm not in the field anymore." He sipped his scalding tea, used it to disguise another pained look. "Well, you're not dense. You can see that."

"So, it really is hopeless. Completely hopeless."

"It's not implausible that Jacob Francis has made some progress. He's a competent enough scientist, I suppose."

"You gave up. I never thought, you of all people . . ."

"Addiction carries a quantifiable social cost. And if I'm able to help a few troubled souls, then I should think it's worth the . . . Oh, Jesus, you try writing NIH grants for twenty years, see where you get."

"No, I understand." I was too tired to explain what I did for a living, that I knew a thing or two about for-profit research. "It helps to have a partner in the private sector."

"Yes," he said miserably, "a real boon." He reached out, parted my bangs, examined the nearly faded bruise on my forehead. "And how is our old friend?"

"She's stuck around way past her welcome."

He mentioned the brand name of the pills. "Have you considered them?"

"I thought you were against that sort of treatment."

"Perhaps one grows accustomed to the side effects."

Do you have some? I wanted to say. Jesus, do you have *anything* I can take? "So what kind of defectives do you have coming here now? Crackheads, tweakers?"

"Grandmothers, housewives, middle-aged middle managers. They go into the hospital with a broken whatever—six months later hooked on an opioid. Lovely business. Get them on the magic pain pill, then sell them the stuff to get them off."

"Must be nice to have your work in demand."

He took another sip of tea, stared forlornly into the mug. He might have had the same manner, but the Dr. Bell I'd known had crumpled and wizened. I watched the steam from his tea curl around his face, fogging his glasses.

"When you look into the brain," he began, "you understand. We like to think we're lugging around the most perfect, miraculous thing in the universe. But try *looking* at the thing. Addicts? We're all made to be addicts. Look at the limbic making the same connections again and again. Automatic behavior probably kept *Homo ergaster* alive. There's reason for it. But if you've seen the neural activity of a schizophrenic, the incessant mental replay . . . Repetition, repetition, repetition. Then there's everything we have no *clue* about. The same neuron fires when I see *you* sip the tea as when *I* sip the tea. So how do I even know who's doing what? How do I know anything? It's chaos. And not divine chaos but the chaos of the bog, the crawling jungle." He balled up his fist and struck it, hard, against his temple. "When you look, when you really *look*, you see only murk, one evolutionary accident after another. Twenty years of people coming to me with the same question: Am I broken? Am I broken? And I want to say, What do you want from me? We're *all* broken."

The steam was dissipating. He put down the mug, took off his glasses, wiped away the fog. "Tell me, how is your mother?" If I hadn't known better, I would've said he was blushing. "A beautiful woman, I always thought."

My eyelids fluttered. An honest laugh, I hoped, not a cruel one.

"I might never have taken you as a patient if I hadn't known I'd see her every week."

"What? I was the best guinea pig you ever had."

"You were too fatalistic. You thought you were doomed."

I started to protest. Then I realized he wasn't wrong. "You could have asked her out. She would've liked that."

"A long-distance relationship? I wouldn't have had the time."

"She's only an hour and a half from here."

"Yes, well, I used to think my research was more important."

"So there's really no getting better from this?" I rapped my fist on my own skull.

"Better?" He looked at me questioningly. "But look at you. That's your car out front, isn't it?"

"A loaner."

"You drove here. I didn't think that would ever be possible. To be honest, I always wondered if you'd make thirty. How old are you now?"

"Right on the money, Dr. Bell."

"You do the best with the data you have." He smiled, dug in his pocket. "Mint?"

I DROVE HOME IN A HAZE. The world was flat and vacant, and I was alone, drifting untethered. Coming into town, the roads were potholed and rough, but I hardly felt it. By the time I pulled into the driveway, I was blinking away sleep. I went in as quietly as I could. But underneath the chalkboard wall, clutching a half-full Peroni, my mother sat at the kitchen table, blinking at me. "You took the car out."

"I just drove around a while."

"That was dumb."

"Yeah, probably."

"You could've answered your phone."

"I know, Mom, but, look, I really need to sleep now."

"Sit down. Get a beer if you want. But you're sitting down."

"Peroni?" I got one from the fridge but took my time about it. "Alden's brand?"

"I told myself I wasn't going to yell at you. I've been sitting here waiting for another call from the emergency room."

"Another one?" I said.

"You know what I mean."

"That call came from the morgue, Mom. From the frozen food department." I started rubbing out one of the walls of the Villa. "Why not yell? Go ahead, do it."

"Oh, quit it, would you? Alden spent a long time on that. He was out half the night driving around looking for you. I sent him home to rest up. He'll be worn out all day thanks to your little joyride."

I swished the beer around my mouth, bitterness creeping back up. "So what happened to all the years holding vigil for Dad?"

"Your father's still part of this house, Daph."

"Well, yes, historically that's been the problem."

"Alden understands. You think we don't talk about the past? Once you get to our age, all you do is talk about the past."

I got up and took another beer from the fridge.

"You went through that quick."

"If we're talking, I'm drinking."

"Do I have to worry about that again as well?"

I sat down, swished around the beer some more. "Fuck it, I'm too tired to work up to this. What happened to Dad? He didn't have a heart attack. There's no way he did."

My mother's eyes startled, then turned as fragile and cloudy as old glass. "That's what your uncles and I told you, what we told everyone, ourselves even. But, Daph, do you really not remember . . . ?" She pressed her cold beer to her forehead.

It was the Fourth of July, she began, and the three of us—her, Dad, five-year-old me—had driven over to the river. My two uncles had brought everyone up from Georgia, the Irvine boys' annual barbecue. That year there'd been added reason to celebrate, though everyone down south had been keeping quiet, to make it a surprise: Jerry, my dad's youngest brother—who'd been through layoffs and back pain and a tree falling through his house—was finally healthy enough to work again and, best of all, getting married to the girl he'd been courting forever. My Aunt Bethany had finally said yes.

"When your dad heard the news," my mom said, "he sat down in a lawn chair, then slowly, real slowly, a smile came across his face. Using one finger he kind of beckoned Jerry over, slowly raised his arm, shook his little brother's hand—weak, but he still shook it. 'Oh, Don's already drunk,' we all said and laughed it off. The truth was we hardly ever saw him smile like that. We figured he *must* be drunk, though he was never a real big drinker. Anyway, he hardly ever seemed to get worked up over anything. 'Stoic,' we called him. He and Jerry finished their slow-motion handshake, everyone laughing about it. Then we all went back to beer and goofing around. If we'd known . . ."

I only half-heard my mother. I was there again, the patchy, sharp grass, the low pulsing cicadas in the trees, the adults all going down to the river to swim. When he came out of his attack, my father must not have been able to resist. Still clumsy and tentative, he kept to the shallows while they all splashed and dunked one another in the cool water and the high, hazy sun. Then, one by one, they all got out to towel off, get the grill going, pop open more beers and containers of food, meat on the grill, the soft breeze carrying the smell, the white smoke, the glad laughter across the water. But he lingered there, the gentle current tickling his toes, still keeping apart from their joy, trying to keep his own pleasure private and small.

"Jerry swam out to this raft chained out in the middle. I guess your dad wanted to be out there with him. We all knew how at home he used to feel in the water."

It came into focus: my uncle on the raft, a couple of wooden pallets lashed to some old blue rain barrels. Jerry sat on the edge, kicked his feet in the water, sprawled out to get some sun. My father pulled himself up, sat beside him, the two brothers together. Jerry started doing cannonballs off the raft, splashing my dad, who put up with it good-naturedly, just sitting there, slumping a little. When the burgers came off the grill, someone shouted for them to come eat. Jerry dove right in. But my dad stayed out there, so happy he didn't want to move, or couldn't.

And there I stood in the shallows, looking out at him. I

raised my chubby arm, waved to my father. Slowly, he stood, waved back, his arm struggling to reach above him but waving anyway. He called out something, the words all jumbled. "Daddy, Daddy!" I cried out, giggling. "You're the king of the river!" He tried again to call out to me. Then he crumpled to the lip of the raft and dropped into the water.

"Before your diagnosis," my mom said, "his death was a mystery, to all of us. When Dr. Bell came along and told us about your condition . . . But I still wouldn't accept it." She rubbed out one of the old notes on the blackboard. "Otherwise, the tragedy was just explained away."

A huge wave of happiness, too sudden for him to stop it. He must have wished he could just let go, glory in the moment, a second or two too long—and then he was in the water. He'd panicked. With panic, there was no easy way out. He wouldn't even have known how to come out of it. But he must have tried, instinctively, to tamp it down. I'd watched him sink slowly to his knees, so that, when he went under, he didn't make a loud splash. Or maybe it was just that no one heard.

"We were toasting your Uncle Jerry, having a great time. Then someone said, 'Where's Don?'" My mom shook her head, her eyes closed. "We went to the riverbank, saw him floating facedown. I was screaming. Uncle Jerry and Uncle Rick had to drag him out. His skin was still pink. He'd only been gone a few minutes. We put you in the car. We didn't want you to see."

"I saw him go into the water."

"Oh, honey."

"Why didn't you ever tell me?"

"I didn't want you to remember. I told myself you wouldn't."

"I do. I do re-mem-ber."

My fingers slipped from the beer bottle. I slumped against the wall. The chalk dust got in my nostrils, burned. I couldn't even sneeze. My mother reached over, wiped my nose. "Take your time. I'm here."

Finally, my tongue came back. "I saw him. I saw him fall in. I could've done something, told someone."

"You were five, honey."

We sat in silence. My mom got up and took two more beers from the fridge. "He was like you," she said. "Just like you. So openhearted."

I scoffed. "Don't bullshit me, Mom."

"You're your father's daughter. You take everything to heart."

"And that's what got him killed."

My mother's face creased, folded on itself. But she didn't. She didn't cry. "How'd we get so far away, kiddo? I remember you and me making bubble beards doing the dishes, drawing a whole little world together on this wall, castles and mountains and whatever popped into your head. Now you're just a little box in the corner of the screen, saying awful things to me."

"Mom," I said feebly, tasting slick, welling tears. "I'm sorry. I'm . . ." I closed my eyes, leaned harder against the wall. I felt it unravel, the tight little knot coming all undone. "I'm coming home, Mom. I'm moving back for good."

"Oh, Daph, that's not what I want."

But it was. It absolutely was. And I couldn't resist anymore. How many more nights alone could I risk? I never wanted to go back into that darkness. Dr. Bell was right—the impulse to survive was too strong.

"I can sell my place. It should be enough to live on for a year or two. If it comes down to it, Eli Lilly is usually hiring. Or I'll find something closer to here."

My mom's face slowly unfolded, brightened. "I do worry about you out there. You're so far away. When I saw you at the airport, and you came out without . . ."

"It wouldn't have worked out with Ollie anyway."

"Why not, honey? It can happen. Why wouldn't it?"

"Because I won't accept anyone who'll settle for a defective product."

"I spent twenty years telling myself: Who wants to date a widow with a kid? Bad questions get worse answers. Don't come back because of me." She smiled distantly. "You wouldn't want to live in your old room . . ."

"Just till I found an apartment nearby."

"Come on, time for bed. You haven't slept, and it's the big meal today."

I let her help me to my room, her arm threaded through mine for stability. I wriggled under the well-worn flannel sheets. She stood over me in the gray early morning light. I could feel her straining to say something. "Mom, what is it?"

"Honey, we were going to tell you tomorrow. Alden and I are moving in together. He's giving up his apartment, moving in here. And we're getting married, next summer."

"That's great, Mom. I'm really glad. Really."

"I know you are. I can tell."

"One happy family under the same roof," I said. "Free stump removal."

"Come on, bedtime."

"Am I already? Am I dreaming or what? Mom . . ."

"What?"

"It's my fault. That he drowned, it's because of me."

"No, it's not. You know it's not."

"It is . . . It is . . ."

"Hush up now, get some sleep."

She kissed me on the forehead, turned off the light, closed the blinds. With the pale phosphorescent stars above me, my feelings bloomed, thick, tangled, choking. I huddled up to the wall, wearily tried to beat them back. The river, the cattails, the willows . . . But now all I saw was my father— my father slipping under the water. All of those years my image had seemed serene, innocuous. Maybe it had really stood in for overload, shock, paralysis deeper than emotion. Yet I could see my dad again. There he was, waving to me. I could finally see him clearly.

MOM WOKE ME at four that afternoon. We got dressed and drove over to one of the new subdivisions on the other side of town, to Alden's ex-wife's house. As we went up the front walk, Mom's nerves jangled the air. "This the first time you've met her?"

"I see her in the Piggly Wiggly. We get along fine. Everything's fine."

Thirty or so people were gathered in the kitchen and living room. Despite the chaos of all the little ones tearing around, it was gentle. No flare-ups, no grudges. After some too-polite banter, my mother ended up kidding around with Alden's ex, making little jokes at his expense, which he suffered with his big, wheezy laugh. Mom kept checking in on me, but I told her I was okay, tried to make a point of socializing. A few people remembered my volleyball days—some glories never faded—asked if I still played. "No, but I think Mom still has my old kneepads boxed up somewhere." They chuckled indulgently, all good midwesterners, who did everything in their power not to ruffle or disturb you, who just wanted to make sure, honey, that you had enough to eat and drink. The rest of my life could drift pleasantly away on this warm tide of decency.

I found myself playing with a little girl, about four, who explained all the features of the doll she'd gotten for Christmas. If she was sad, she turned dark blue. Happy, bright green. Excited, an even brighter yellow. And you only had to coo softly and tickle her belly, and she laughed and burbled and sang and lit up all colors.

"Do you know how come?" the little girl asked me. "How come she works?"

"You'll have to show me again," I said. "Show me how you make her happy."

TWENTY-SEVEN

T HE NEXT MORNING I SAID GOOD-BYE TO MY
mother on the front step. I was surprised she wasn't
going to see me off safe at the airport.

"Alden's going to drive you. I want you two to have a
little time."

"Mom, there will be plenty of that later."

"Text me when you land, okay?"

I yawned. I could've slept another night through. "I'll
probably use the same agent," I said, thinking aloud about
my apartment. "She worked her dark magic on me."

"Hold on, I've got something for you." My mom disappeared back into the house for a moment. "I don't know if
you'd want this yet . . ." It was one of the framed photos of
my dad. "You can tell me I'm crazy for even—"

"Don't worry, I'll be back in a month."

"Then hold on to it till then." We hugged, and she whispered in my ear. At first I thought she said, "Be careful," as she always did. But, no, she said, "Be good to him."

Alden was waiting in his pickup. I rode next to this large, unfamiliar man all the way out to the highway before either of us risked any idle chatter. "So, tell me"—I tried to let a little good cheer into my voice—"what's the biggest stump you've done?"

He looked at me cautiously. "Sorry, I didn't get born with the sarcasm gene."

"No, I'm really asking."

He rubbed his chin. "Has to be this old oak down in Martinsville. I drove down, took a look, knew we'd need two trucks. The big ones, diesel, four-wheel drive. But that stump didn't want to come. Tree must have been two hundred years old, I lost count of the rings. Two hundred years, those roots go deep, and the earth is clay, sometimes stone, and those roots have to push down through it all. You're pulling up a couple of tons of dirt and rocks as well. Sometimes a winch will get you nowhere. You've got to do it in a series of yanks. But watch out now! You'll wrench a truck's whole frame if you're not careful. You've just got to keep steady and listen, listen to the way those roots start creaking up. Slowly, slowly. Each big pull, they get looser and looser. Then you feel it. Takes a whole afternoon, but comes a point all you got to do is keep pulling."

"Bet that feels good," I said softly, "feeling it all come free like that."

He looked over at me again. "I'm aware of your ailment. Your mom told me."

"Better that I don't have to educate for the millionth time."

"I understand if it makes it harder for you and me to get to know each other. I'm sorry if I wasn't sensitive enough of that."

"I'm the one owes you an apology. It's not an excuse."

"The holidays. We all go a little haywire." He shifted lanes to pass a semi. "How's the weather out there in Frisco?"

I thought to correct him. No one but tourists called it that. "January rains are coming," I said. "Be nice to miss those."

"You don't want to come back here. If I'd gone to Rome when I was younger, I'd never have come back."

"I have to. We're talking life or death."

"Your mom told me about your job, too. Must be hard. I love dogs."

"Me, too."

"Your whole deal sounds kind of hard," he said.

"Well, I guess you just keep pulling."

He laughed, somehow both mournful and content. "So, think I'm too old for your mom?"

"I thought you were about the same vintage."

"Nah, I got a few extra rings on me. Want to hear a joke my dad used to tell?"

"Only if it's a bad one."

"Old man comes across a frog one day. Frog says, 'Kiss me, and I'll turn into a beautiful princess.' Old man picks it up, puts it in his pocket. Frog says, 'Hey, didn't you hear me?' Old man says, 'Sure did. But at my age, I'd rather have a talking frog.'" Alden broke into his big wheeze.

I slumped forward. The seat belt held me up. Oh, God, dad jokes and everything.

WHEN I WOKE, my flight was passing over the golden rills of the Sierra Nevada foothills. The land grew verdant. The iridescent labyrinths of the salt marshes at the tip of the bay crawled into view. The plane's wings tilted to descend into SFO, and I saw the Berkeley Hills and the Bay Bridge glowing in the late afternoon sun, a steam train of pure white fog chugging toward the city, the sky above a high, heartache blue. But no one stayed in San Francisco. It was a place you were meant to leave and miss for the rest of your life.

Coming off the plane, I felt purposeful, unfettered, the taste in my mouth cool and clean as peppermint. Only on the train did I think to turn on my phone. I expected my mom to have already left a text or two. But there was only a voicemail, from a number that didn't come up with an ID. I played it. "Daphne"—an unfamiliar voice—"sorry to disturb you. This is Carianne, Bill's wife. Bill, from your group . . ."

I should've waited till I got home. Instead, foolishly, I did as she asked and called her right back. She picked up, asked if I was sitting down.

"Sort of," I said. "I'm on the train."

She was saying something about Miranda. Miranda had

gone by Sherman's to drop off a fruitcake, like she did every holiday season. Sherman had missed the last meeting. That close to Christmas, the few of them that showed up figured it'd slipped his mind to cancel. They'd called, and he said, yeah, he'd forgotten, sorry. Sorry, everyone. Two days later Miranda, fruitcake in hand, knocked for a while, thinking maybe, of all things, he'd gone out. Then she got a strange feeling, went downstairs and knocked on the neighbor's door. The guy turned out to be the landlord, and . . .

"Oh, Jesus," I said. "I'm not ready for this."

When the landlord let them into the apartment, Sherman was on the couch, head lolled back. His skin was ashen, and when they touched him, cool and dry, papery almost. He'd taken a handful of the pills and tried to wash it down with a fifth of Gordon's gin.

"Bill thinks Sherman must've switched off before he even got past the neck of the bottle," Carianne said. "That he must have dropped the gin but got down enough pills."

"Ah, fuck, I . . ."

"Bill says the percentage of people who do it around Christmas is—"

"Have we called his family? Do they know?"

"His sister was listed for emergencies. She's flying in tomorrow. He also listed you, Daphne."

"He did?"

"We thought we'd try the sister first."

"Right."

The news delivered, Bill's wife got off the phone. She said he needed to call everyone else in the group, even those who hadn't attended in months or years. She said Bill wished he could do it himself. But he was just so upset.

My fingers could barely end the call. I sank back into the seat, head against the scratched Plexiglas window, went right past 16th Street and several stops across the bay before I had it in me to get off and change to a train back into the city.

I feared the moment when I opened the door to my apartment and felt again how empty it was. But when I got home, I just stood on the threshold, staring at all of the beautiful, anonymous furniture, the national parks prints that had nothing to do with me, the group of hand mirrors that reflected back eight different Daphnes, none of them complete. My "Cozy Roost." Why had I ever cared so much about this finely wrought cage? I wandered the apartment, picking things up, putting them down. All I could smell was my old childhood room still clinging to my skin.

I WENT TO WORK. I was supposed to have the week off, but what else was I going to do? Anyway, the lab was quiet. I'd decided to go to HR on Friday and give my notice. I'd tell them I didn't want to run hardware. It was further from the reality of what MedEval did, but it wasn't far enough. I'd tell HR that, with thirteen years' experience, Byron was the only reasonable choice to take over the lab. If they thought *I'd* kept the budget tight . . . But there was a little flu outbreak among the dogs, and the night-shift techs and I had to quarantine and treat the sick ones, make sure it didn't spread to them all.

Pin came in and spent an afternoon helping us. She and I took a break, went over to the café. I couldn't bring myself to tell her I was quitting. But I also couldn't resist a confession. I told her all about the condition, gave her the well-rehearsed speech. What did it matter? I wouldn't have to deal with the aftermath. Pin nodded slowly as I spoke, as if none of this were a surprise.

"Oh, Christ, Byron told you. That prick."

"No, he has never said anything. It is just that we notice your . . . We call them your 'Wednesday faces.' You get them more in the middle of the week."

"You all probably think I'm a real dragon."

She was weighing her answer carefully.

"Go ahead," I said. "I can take it."

"We give you the doubt benefit. Always doubt benefit. Not easy to be the boss."

It took a moment to untangle the idiom, and then I liked it too much to correct her.

I SPENT THE REST OF THE WEEK with the dogs. By the time Saturday came around, I just had time to take a car to the mall, buy a black dress, and make it to the funeral. The parlor was on Geary, not far from Sherman's apartment, the exterior an anachronistic seafoam green. Inside, however, it was all dark wood and organ music playing quietly from hidden speakers. I looked for everyone from group. They were, prudently, sitting in the back, the small clutch of them together, some already with heads bowed. We headbobbers were naturals at funerals.

The viewing line curled all the way around the room. How had a guy who'd barely left the house known so many people? Maybe these were all family or internet friends. I thought about going straight to join the group but got in line instead. Finally, I came to the casket. The top half was open, and there lay Sherman. Or some waxen replica of him in a nondescript suit, without one of his loud, sharply pressed shirts. I reached out to him, then stopped short and gripped the edge of the casket. Turning away, I made an effort to shore up my knees. But there was no need. Grief was too bewildering, too tangled. It pulled you in every direction at once.

A Universalist priest led the service and said comforting, only vaguely religious things. I sat next to Miranda, who halfway through let her head droop on my shoulder. The priest invited anyone who so wished to say a few words in remembrance of Sherman Allen Steward. His sister, a petite woman with a stylish, chopped hairstyle, spoke first. Next came two childhood friends. Then Teshawn was at the podium, talking about everything Sherman did for the group and for the online community, how much of a difference he'd made. Everyone else must have heard him speaking with the barest inflection, like he was reciting a script. But I could hear him struggling, pushing every word past the thick murk of the pills. "The people who remember you," he said, "are the people you looked after." Miranda's head on my shoulder grew heavier. Then the organ music came back up. The coffin lowered into the floor.

People started to leave. The group stayed put, heads lolling forward or back, arms hanging at their sides, jaws drooping, eyelids going up and down like window shades. I was the only one fully upright. Consciously or not, we'd pushed our chairs out into a loose circle.

"Well, that's the end of us," Miranda said.

"Someone can take it over," I said. "Maybe share the administrative stuff."

"And who would that be?"

"I don't know, Bill? He's organized. Or his wife is."

"Bill didn't even make it today. He had 'child care conflicts.' And, Jesus, letting Carianne make all those phone calls . . ."

"We could just migrate over to the web forum," I said. "That's easier all around anyway. And I'm sure someone on there would take over the hosting."

"Group's the only thing getting some of these people through the week. It disappears, they're going to dry up and blow away."

Some of these people. Miranda was talking about herself.

"Well, go for it," I said. "If you want to keep the thing going."

"Yeah, Miranda," Teshawn said, "teach us. Give us that professor thing."

"I won't have the time," she said. "I'm going back on the job market."

"Oh, you didn't get—"

"The war on academic freedom continues. Anyway, no one listens to me. The only one they listen to besides Sherman is you, Daphne."

That's when I told them all I was leaving, moving back home, back in with my mother. Surprise flickered over their faces. Miranda's expression sagged. I wouldn't have believed it if I hadn't seen it. Did she actually care whether I stayed or left? I listened to them all halfheartedly debate replacements for Sherman. At one point, a beautiful young woman came over and embraced Teshawn. My heart boomed out for him—a girlfriend?!—then he introduced her as his cousin. After a time, I pulled my shawl over my shoulders and readied myself to slip away. Sherman's sister caught me before I could.

"You're Daphne, aren't you?"

"Sorry for your loss." The words came automatically. "Sherman inspired us all."

The sister had the same shy smile and kind eyes as Sherman, but she was a tiny thing, as delicate as he'd been bearish. I was wary of her. What if, any second now, her tears came shuddering through?

"Daphne, I'm sorry to be so brief. There are so many people to talk to. Could you come by Sherman's apartment this evening? There's something he wanted you to have. Do you know the address?" I said I'd dropped him off there once. "Oh, good. It's a relief that you can come."

We agreed on six o'clock. I kicked around the Grove for a couple of hours, then took a car out to Sherman's place.

The fog had already come in, covering the whole street of pastel houses in gray, shimmering haze. I asked the driver to wait for me.

The sister let me in. She wore jeans now and an oversized cashmere sweater. "Oh, thank you for coming, Daphne. I know it's an inconvenience."

"None at all."

Almost ceremonially the two of us sat on the couch, right at the edge, as if poised to get up and check on a roast. I looked around. The apartment was smaller than I'd imagined it. Sherman had been tidy, everything tightly shelved, the books and CDs all lined up by color. The furniture and accents were masculine without being overly restrained, the whole place tastefully, impeccably done. So, I wasn't the only one.

"How are you?" I tentatively asked the sister.

"It's not real yet. Even seeing his body didn't make it real."

A question lingered on my tongue. "Are you . . . like him?" I gestured at myself. "Like us?"

The woman seemed to have a very inward glance, as if she were off somewhere pondering some nagging, eternal question. "The mysteries of inheritance. It missed me."

"That's lucky."

She pondered further. "But sometimes, you know, I was envious of him. He knew himself so well. He was so careful about his feelings. But he was generous with them, too. Whenever I was going through something, he always knew what to tell me. He just knew. I think the condition made him, I don't know, in awe of what it is to feel."

I nodded. "He was . . ." Something was pushing its way up: a laugh, a shout, the urge to vomit maybe. "He was so . . ."

"No rush," the sister said. "Take your time."

"I undermined something that meant a lot to him. He put a lot of faith in it, and I just shit all over it."

"The Stanford study? He knew those things were Hail Marys. He struggled. He always struggled. I don't think there's anything any of us could've done. I'm angry with him. Furious. But I understand why he did it, as much as you can understand these things."

"A lot of them, the group, they're really shaken."

"And you?"

My throat was so tight I could barely swallow. "I'm getting by."

"He left a note, just instructions really. He never had a real will drawn up."

"You never think the moment will actually come," I said and hoped the woman didn't hear the hitch in my voice.

Prince Hairy slunk into the room, even more alien and hairless and desiccated in person. Wizened, I thought. Wizened, shriveled, shriven, shrimpy. My thoughts were all over the place. He butted at the sister's leg, asking to be fed.

"Good timing," she said. "I was wondering where he got to."

Then I understood why she'd asked me to come.

"I can't," I said. "I really can't. I'm moving."

"Of course. Sherman said, 'A long shot, but maybe Daphne Irvine would want His Highness.' He's been declawed. That's about the only thing easy about him. And no fur to get all over everything."

"He always looks like he has about a week left."

"Since I arrived I've been expecting to find him belly up. Sherman kept preparing himself for the day he'd finally go. Who knew he'd last longer than—?"

The sister put her hand on her chest, which heaved underneath it. She looked like she was going to hiccup. Then she was in my arms, her sobs thrumming through me. I resisted a moment longer, and then they became my own. She held me up. She'd done this before.

"You really don't have to," she said when we'd pulled ourselves together. "I've spoken with the SPCA. They're full. But they'll make it very humane."

"I know. They're good. They do good work."

Prince Hairy was lying on his side on the rug, blinking slowly in a ray of sunshine. He was so skinny he looked translucent. He turned his head and looked at me haughtily, aristocratically, as if he'd already made the decision for me.

I SPENT THE NEXT WEEK staging the apartment, trying to make it look its most inviting, like someone else's home. I called my broker. We agreed on a listing date. "And should we choose a day for me to come over and take some pictures?" the woman said.

I laughed ruefully. "Ah, no, I've got that taken care of."

New Year's passed quietly. Brook and I watched a couple of movies on my flat-screen, British comedies that came out when we were in college, more wry than hilarious, more adorable than moving. It didn't matter. I spent half the night with my head lolled back on the couch.

"You can't go," Brook said.

"I don't really have a choice anymore. Not since that bath."

"You can't. I won't let you."

At midnight, we popped a bottle of prosecco. "Don't you want to go out?" I said. "Isn't there a club or a secret warehouse party or an orgy you should be getting to?"

"There's at least five."

"Well?"

"I already have enough regrets for the new year."

I went over to the dresser, pulled out a vacuum-sealed package. "Here, a belated Christmas present." Her pajamas.

"Those are yours, not mine."

"Then keep them for me," I said. "For when I come visit."

THE NEXT MORNING I was woken by Prince Hairy sitting proprietarily on my chest. I shooed him off, and he emitted one plaintive cry, the first noise I'd heard him make. He looked at up at me reproachfully. "Happy New Year to you, too," I said groggily.

I rolled over for my phone, opened my in-box, and there it was: an email from Ollie. "hi," the subject read. My finger hovered over the screen. I could open it. If it was just more spam . . . But, no, I couldn't. Not yet.

To distract myself through the morning and early afternoon, I thumbed through *The Return of the Native* on my phone. But I couldn't concentrate. It was all I could do not to open the email.

At two-fifteen, I felt myself growing anxious, the old familiar acid and twitch. I called my car service. Half an hour later, I was outside the church. The boys from AA were just going in. The action figure held the door, raised his coffee. I wished him a happy 2012. He gave me a red-eyed, bleary wink. "Party of the decade last night," he said, still drunk.

When I went in, they were all arranged in their circle, in the same spots as always. We looked around at one another. No one knew what to say. We were going to have our own little memorial for Sherman—the only reason, I told myself, I'd come today. But, finally, I couldn't take the silence.

"Okay, then," I said, "where should we start?"

I CAN'T SAY EXACTLY when it was. Somewhere, perhaps, in the middle of Miranda telling us how Sherman had once talked her through her brother nearly dying in surgery after a hit-and-run. On his end of the line, Sherman had waited nearly forty minutes for her to come out of an attack, murmuring words of encouragement the whole time. "He would've waited hours," she said.

Or maybe it was on my way home. When I came out of the church, my car service was waiting. We'd gone long, and I apologized to the driver, gave him forty extra bucks for his trouble; I was going to walk home. I went through the park, taking the same route I had all those months ago with Ollie, wandered down the Panhandle, through the Haight and Duboce Triangle. The same concerned-looking joggers, the same casually, expensively dressed people with their pampered, happy dogs, but somehow the very city seemed to glimmer and hum. The afternoon turned misty, the chill, heavy mist that comes before several days of rain, the air so raw it made me shudder with something like anticipation.

So maybe it was then that I knew: I wasn't leaving. I couldn't. As hard as it had been to make a life here, as hard as that life was, I couldn't walk out on it now. Not on Brook, not on my group or my workmates. Not even on the dogs.

I was so lost in the realization that, without looking, I stepped out into an intersection. A silent, stealthy Prius squealed to a stop, blasted its horn at me. The buzzing leapt up. My knees started going out from under me. *Diamonds glinting on the river, my father, my father waving to me*—the image slid right in. It should have brought terror, shock, grief. Instead there was only something clear, hollow, and still. And I tasted sorrow, but only faintly. I stayed on my feet.

The rest of the way, I wanted to look at my phone, open

the email. But I would save it till I got back to the Grove, back to the couch. Whatever it said, it could wait at least that long. As I came into my neighborhood, the fog had started to gather, blurring all the lighted signs. PERFECT DETAILING. My sign burned out of the gray evening. For a moment, it blinked off, faltered. ERFECT.

And then it blinked on again.

ACKNOWLEDGMENTS

MY ENDURING GRATITUDE to everyone who read, listened, and helped me along the way, especially:

Ann Beattie, Ryan Bieber, Kat Carlson, John Casey, Deborah Eisenberg, Tom Franklin, Gail Hochman, Leslie Jamison, Drew Johnson, Jody Kahn, Jason Labbe, Catherine Lacey, John L'Heureux, Paul Reyes, Erin Saldin, Caitlin Satchell, Elizabeth Tallent, Ted Thompson, Chris Tilghman, Gemma Trevisani, Tobias Wolff, and Cutter Wood.

For all of their passionate, intelligent work and guidance in bringing *Daphne* into the world:

Jin Auh, Jessica Friedman, Alba Ziegler-Bailey, and everyone at the Wylie Agency. Cordelia Calvert, India Cooper, Gina Iaquinta, Phil Marino, Peter Miller, and everyone at Liveright. Ka Bradley, Sarah Wasley, and everyone at Granta Books.

My brilliant, insightful, and patient collaborators: Katie Adams and Max Porter.

ACKNOWLEDGMENTS

For the generous support of these institutions and individuals:

The American Academy of Arts and Letters, the John Guare Writer's Fund, Dorothy and Lewis B. Cullman, Michael Collier, Noreen Cargill, the Bread Loaf Writers' Conference, Martin Pick, the Charles Pick Fellowship, Stanford University, the Truman Capote Literary Trust, the University of East Anglia, the University of Manchester, the MacDowell Colony. The University of Chicago, the American Academy in Rome, and my friends and colleagues at both.

Finally, I want to acknowledge the support and love of my friends and family. I'll never be able to thank you enough.

Keep in touch with
Granta Books:

Visit granta.com to discover more.

GRANTA

Also by Will Boast and available from Granta Books
www.granta.com

EPILOGUE

A Memoir

A BBC Radio Four Book of the Week

'Each tiny piece of this story is so sweet and heartbreaking I couldn't stop reading it. It's brilliant. It will make you cry. I have never met Will Boast, but I'm so proud of him' Nina Stibbe, author of *Love, Nina*

When Will Boast's father dies he is alone in the world: an American with English roots, orphaned and derailed by grief. Everything he thought he knew about his parents unravels when he discovers he has two half-brothers living in England. In exquisite prose, Will Boast sets about piecing together a new sense of himself, attempting as he does to understand, forgive and heal the mistakes of his father's past.

'Riveting, soulful, and courageously told, Will Boast's memoir is a gorgeous meditation on grief and family and also a deeply personal account of his coming-of-age under a relentless bombardment of tragedies and revelations. Never has a story of loss been so full of life' Maggie Shipstead, author of *Seating Arrangements*

'Blew me away and kept me riveted, absolutely locked in its orbit for days'
Leslie Jamison, author of *The Empathy Exams*

'Heartbreakingly raw but gracefully constructed' *Independent*